A LOVE DESTINY

Mary's Unusual Love Story That Transcended Time and Space

---

by

Sue Liu Maisano

and

Charles Rappaport

Table of Contents

Preface

This book you are reading was written by consciousness.

I know what you are thinking.

Aren't all books written by consciousness?

Yes, indeed.

But this book was written by consciousness that you cannot pinpoint in a physical body. The authors, me and Charles Rappaport did not come up with the wordings of this book. It was created by the collaboration of us through a method of meditation, which you may call channeling.

Channeling may have the connotation of letting spirits talk through you, but that is only the tip of the iceberg.

I believe all thoughts are coming from higher planes, higher dimensions if you wish. Our mind is a channel, a bridge, a conduit that receives certain thoughts because we are a vibrational match to their energy. In that sense we are all channels, unconsciously.

All information, including ideas for fictional stories, is out there in the ether, the Akashic Record, spiritual plane, higher dimensions, higher realities, higher frequencies, intuition, however you want to call it.

Perhaps what we are more familiar with and can easily accept is the term intuition. Where do you think intuition comes from? Higher consciousness.

In moments when what you perceive from higher consciousness can be somewhat sensed/felt in your conscious mind, that's when intuition occurs. We call it hunches, gut feelings, inner knowing, or even Divine Intervention. Not all thoughts from higher source are sensed however.

We live in a world of distractions. There are many random thoughts going on. How do you know it's your intuition v.s. wishful thinking, daydreaming, or simply nonsense?

Then comes meditation and channeling where you directly connect to higher consciousness to withdraw information purposefully. You can think of it as the ultimate intuition, where the information is so undeniably real. It is a natural phenomenon, an innate ability we all possess, which may require training to initiate from our socially trained blocking.

We chose to use this form of meditation, channeling, to create this fictional story.

When you think about it, when writers work on their masterpiece, they "drift" into a state of being where words can flow effortlessly. Sometimes the character within the story became live and even dictated their destiny. What do you think is happening?

There is a higher source for all information. Our mind establishes the connections to the "source" to withdraw that information and bring it forth to physical creation. We want to demonstrate this amazing ability of our mind in its barebones through writing of this book.

Not only the way this work was created was fascinating, this fictional story itself is equally captivating.

Mary's unusual love story was inspired by a real story where a famous American Hollywood actress fell in love with a much younger Chinese man, changing the lives for both of them.

The original story told was about a Chinese man named Chunping Li, a philanthropist in China, who inherited his vast wealth from his late wife, a late famous American actress 38 years older than him.

Even though Chunping Li allegedly never loved her back, this American celebrity actress loved him dearly. She brought him to America as her adopted son/lover and so began a secret love for over a decade. Right before she passed away, she married him so he could inherit her wealth. She had him vow to never reveal her true identity and also never marry again. Ironically, he became infertile. If this unlikely story is not destiny, I don't know what is.

From the point of view of this American celebrity, the love was genuine and deep. It's worth telling even though it's forever a mystery who she really was.

This is where we got our inspiration from. We simply made a decision to tune in to a fictional story of such nature through Charles Rappaport's meditation, and the words flew out automatically to dictate the story you are about to read from the viewpoint of an American actress.

I believe creation of any kind can be effortless, if you allow it.

We started our first meditation session in February 2018 and finished within two months. Each session lasted twenty to thirty minutes depending on how much time Charles could take from his lunch breaks. Most sessions were recorded with Charles sitting in his car in a parking lot outside his workplace, trying to avoid onlookers.

You can find out how we did it in this article (http://mindrealities.com/benefits-of-channeling/).

Mary's love is not a story of sensuality but one of tremendous healing. She went from fear and self-doubt to trusting and embracing this unusual relationship, eventually seeing it as her destiny.

Embark on this journey with Mary as she tells her story of love that transcends everything.

INTRODUCTION

Can we know that love spans time?

Can we know where love comes from?

It's not for us to judge to whom and where this happens—it's only for us to accept and embrace love.

I used to have everything—money, fame, possessions... You name it. However, the end result was that I was miserable. I just had a feeling of emptiness and I didn't know what caused it.

I didn't set out to understand what love meant, but, somehow, *it found me*. I couldn't do anything but embrace it.

Love conquers everything, and soon you will know why and how this happened to me.

Many thought I was a fool.

Many thought I wasn't able to give love the way I needed to receive it back.

They were wrong.

This was, indeed, the love I had been searching for all my life. And those people needed to understand. If they couldn't, so be it. But I truly had that love.

When you read my story, you will see it went beyond time and space. I know this may sound foolish when you read this, but it did happen to me.

I can begin the story way back when I was a child and first did acting, and you will see that throughout my life I never had a need or want; I had it all. And yet I missed the very thing I needed.

Have you ever felt you were not complete? Not whole?

Is there anything missing or gnawing at you?

I bet there was. At least once.

For me, it was that elusive love.

I had searched for it through the pleasure of others and monetary possessions.

And yet, I never felt either complete or whole.

People would come to me and say, "Why? Don't you have it all? I mean, look at you. You have every acting job in the world. You have many men, you have many possessions, you have many things, and yet you are miserable."

I didn't disagree.

They were right, but I didn't know why.

I tried to suppress everything. I tried to bury everything. I tried to do it again and again. And yet, every time I did, I felt the misery increase, as if the Universe was telling me I was missing the very thing in life that I didn't know I was.

This is my story. The story that began many moons ago. The story that ended up spanning space and time. The story that eventually led to happiness, which I'm sure no one would ever understand.

Not even me.

Yet I finally felt complete. Whole. I was able to move on in my life and live the last little bits of it in peace.

If you think you know my story, think again. Because maybe you don't know all of it. If you knew what was missing and what completed it, I bet you'd be surprised.

Hear my story and understand, and you will be fascinated. You will be riveted. You will think this wasn't real.

But I tell you that it was.

It was more real than a pair of booted feet stepping upon the earth. It was more real than the air you breathe, and it was more real than anything you've ever felt.

Are you ready?

Here's my story.

CHAPTER 1
Making Our Way to Hollywood

My story happened in the most unlikely of circumstances.

It started when I was a child and ended with happiness attained before I died. I remember the moment before closing my eyes, saying this was the most unlikely story that had ever happened, yet I wouldn't trade it for anything else in the world.

In order to know how I got there you must know how it began.

You see, I came from a family and a life of means. I was an actress in Hollywood.

I was born in 1911. When I was a child growing up in Texas in the 1910s, my parents were hard-working people. They made their lives in Hollywood, but it wasn't what you think.

They were not actors or movie producers. They were working on the sets of Hollywood's most famous films.

If you have ever seen a film starring the Hollywood greats of yesterday—like Cary Grant— the set was probably built by my father.

You see, Hollywood needed set designers to make things to come to life. It was the set designers and costume designers that made the movies so real. I grew up in that era.

My father, Patrick Maddin, was tall and strong, with silver hair and brown eyes. He was very kind and always loving toward my mother and me. He started off as a carpenter, learning from his father who came to America from Poland. His father taught him to be a carpenter capable of building anything. My grandfather was a kind man. I remember him so well.

My grandmother was a tough one, always very serious. But the reality was she was just trying to protect our family. From what I never exactly knew, but I did know that she was always there, trying to be the rock.

My grandfather worked very hard, and he taught my father well. My father really could build anything. Our family moved to California when I was nine years old because my dad wanted to seek better job opportunities. One day he saw an ad for Hollywood set design, and he answered it.

He told my mother, "It could be good money. It's a lucrative job and we could use the income."

He went for the interview. The movie producer, whose name was Mr. Jones, looked at him. "Tell me sir, what can you build? Why should I pick you? I got ten other men here today who want the job just as much as you do."

"Well, sir, I need the job because I want to provide for my family. And well, if you tell me to build something I can probably have it for you by tomorrow."

"That's pretty funny."

My father said, "No, I'm serious."

"All right, big talker. I want a Hollywood backdrop like I'm in a forest. If you build it by tomorrow, kid, you get the job. If you don't, don't bother coming back."

My father simply said, "See you tomorrow!" and walked out with a smile.

I don't think he ever told my mother what he did. He didn't tell me until many years later. All he said to my mother was, "I've got to work hard tonight. I'm not coming home. I got to get this done. If I get this done, I get the job. If I get this job I get paid. This is a really good paying job for us."

My mother, being the great wife she was, said, "Okay, honey. What can I get you?"

"Nothing. Just let me get to work."

So he went and he built the set.

By the time my father was done he built the most amazing scene you've ever seen, and he built it in his factory. It was a grassy path with majestic trees on either side. It was as if you were walking down the path in a forest. It looked so real.

He called Mr. Jones. "Mr. Jones, guess what? The set is ready."

"Yeah, right," Mr. Jones scoffed.

"Here's the thing—you've got to come to my factory."

"Kid, you better not be pulling my leg."

After Mr. Jones looked at the set, he said, "You know what I think, kid? I think you didn't build that—you always had it."

"Of course it was me. I built it as you requested."

Mr. Jones paused for a minute. "All right then," he said. "You got the job! We need a small budget set." He gave my father all the details. "We need it in two weeks."

"You'll get it in two days."

Mr. Jones shook his head. "Are you kidding? We don't need it in two days. You just build it right and build it well. We will take from there."

That's how my father got started in Hollywood.

My mother was of Irish descent. She had a beautiful oval face, with blond hair and fair skin with a few freckles. Pretty looks aside, she was strict. She was the parent who disciplined me while my father always treated me like an angel.

My mother was a costume designer. She didn't have any aspirations for that kind of work at the start. She became a seamstress because we needed to have clothing, and it was cheaper to make our own.

My mother bought material and made such beautiful things. She made everyday clothing and formal dresses. She loved to learn new skills. She became good at making dresses with different materials and fabric—cotton, silk, and many more. She loved to explore different patterns, colors, and designs and she was good at it.

I loved wearing her stuff, it was so amazing. I was a lucky kid whose clothing was admired in school.

My mother often used to go to a nearby clothing store where she observed the latest and trendiest designs. She became good friends with Mrs. Cindy, the owner.

One day Mrs. Cindy said, "Margaret, you make such amazing things. Why don't you sell some of them to us?"

My mother shook her head. She had never thought of selling her dresses. "I don't know… I don't know about my stuff."

"Just try it. Don't be humble. You are really good at it. People will love your stuff!"

So, my mother decided to try it.

Guess what? The customers really liked it!

Her designs started to sell. One day a Hollywood actress named Virginia walked in and asked whose dresses they were.

Mrs. Cindy simply said, "Well, I'm the one who *sells* them."

"I know," Virginia replied, "but who *makes* them?"

"A friend of mine. Her name is Margaret Maddin."

"Well, I have to meet her."

So Mrs. Cindy introduced Virginia to my mother. Virginia said, "You must make me some dresses."

My mother shook her head. "I can't do that. You're a Hollywood actress."

"You simply have to do it. I really love your designs!"

When Virginia got the dress my mother made for her she was awed.

Soon other actresses and movie producers saw the dress and said, "Wow! Who makes that snazzy stuff?"

At first Virginia didn't want to tell them because she didn't want to lose her secret seamstress, but then she realized she may soon change her style and have nothing for my mom to work on anyway. She said to my mother, "Hey, Margaret. I got this opportunity for you and you simply *have to* take it. It's such an amazing thing. If you do it, you may even be able to become a Hollywood actress yourself someday."

My mother said, "No, I wouldn't. I wouldn't want to."

"Suit yourself. But at least go make their costumes."

"Sure. I could do that, because we sure could use the money."

Soon after, my mother started making dresses for all the Hollywood actresses and for other people with a good reputation in the industry.

The industry communicates within itself. Reputation is everything. Once you became somebody, you were gold. That's how my mother got started as a dresser in Hollywood.

She made whatever the cast needed because they knew she was amazing and could do it. That's how my mother got her start.

Which is how I got *my* start.

Once my father and mother were both in Hollywood the money they made was good. We lived a decent life in California.

They worked incredibly long hours. People don't realize what goes into making a Hollywood movie. They think Hollywood actors just show up and *vroom*—it's there. That's not how it works. For writers, set designers, costumes designers, and the rest, there is so much more than what you realize. But my parents worked hard, and they made good money.

I was a beautiful kid, with light brown curly hair. My eyebrows were always trimmed thin and curvy to show off my eyes. I was always secure and happy. I loved to talk to different people. Being the only child in a nurturing family, I always thought I could achieve anything I set my mind to.

Being exposed to Hollywood in my early teens, I was inspired and a little starstruck by the actresses I saw. I wanted to be one. I wanted my name to mean something like those big-name actresses' did.

My parents didn't think it was a good idea, but they'd never wanted to discourage me from doing something I was passionate about. They always inspired me to reach out for my dreams like my life depended on it. So my mother and my father allowed me to get into becoming an actress even though they rejected the idea at the start.

I didn't know how I would get my break, but I practiced lines from different screenplays all the time. I'd see the actresses on-screen and tried to act like they did.

To me, it was all about becoming an actress. It was the most important thing in my life and I'd do anything to get there.

Eventually, a guy named Robert, an admittedly smallish producer, was looking for an extra. It was a backup situation in those days. In case someone forgot their lines, they needed someone to help.

We didn't have teleprompters, although they would have been as helpful then as they are now. Back then people would help an actor memorize their lines. Funny, the way the world once was, though it seemed to work.

So, back to being an extra and getting my big break.

How'd it happen, you ask?

Well, the actress for whom I was the backup, Irene, was pretty drunk on set.

The fact is, in those days, *everybody* had a vice. Sometimes they were drunks, sometimes they were gamblers, sometimes they were drug-users, sometimes they were things beyond your imagination.

Irene, she loved to drink. She would come in and forget her lines all the time. But she was so famous everybody wanted to know what her line was. They needed to keep her around, so Robert said, "Anybody love to be the extra today?"

Usually people were lined up, but for some reason that day it was quiet. I knew this was my chance, so I raised my hand and said, "I will be the extra. I can do it."

"You're pretty young, kid," said Robert.

"When I say I can do it, I can."

Robert, surprised by my confidence, said, "Let me test you out."

I memorized all the lines. Once Robert and his crew were done testing me they said, "Oh, this little kid could really do it! She's got it!"

Like father, like daughter. And that's how I ended up being a movie extra.

Irene forgot so many lines it was pathetic. But guess what? It helped me.

Robert liked the way I spoke, the way I acted, and the way I helped. "Kid, I'll give you an extra position for my next film."

"I'll do anything you need, just give me the line."

"All right, kid, in my next movie you'll get one line, *if* you can do it. The line is, 'Can you help this guy?' You're going to be a lady who works at a hotel."

"You got it!"

Once I made the most of that one little line Robert put me in another movie where I had several of them. From there I started getting bigger roles with more and more lines. Other movie producers started noticing me, leading to even bigger roles from bigger, better producers. I wasn't picky, so I accepted any type of movie, ranging from romances to the ones they made for kids.

I was building quite the résumé. I wanted to attract movie producers with a broader range of interests so I could keep getting cast in all sorts of films. Films were everything then. I really wanted to get my name out there, so I would take any and all opportunities that came my way.

And that's how my introduction to Hollywood began.

And how did I meet the man of my dreams?

That's the next part of the story.

CHAPTER 2
A Chance Introduction

I made seventeen movies in the next several years and by the time I was twenty I was a reasonably well-known Hollywood actress.

At twenty, I was living the high life in California, where I was well connected in the film industry. It was then that a big producer named James approached me. "This is your chance to go to the next level," he said. James was a stocky guy who always seemed so confident. He had many connections in Hollywood.

I laughed. "Next level? I make so many movies I get to turn down some roles. What do you mean next level?"

"You get a chance to travel and make an overseas film."

"I don't need to go. Hollywood has everything I need. I have twenty scripts on my desk I can choose from. Producers don't tell me what movie to be in, I tell them. I'm so popular I could go anywhere I wanted." I raised my eyebrows with pride.

I had never thought about going overseas. I never felt the need. I had so much money at my disposal I didn't need to go out of my way.

But I decided to listen to James. Something inside me said if I did it would be for my benefit. I didn't know why at the time.

Eventually I told James, "Okay. Let me read the script."

"It's called *Dreams in the Orient*. A Western traveler meets a handsome gentleman in China. They develop a relationship, but it doesn't work out because of cultural differences."

I was awed and overwhelmed. A romance film with an Asian guy? It wasn't the type of story I sought out. After all, I was someone rooted in the Western culture who gave little thought of the Orient.

"Okay," I said, playing it cool. "Sounds interesting, but how can it benefit my career in America?" I gave a quick bark of laughter.

James continued his pitch. "You see, if you want to be something special you have to be willing to show them you can do anything. When you go overseas you show them you can play in a movie anywhere. That's when all the top-shelf offers will come in."

I didn't necessarily agree with him, but I said, "Okay. I'll travel."

Then I talked to my parents and asked them if they thought it was a good idea. I still thought their input was important in my life.

My parents weren't thrilled. While my mother was typically the one giving out discipline and advice, this time she was silent. My father, always so protective, let out a sigh. "Mary, you are still young, and you have large room to grow here. Why go to China?"

"Why not?" I asked.

"Because you have everything you need right here."

"I know that, but something keeps calling me to go. I feel like it's destiny. Like it's my fate to seize this opportunity."

There was silence for a while. I could feel that part of the reason they didn't want me to go overseas was because they still thought I was a child and since I was their only child they wanted me to stay around them as long as possible, even if they didn't agree with me being an actress. They were shocked that I was talking about my feelings of going on this trip being my destiny.

Also, I would have to go overseas for at least three months, and that was a long time. It was the 1930s, and travel by ship and going overseas in their minds was unpredictable and I am sure they felt frightened.

After a long pause and a lot of sighing, my mother said, "Then go and follow your dreams."

My father shook his head. "Do what you need to."

My mother wished me well.

I began packing and asked James how long I had.

"About two weeks."

I prepared myself as if I was going away forever.

Betty was a sweet girl around my age who lived near me in Hollywood. Since we were close I told her where I was headed.

"Whoa! China! That's a long way away!" Her eyes went wide, filled with excitement.

"Yeah, this is either going to make me or break me," I joked. "I'm going to come back like a really powerful Hollywood star, or just another girl trying to make it in a big, unfriendly place."

"I understand. I wish you well," she said softly.

"Thank you. I have a feeling that this will change my life."

Little did I know just how right I was. It would change my life forever.

When you are young in Hollywood, with a lot of money, a lot of fame, most people didn't know what they really want. They are either depressed, drinking or doing who knows what.

What I soon found was that I was missing love.

I dated a lot of men, but I never found anybody right. My longest relationship probably lasted a month, and even that was fake.

I dated one guy who was in and out of my life. I called it a casual romance. It never seemed to last for long. We never could be serious.

Another time I was dating a movie writer named Steve. He knew the Hollywood game and so did I. Neither of us really took it seriously. We'd go out, we'd spend time together.

We talked about a lot, but never about a life together. We never talked about what we wanted or having a family or our future. We just enjoyed each other's company and let the chemistry run its course until the physical attraction was gone.

There was no man in my life to make me think, "Well, maybe I should stay." So, when the opportunity came to go overseas, it was natural that I said yes, despite initial doubt.

I packed up, readying myself to say goodbye to my parents, Betty, and a few others I thought were important.

Then, when I thought about it, I realized there weren't many at all.

You see, everyone in Hollywood calls the town a fake and you know what? I would really agree with them, because the reality was you would go over to somebody, hug them and kiss them on the cheek or whatever, pretend you knew them and say, "Oh, I know this one. Yeah, I met that one," but the reality was there wasn't anybody to say goodbye *to*. My parents, my friend Betty, and maybe my agent Mike. That was really it.

Mike had been my agent since I first started acting. He was a typical agent, always looking to get the most bang for the buck. Agents took ten percent of your salary. I guess they got paid on volume because Mike was always shoving another script down my throat. It didn't matter if it was good or bad. It didn't matter if it made sense or not, he was always chasing a script. Maybe the agents were afraid that the producers would stop sending them business. Maybe they thought if they said "No" the producers would send the scripts to other clients.

Even though Mike was a workaholic he didn't push his clients as much as most of the other agents. However, he was willing to kick butt whenever he felt it was necessary. He did it in a friendly way though, and I liked him being so frank. He was someone I could trust in untrustworthy Hollywood.

So, I got on the boat. I was booked a first-class suite. In those days the boat took a while. You got to get through different countries and make pit stops. There was no direct flight or direct anything.

It was a two-month journey to get there. Stay three months and two months coming back. That's over half a year right there.

I saw different countries along the way including South Africa, Singapore, and Hong Kong. We made stops, some for days, some for a couple of weeks. It was very pretty and very inspiring, places that I'd go back to again.

Finally, we got to Shanghai, China and I prepared to get off the boat. The landscape and people were so foreign. There weren't a lot of wooden houses. They were all made out of brick. Houses had walls surrounding them in a square, boxing them in. Men and women wore long dresses. Women had their long hair braided. I felt that everything had to be straight, squared, or something that resembled order. I felt kind of out of place. It took me a little while to get used to my new environment.

Waiting at the dock were the producer, the set agent, all of the helpers, and some of the cast. The entire crew looked not very big, but who was I to question? As I got off the boat though, I did wonder about it.

I went over to the overseas producer, William, and said, "Hey William—tell me something. For a movie that is going to last three months this doesn't seem like much of a cast and crew."

William turned with a grin. "Kid, guess what? There is more to the cast than meets the eye. There are a lot of men, many of whom are locals."

"Okay, William. Sounds good. I'm sure you know what you're doing."

We went and made the film. Starting on day one.

I put all my effort into the movie. All my effort into the set. All my effort into my lines.

The director was a snob. He would yell out loud if you made mistakes. But for Hollywood that wasn't surprising. I had met plenty worse than him. I saw right away he'd be difficult to work with, but I knew my lines and I knew my role, and I knew my job, so I did it well. As long as he did what he was supposed to do, no one really questioned it.

On the third day of filming *Dreams in the Orient*, a young man I'd never seen before walked onto the set. A very handsome man. I was instantly shocked by how handsome he was.

He had a square face with pitch black hair and very thick eyebrows. His black eyes radiated friendly warmth and he was always smiling. I loved how cheery he looked. And it wasn't just me—everyone around him would be instantly boosted to a better mood.

He was local, I assumed. Bringing him over to meet me, the director said, "This man is going to be filmed in the scene. The scene is going to be about you coming to a wine vineyard and he'll be the man to show you around."

I could feel my heart beating faster with excitement. "All right, Mr. Director. I know the scene you mean. I memorized my lines. I didn't know who the man was going to be to show me around, so now I guess I know."

I turned to the new guy and said, "Hello there. What's your name?"

"My name is Ming. What's yours?" he replied with a genuine smile.

"Mary Maddin."

"Nice to meet you."

I smiled. "You as well."

We hit it off well, and our working together was very pleasant. I walked away after the director's final shout "Cut!", thinking that Ming was someone like I had never seen before, someone I had never imagined.

I don't know if it was because he wasn't the Hollywood type. I don't know if it was because he was mysterious and Asian. All I remember is that I just felt drawn to him.

I felt so drawn and yet so far. I felt I wanted to get closer to him and get to know everything about him. I was eager to learn more about him. But at the same time, he seemed so foreign and mysterious that I felt I could never understand him.

I knew in my heart it was something very different. Something I had not experienced before. During the day, I was too focused on my role to notice what I was feeling, but I thought about it after I went home for the night.

Three months of shooting flew by fast. When I was done filming, I went to Ming and said, "It was a pleasure working with you. I don't say that to many actors. I find them to be very self-absorbed."

Ming smiled. "I had done local roles in my country, but nothing like this. I found working with you to be a very eye-opening experience."

I sighed. "Yeah, me too. I wish I could stay longer."

His eyes lit up with joy. "That would be very pleasant for me too."

But it wasn't meant to be. Little did I know, this would only be an introduction to a love that would happen much later in my life.

I got back on the boat. I knew something had changed but didn't know what. I thought about it often at night as I lay in bed on the boat.

When I got home my parents were excited to see me. They gave me a big hug and said, "I'm glad you made it back!"

I shrugged. "I hope the film came out well, because in the end it was a long trip, so many months away. Hopefully, it was worth it."

My parents were simply too excited to see me back to care much about how the film would pan out. To them, me coming back safe and sound from China was the biggest deal.

I went home to my apartment to sleep. I was forever changed.

I went to see my agent Mike in his office the following morning.

Mike asked me how *Dreams in the Orient* had gone, to which I said, "I hope it went well."

Mike raised his eyebrows. "So many roles have popped up since you've been gone, I think you should start on something right away."

"You know what? I think I need a break." I let out a deep sigh to show him I was serious.

Mike shook his head and laughed. "Kid, you're twenty-one. Most actresses go like mad until about thirty. If you think you're going to be able to go on forever, I'd be shocked."

I shrugged. "Don't be. I think I will. As of now, I'm pretty good." I was young and ultra-confident in my career.

"All right, kid. I guess it's up to you." Mike said matter-of-factly.

"I don't need much of a break. Maybe a month. You can give me the scripts to go through in the meantime. I'll let you know what I think about them."

He handed me the scripts and said, "All right, kid—but don't take too long. I need to get back to these producers. You know how they are."

I winked. "Yeah, I know how they are, trust me."

I don't know what Mike was thinking, but I know one thing. Some of the roles I read were ridiculous. There was one about being a banana salesman.

I couldn't stop laughing. "Are you kidding me? After all the films I was in? A banana salesman?"

"Look, kid, I just got the script," Mike protested. "I know that it's ridiculous. I tried my best not to give you the bad ones, but hey—there's a big producer working this banana idea, and you want to stay on his good side."

I remember laughing and saying, "I don't know where his good side is, but if he thinks that this is the role I should be in then I don't want to know. You can tell him from me not to bother sending another script."

I don't think that was what Mike told him, but I know I didn't take that role. Smart.

Anyway, I went through the scripts and it was amazing. Some of them were really good. Some of them were definitely bad. I picked the three that made the most sense. One was about love, time, and destiny in the Orient.

The minute I read it I got wrapped into the script because I thought back to what I had seen when I was in China. That this man I met named Ming was amazing, but I could never say why.

I only saw one problem. The script was way too long. I thought, *Man, this movie is going to be four hours long. There is no way we could make it.*

I am going to have to cut that down to an hour and a half. Anything more people will never get to see it. They'll be bored enough to cry.

I read it over and over.

I went back to my agent four weeks later. "Mike, this is the script I want to do."

"Why? What about the other eleven I sent you?" Mike raised his eyebrows.

"Only three were really good. This one specially. It really caught my eye."

"You got a thing for the Orient now, don't you?" Mike grinned.

I knew Mike was teasing me. He liked to spice things up. I laughed. "Well, maybe I do, maybe I don't. I don't know. What I do know is that this script makes sense."

"Yeah, it's funny. This producer is new," Mike said, "But he's getting a lot of attention. We got to get in good graces with him, Mary."

"You're my best friend, Mike!"

"Your what? I don't think best friends could have sent what I send you!" he said. "The producer likes your work, your attitude—especially that you went overseas. You would be a great fit for his new role. I'll send him over your stuff."

"All right, let's do this. I'm in!" I felt like I wanted to jump up and down with joy.

About a week later, we found ourselves sitting in a studio office in front of the producer, whose name was John. He had just finished a shooting session when we met him. John was in his late twenties. He had long brown hair and a neatly trimmed beard. He seemed good-tempered and very knowledgeable, despite being young.

After we greeted each other, John smiled. "Mary, you are the gal I need for this film!"

He looked so friendly anyone would feel comfortable around him. I laughed. "Really? Why is that?"

"Because I'm making a movie called *The Man's Fortune*. It's about this Asian guy who comes to America. He's a humble worker from a poor family who meets this rich American girl, and you are the girl. This is going to be a love story."

"All right, John. I'm game." I paused and then asked, "Does it pay well?"

"It pays outstanding, but it's not about the money."

"Oh, it's about the money." I nodded and said, "It's about the money and the story, but it's always about the money, don't ever forget that. I know you're young. I've made a million films. I haven't met an actor or actress yet that is not about the money. Just remember that going forward and you'll be fine."

John laughed, though he was probably shocked by the way I talked. I doubted he had ever had anyone speaking to him as frank as I was. "That's why I like you, Mary—you're direct."

"Hey, you learn to be direct in a hurry in Hollywood," I said with a grin. "You don't get anywhere by *not* doing it. You know, you got to kiss people's butts, but you also got to know when to be direct. I learned it all."

"All right, then. I'm game if you are," John said excitedly.

After about two weeks of filming for *The Man's Fortune*, I realized the story really was great. I thought it should have been played by somebody older, but like I said I liked the story a lot. The man opposite me was an Asian named Wei.

Wei was a pretty good guy, but for some reason I never felt the same way I did with Ming. He was a nice enough fella, a pretty good actor who'd been in quite a few roles. We hit it off well. In fact, we even dated a couple of times outside the set, but it never was the same.

I don't know why. I tried to make it the same, but I just didn't feel it. I don't know if he did. He never talked about it. A couple of times on a date it felt like we were really hitting it off. You know, we even slept together now and again, but at the end of the day, it just wasn't there. I finished the film and left.

In the meantime, the film I made in China, *Dreams in the Orient,* was coming out in theaters. I went to see my agent, "Mike, what do you think?"

He winked. "It's going to be a hit. As if you didn't know it."

"All right, Mike. Maybe yes, maybe no. I have no idea."

Turns out we were right. Everybody wanted to see it.

From there, I got an offer from Broadway. I had never done Broadway—I'd never even seen it—but a big New York producer called and said, "I got a part for you."

Something you should know. In those days, Broadway paid well. If you could show them you could do Broadway, you could do anything, and people were really interested when you had connections to the big-name, famous Broadway producers.

I went and told my parents I was going to New York. They were concerned and said, "Are you leaving Hollywood?"

"Only for a while, maybe a month or two. It's not like I'm going to China."

"All right, you do what you have to."

"Yeah, I love to sing, I love to dance, I love to act, I love to do it all." I was such a character I wasn't afraid of anything and loved to try new things.

So, the next phase of my life was going over to Broadway—the next stop on my story.

CHAPTER 3
Off to Broadway We Go

I took trains to Broadway. I could have flown, but the planes were kind of new back then. I was a big star, I could have done anything I wanted to, but I decided I wanted to see the country.

I had been to China, to Alabama when I was a child, to Hollywood, but I never really saw the country and I decided to make a trip out of it.

I went a little early. Rehearsals were still a month away. I wanted to cross by train, which would take two weeks. I made a few stops in a couple of cities along the way. I stopped in Ohio and in Pennsylvania. I felt like it was a nice time to see everything.

I met some people there, some men even. I kept on searching for love, all the while secretly afraid it was never going to appear.

I eventually got to the coast. New York City was so big and bright! It was amazing. It was the biggest thing I had ever seen. I mean Hollywood was big, but Hollywood was also spread out. New York City, especially Manhattan, was something all its own. Full of tall buildings and bright lights—so many people in such a tiny place.

There were skyscrapers everywhere. The fancy hotels, restaurants, the shops, the streets, the bridges were bustling with traffic. People seemed so busy and on the go. *All the time.* It was inspiring and mind-blowing, and it showed you what really being rich entails.

Wow, I said to myself, *I could learn to fall in love here.* I don't know if I said it to fall in love with a man, or fall in love with the place.

I went to meet the producer of the Broadway play, whose name was Richard. Richard was in his mid-fifties with a large frame and stern face. I wasn't sure if he had ever smiled, or if he ever cared about making people comfortable around him.

I said, "Here I am."

Richard looked me over and handed me a pile of documents. "Good for you! I'm glad you finally made it. Here are your lines. We begin production training tomorrow. Don't be late."

"Is that your standard greeting for someone like me? Who just came all this way?" I tilted my head.

"Kid, if I had to greet every person who came through here, I'd never get anything done," Richard said impatiently. "So, this is my way of saying hello. Now, memorize your lines." He handed me a piece of paper with information written on it. "Here's the place you'll be staying. The man who will be taking you there is waiting outside. Make sure to memorize your lines. You'll do a great job and I am sure you'll be on your way."

I shook my head at him, took the paper, and left.

The driver, a man named Harry, was a nice old man. He had rough skin and gray hair with beautiful green eyes. He seemed so tired, but he was very calm and knew Manhattan well. "First time in New York City, kid?"

"Yeah, first time."

"Hey! Let me show you around."

"No, I have to go home. There will be time for that later." I waved my hand. "I have to memorize my lines."

"You sure?"

"Yeah, if I get it wrong the producer will kill me."

Harry laughed. "Actually, I have worked with Richard for many years. He is a bit of know-it-all, real serious dude, but down deep inside he's a good person."

"A good person? I don't know. I have to memorize my lines, or I'll be in big trouble."

"All right, off to your apartment we go."

He pulled up to a luxury apartment building. The building was fenced in and a bit secluded from the outside traffic and noise. There were seven floors in a semi-circle with a large fountain in front of the entrance. There was a circular driveway before the doorway where a uniformed doorman greeted everyone who entered the building. People going in were all nicely dressed; they seemed important.

"I'm not staying in a hotel?"

"No, this is cheaper, but don't worry—it's top-of-the-line. Doorman, elevator, plush apartment, beautiful chairs, comfortable couch. You are going to love it," Harry said. "Let me help you with your stuff."

"All right."

I had a couple of suitcases, nothing too fancy. We took it upstairs through the elevator and off we went.

Next thing I knew, I was sitting on the couch with a bunch of lines to memorize. Broadway plays are not like being in Hollywood. In Hollywood you got a script that was easy. Slug line here, dialogue there. It was easier to read.

On Broadway, you had to memorize the lines for sure, but don't forget there was also song and dance. I had signed up for a musical, a musical by Broadway standards.

With music you got to practice. Not only did you have lines, but you had to dance. So, you have to memorize the lines and when to dance, and when to move, and when to stop. It was something I hadn't done before, though I had always wanted to dance.

I started to memorize my lines and shook my head with each step. It got me to another level. *Oh, this must be when you dance, this must be when you sing.* But either way I focused on my lines and did the best I could.

Next morning, Harry arrived early and met me in the lobby. He leaned forward. "Good morning, Mary. You ready?"

"Ready? I don't know if I'm going to do a great job with this; I've never done it."

"Listen. Throughout the years, many people who knew less than you came through this place. They did great. You're a professional actress. You can do even better than them."

I smiled and said, "Thank you. I appreciate that."

"Hey, I just tell it like it is."

While we were in the car I kept memorizing my lines and we finally pulled up. Richard looked at me. "Hey. Did you memorize your lines last night?"

I nodded. "The best I could."

"This best of yours better be good enough, because 'A Connecticut Yankee' is one of Richard Rodgers and Lorenz Hart's Broadway hits."

"All right," I said. "I'm game."

"No, you are not game. You've got to get it done," he said. "I hired you because you are a professional actress. I said I'm going to get a big person for this part. The director said we want the best and I said I'm giving you the best. So, kid, you better produce."

I thought, *At least in his eyes I'm a star.* Out loud I said, "Hey…"

I don't know what I said after that. I went out and I saw the set—and it was big! I'd never seen anything like it in Hollywood. I had seen big sets, but I hadn't seen anything like the one for a Broadway play.

So many cast members, and so many costumes.

"Go on and get the costume," Richard said.

While I changed, a costumer helped me. I had been in many costumes before on Hollywood sets. I don't know why, but this felt different.

Richard motioned me to go forward. "There you go, kid."

"All right, then. Let's start," I said confidently even though my hands were sweating. As I finished dressing, I noticed the leading man—another Asian. I murmured, "This has to be a coincidence, right?"

Richard asked, "What are you talking about?"

"Never mind. I'm talking to myself."

Richard told me that his name was Fanyu. Since we were still waiting for everybody to arrive, I decided it was a good opportunity to approach him. I walked closer, looked into his eyes and said cordially, "Nice to meet you, Fanyu."

"Likewise."

I whispered, "I feel like I know you from somewhere."

He smiled, leaned back a little and said, "Not that I know of."

I felt Asian guys had their stereotypical traits and it was hard for me to tell the subtleties. Perhaps Fanyu reminded me of Ming. I didn't want to raise his suspicion that I was judging, so I took a step back. "All right."

The rest of the cast circled around me and introduced themselves. They all made some light introductions and had a laugh.

Giving them my biggest Hollywood smile, I shouted, "Let's begin!"

"All right, then. Let's do this!" Fanyu yelled.

I read my lines and he read his. The director waved us over and said, "Hey! This is when we dance. We are going to learn some dance moves."

So, he taught me the day's dance moves. All I can say is, I really tried my best.

The director shook his head. "You made a few mistakes, kid, but for the first time learning dance you were doing pretty good. You are going to have to learn how to make your lines with the dancing."

I frowned. "I've never done it before."

"I know. That's why we are going to have to do it in stages—you are going have to do the dance separately, and then the lines." The director was being very patient with me, which I appreciated.

Eventually, I got it right. I practiced and practiced, day after day.

Fanyu and I practiced so often, you would have thought I was a regular dancer. I was not in any way a *real* dancer, but I kept on dancing anyway.

The show was a great big hit on Broadway, and so were Fanyu and I. I was ever more of a star. Important people invited me to all of the city's most fabulous events and parties.

I never thought of myself as a party girl, even though in Hollywood I went to them all. And the events—Oscars, Golden Globes—you name it, I was probably part of it.

Yet, in New York, it was a lot different. I found myself at more and more parties. Maybe because I was so lonely.

I tried dating, but nothing seemed to work. I told myself I was happy when I wasn't. Every party brought me the opportunity to distract myself from my sadness. I just couldn't meet anybody who made me feel special and whole. Every time I thought I could get closer to happiness, but I never did.

The play had been running to sold-out houses and rave reviews for two months when I decided to talk to Richard.

"I'm miserable. I want to go back to Hollywood."

His eyebrows began to rise until they actually curved, nearly touching in the center of his forehead. "Kid, this play is the best thing that's ever happened to us."

"I know, but I'm miserable." I kept my head down to avoid eye contact.

"Well, then… I'm going to keep it going and replace you. But I'm going to need some time."

"Do what you have to, but I've got to go home," I said with relief.

I tried my best to be patient, but after another month I just couldn't do it. So Richard made the switch. On the drive back to my apartment I said to Harry, "I need to tell you something, I'm going home tomorrow."

"I know." Harry nodded with sympathy.

"You're not upset?"

"I'll miss you, Mary. You're kind of fun to drive around with, but I understand."

"Tell me… do you know many people like me who are so completely miserable?"

"I've met plenty that are more miserable than you. They thought they weren't, but really they were," he said. "You can really act, you got it together. But at the end of the day, I don't know what it is, but you just didn't feel right here. Tell me if I'm wrong."

"No, of course you're not. You are far from it. I don't know why I don't like it here."

"Hey! Each of us has to do what we got to do to make ourselves feel special and whole," Harry said.

The next day I was on a train back home. I didn't know why, but I felt like it would make me whole. I asked myself, "What's going on with my life?"

I went to Hollywood, I went to the Orient, I knocked them dead on Broadway, but I never felt complete. I didn't know why, but New York wasn't the answer.

Maybe this Hollywood thing wasn't for me. Maybe something in my life was completely void and completely not whole.

From there I went to my agent, Mike, and said, "All right, I did the Broadway thing. Now what?"

"You tell me, Mary. I got another twenty scripts that have your name on them. You want to do it all again?"

I shrugged. "I don't know about that, but I've got to do the thing that I know best."

He paused and stared at me. "Tell me something, Mary. Are you happy?"

"No." I didn't even hesitate to answer. After a short pause, I asked, "Who is happy in Hollywood?"

Mike shook his head. "I don't know, perhaps no one. But you can keep going through life like this or you can find out."

"No time for that, Mike. I'm just going to keep on going."

"All right, kid." Mike handed me a pile of scripts. "Get reading and let me know what you like."

I took a deep breath in and out. "All right, then, that's what I'm going to do."

I felt like I was drifting without touching the ground. I felt like I was screaming inside a sound-proof enclosure where nobody could hear me, eventually not even myself. I felt tremendous pain and totally numb. I felt something was missing in my life, but I just couldn't find out what it was. I couldn't find happiness in my possessions nor the countless men I dated. At the same time, I felt helpless.

There seemed to be nothing else for me but my acting jobs, which distracted me from my pain without curing it.

CHAPTER 4
Acting in My Marriage

I kept reviewing scripts and they kept on coming in. Script after script, movie after movie. I probably could have done this for another twenty-five years, but eventually something inside told me I had to start a family. Like every gal and guy out there, I knew that maybe that was the answer to why I was always so miserable.

I was looking desperately for the man of my dreams. I had been to many dances and formal events, looking for Mr. Right.

I was able to date any man I chose. So many dates through so many films. I dated actors, producers, and writers. They didn't give me what I searched for. On every date I thought I got closer to the love I wanted but I found myself further away.

There was a handsome man named Donald with whom I went out on a beautiful date. Donald was tall, with a muscular body. He was fun, outgoing, and very attractive. One time, we went to a busy restaurant. I could see everything, hear the conversations with him, but it was as if I was talking to someone who wasn't there.

"Donald, why is it that you don't have any interest in what I'm saying?"

He shook his head. "Honestly, Mary, I don't know, but I find you very attractive."

"Thank you, I appreciate that. But that's not all there is to me. There's so much more. There's my mind, my heart, and yet you don't pay attention."

Donald was quiet for a few moments. Then he said, "You're right. I didn't want you for those reasons. Perhaps we're not compatible."

I laughed and actually felt a bit relieved. I felt that he was shallow, and it was impossible to engage with him in any deep conversation. At least he admitted that we were not compatible. I smiled. "You're right. We aren't meant for each other." Then I got up and left.

There were many men like that, who didn't seem to care about who I really was. Men only interested in superficial things, like my looks or my money. I felt so disconnected with the men I dated, even the ones I had intimate relationships with. I almost gave up on romance.

Eventually, at the age of thirty-six, I settled.

I had to, because I wasn't getting any younger, and I felt with each passing year my options becoming more and more limited. I really wanted to settle and start a family. So I settled on a man I knew.

He was an agent. His name was Derek. I had met him at one of those parties. I thought he was cute enough to fit the part. Play the role. So, I dated and eventually married him.

We had one of those big fancy weddings the tabloids love to cover. My parents were so happy their girl was finally settling down.

And I did settle down, eventually having two kids, named Bobby and Bo.

We were still living the Hollywood lifestyle, even though we were parents.

Maybe we had less parties, but at the end of the day, we still went to a heck of a lot of them. Still dressed for the part, still looked the part, still acted the part. I acted even when I wasn't acting.

I was never happy at home. My husband wasn't either. I'm sure he had more than one affair while he was with me. I never did the same. It never felt right. I just thought that if you are married you might as well stay together.

Acting still made sense. I guess that was my way of dealing with things.

I focused on my family and my work. That's what kept me busy. Derek focused on meeting other women. I guess that was *his* job. We both had our jobs.

I never had a deep connection with Derek, nor him with me. But I stayed with him, so my children would have a family that wasn't broken. From the outside anyway.

But then, after twenty years, I finally had enough. The boys were old enough to make their own decisions. We both had enough money.

One day, I said to Derek, "I want out."

Derek didn't argue. "I'm surprised it took you so long."

"Tell me. How many was it?"

"I have no idea what you mean." He tried to play it cool but his eyes were wide.

"How many did you sleep with?"

"I don't know, Mary. I lost count after twenty." Derek grinned. I guess he was proud of what he'd done, and he reckoned there was no point keeping it a secret anymore.

We were finally done pretending.

"Really? That's kind of funny, because twenty is how many years I've wanted out of marriage and you can barely count to twenty." I laughed. "I guess I made the right decision."

"Hey, I would have left twenty years ago, except I didn't care," Derek said, his voice full of bitter retaliation. What a shame I stayed with this guy for twenty years! Twenty years that I couldn't get back.

"Me neither, Derek. I've been acting out the part."

"Me too," he replied.

This was probably the most honest conversation we had ever had. It's funny that it was about how much we both wanted it to end. We knew we didn't even hurt each other anymore by saying things this harshly and openly. I did feel relief, at least on some level. I was sure he did as well.

I asked him, "Who's going to tell the kids?"

"You're the actress. You do it." He nudged me.

"All right, then. I'll do it."

I went to the door and shouted for Bo and Bobby. They were home from college. I said, "Your father and I are getting a divorce."

They just looked at each other, rolled their eyes, and said, "Why'd it take you so long?"

"Tell me, boys, you knew?"

Bobby nudged Bo. He was so much like his father.

Bo nodded. "We didn't ask Dad what he did. We just knew if anyone is in Hollywood it's a matter of sooner or later. That's why we don't want anything to do with this business."

"You kids… it's funny. I never let it stop me, even though your grandparents said, 'Don't go to Hollywood, don't be an actress.' I never listened to them. Because I never listened, I guess I paid the price. You kids, though. You are going to listen. You're going to finish college."

I looked at Bobby and asked, "What do you want to do?"

"I want to be a doctor." His voice was filled with pride.

"Doctor? Not a bad profession." I turned to Bo. "And what about you? What do you want to do?"

"Well, I'm thinking engineering. I kind of like math."

"You do whatever you want," I said with relief. "Just don't go to Hollywood."

"Don't worry about that, Mom," Bo said. "We definitely never will."

They were true to their word. Neither of them did anything remotely related to Hollywood. At the end of the day maybe that is one of the best things that ever happened to me. My kids never went into the business.

Derek and I went in separate ways. He didn't ask for money, even though I could have paid him twenty times over. He made enough money as an agent he didn't even care. Besides, he knew he slept with so many women he'd never get a dime.

He moved out of the house and the truth is, I maybe saw him twice for the rest of my life. Go figure—a big Hollywood agent who I saw twice after being married to him for over twenty years.

The next few years of my life flew by fast through my fifties and into sixties. In my late sixties, the acting work was drying up. There were still jobs, but they weren't the same.

You see, in Hollywood, when you are young and pretty and beautiful and attractive that's when you make the most.

My agent was right. Mike said, "You only got about twenty good years, and then it goes." I lasted well into my fifties, so maybe I defied time, but eventually time caught up.

Oh, don't yell. I still had jobs.

I was the older grandmother. I was the wise old aunt. I was the old principal. You know the roles no one ever wanted? Those are the ones I took. The ugly roles! The roles that Hollywood has to cast because you've got to have the story. The roles that if you asked any Hollywood actress they would throw up before they would take it.

So why did I take them, you ask? If I had plenty of money, why would I stoop so low? Simple. I took them to keep busy. I had the wealth, but I was sad. Because I was miserable, I wanted to do something constantly with my life.

My kids were older, they were out of the house. They came by occasionally, but at the end of the day I was alone.

So, I kept going and this is where my story really began. The story of love. The story that transcended time. The story that made this book.

CHAPTER 5
A Chance Meeting

After my divorce I thought I'd given up on men.

Though I didn't do anything like become a nun, I thought all men just wanted one thing. I don't even have to name it. But I believe somewhere along the line that changed.

I used men at first, just like they used me. I reckoned, "Well, if I wasn't married and I slept with that many people I guess that was fair."

So, I just went out at an older age and flaunted my money.

I could have anyone I wanted. Being rich buys you a lot.

The boys thought I was nuts. I could tell they felt sorry for me. They said, "Mom has gone off the deep end."

They started to have their own lives, graduating from college, getting jobs and starting families and lives of their own.

They would visit poor old mom, but at the end of the day they really just wanted my money like everybody else.

At least that's what I believed.

I never told them that, because I knew as a mother I didn't want to mess things up with them. I'd seen too many Hollywood actresses who had children and somehow left them or worse. I didn't want to be one of those mothers.

For me it was about "keeping up the act." So, I would go and visit their families every Thanksgiving, Christmas, and all the other holidays. I would smile at their wives, pretending to be their best friends, even though we weren't.

Not even close.

I had four grandkids—two girls, Carol and Nancy, from Bo and two boys, Larry and Thomas, from Bobby. I held my grandkids; I did enjoy that one.

Holding my grandkids was special; it meant my line would continue. It meant my kids did something right. They had a normal life, something I never had or never would. Even if I found love I wouldn't call it normal, I would call it whole. But I would say it was special, and that's what I want to relate to you now.

When I played the grandmother and all those other elderly acting roles I never felt like I was totally complete. Like I said, I never found love until later.

My agent Mike was getting on in years. One day he called me into his office in downtown Los Angeles and said, "Mary, I don't know how much longer I'll be doing this. I've got to be honest, my knees are killing me. My hips are hurting and frankly most of the time I find myself asleep."

I laughed. "I could commiserate."

"Really?" he said. "I have money. My wife passed away, and I'm not very close to my kids. I'm probably going to die alone somewhere, probably on a bar with my head across the counter. At least I won't feel nothing when I do."

"All right, Mike. What are you getting at?" I tilted my head.

He sighed. "Yeah, I'm going to retire in a few months."

"Retire? Who retires in this business? We usually drag them out on a stretcher after they die."

Mike laughed. "Mary, listen to me. You're too good for this business. Maybe you became like one of them but you're probably still acting, you're too good for it. I tell you you're the most honest woman I ever met in this business. Don't change. My kids never got into acting. Let me tell you something—if they did go into acting I couldn't forgive myself. I never opened my mouth because I didn't need to. Mary, as someone you can trust I got to tell you that you need to get out of this business. You have enough money, do something else, get a hobby, collect stamps, just do something that isn't this."

I shook my head. "No way, Mike. This is what I was made to do. When I was a little kid I was made to do this."

"So be it, if you're that determined." He opened his desk drawer, pulling out a stack of scripts. It was way thinner than it used to be. "I have three for you. One of them is overseas in China, maybe that's what you need—another overseas vacation. You never took one since that time I sent you over there and you met that Ming guy. Do you know what happened to him?"

I shrugged. "No. I don't know what most of the men I dated or most of the men I actually worked with did after I left. I never kept up."

"Why don't you go find out?" He winked.

"I don't want to take a trip overseas. It's too long a journey."

Mike said, enthusiastically, "It's not that long with airplanes. The world's becoming smaller and smaller."

"I know, Mike. But I still don't know if I want to go," I said without expression.

"Well, think about it. Take these scripts and go home."

I said reluctantly, "All right."

And that's what I did. I went home and looked over the scripts.

One was about a family whose children hated their parents and wanted to live with their grandmother. I would be the grandmother. I read the script and looked in the mirror. "What happened to me?"

I was famous and always the spotlight. I was the most popular actress in the world at one point and now I was playing some grandmother. That was script number one.

Script number two was about the principal of a school for girls who played volleyball. They were an all-girl volleyball team and that's all they did—play volleyball. It examined each of their lives and showed how each was different than the next. Some had normal families, and some didn't. Through it all, all their principal had to do was guide them and help them. You guessed it—I would be the principal.

I kind of liked that script. It had the potential to be the feel-good film of the year.

And the third script, of course, was the one my agent said was about the woman overseas to which I said, "I don't know if I want this." But Mike called me that night and insisted that I at least read it.

I read the script, and it blew me away.

It was about an ancient Chinese culture where there were warriors who went to battle. This woman I would play was the wife of a man who was long ago gone. It was a script which had a spirit that spoke to this woman. The spirit of a young man she probably met back in the day.

I couldn't believe what I read. Maybe it reflected my own life, but I didn't know how. I was drawn to it and couldn't put it down. I stayed up the whole night reading it over and over. I never did that before.

Sometimes I had to spend long nights memorizing a lot of lines, but to stay up far into the night reading a script for the first time, I never did it. I was such a big actress I never had to.

I couldn't put it down. By the time I did it was morning.

I called Mike back and said, "I really need this part. You have to get it for me."

Mike pretended to be surprised. "Really? You're going to go overseas?"

"Yes!"

"Mary, I tell you—I've got a lot of scripts for you even nowadays when you're a bit older, no offense. And I put down each one and I said it's not going to be for now, for this reason or that. You're not going to play extra number five in the back room sitting on a bench somewhere. No, you're not going to be the cashier with no lines in a convenience store. So many scripts I turned down but this overseas one, that I thought you would do. I thought from the start you would do it. I was convinced you would do it and I'm glad you are. I don't know if it's fate or destiny, but I do know one thing, I know that you're going there and I'm sure you'll come back very different."

I said with relief, "Thank you, Mike! I know I need something, and this seems like the opportunity of a lifetime. Do your best to get me the part."

I had to wait two anxious days, but the call came through.

I was going to go to China again, and I was never happier.

This time, I got onto a plane. I was in first class, and let me tell you something, first class on a boat and first class on an airplane are very different experiences.

On a boat you get a suite, a suite that's tiny. A suite you can't flush the toilet in, a suite where you have to go outside to use the bathroom. That was the suite. The food was old and dated. You were lucky if you had any. Even the suite wasn't a suite.

In a first-class seat on an airplane you get a big chair that folds into a bed with a hot towel and your own private cabin. Today you can even shower on a plane. It's so different.

I got on the plane and they said, "Miss Maddin, is there anything we can get you?"

I was glad that I had so many options. I chose a glass of champagne. And they said, "Coming right up. Any drinks, any snacks, you name it, we'll get it."

"No, thanks. That's all I need for now." I felt so comfortable on the plane, it made me feel lighthearted and joyful. Sipping the champagne, it felt so right to be on this trip. A few other cast members were on the plane as well.

I sat down in my seat and looked over my lines. It was a long ride to China. Fifteen hours, I think.

As I was reading the lines again it just caught my eye, surprising me how much I was drawn to this script. There were so many layers to it, so many aspects of love.

I said to myself, "That's not a coincidence. Well, it mustn't be—are you seeing any other signs?"

Next thing I knew to my left I saw one of my daughter-in-law's sisters sitting a few rows behind me. I said to myself, "Wow! How amazing!"

After a brief chat with her I sat back and memorized my lines. I fell into a sleep, woke up and memorized my lines some more. Eventually we landed in China.

When I got off the plane in Beijing and pulled my baggage to the terminal receiving area, I saw a local Chinese man holding a sign with my name on it. I walked up to him and greeted him with a smile. His name was Yong. Yong nodded, matching my smile with his own, took my baggage and told me that he was the assistant to the producer who was going to greet me.

I nodded and said, "No problem."

"In Beijing, one of the things we planned for you was to meet some of our younger military members as a proper introduction to our culture." Yong talked as we walked to the side of the terminal where it was much less crowded and a lot quieter.

I was shocked by the arrangement. "Wow, it's changed a lot from the last time I was here."

He smiled, "Perhaps, but that is what we do to greet important international figures."

"Okay then."

I felt that it must be an honor to receive this type of greeting. Being an actress, I couldn't believe I would encounter such treatment. I thought those rituals were reserved for important political officials only. But of course, I wouldn't complain if they thought I was that important. I welcomed it.

I was taken to a lineup of men, and some of the other cast members and I went shaking each hand. There were about ten men in the line, some of whom were in uniform. Eventually I got to the end of the line and I saw the most handsome man I had ever seen.

He was in his army uniform standing tall and perfectly straight. His face looked serious and his eyes were filled with energy, but he wasn't looking anywhere in particular. He seemed like a statue but was also ready to take a stance for whatever was coming. He was poised and calm.

He turned his head my way and looked me in the eye with a soft and friendly gaze. He made a formal salute to me and then shook my hand. I looked at him in the eyes and smiled. He said, "My pleasure to meet you."

I felt my heart beating faster in front of such a handsome young man. It seemed that feelings buried deep inside of me had been triggered, feelings that been quenched for decades waiting for discovery. I was overwhelmed and almost lost my words until I stumbled out, "No, the pleasure is all mine." I quickly calmed myself down and asked, "Who are you?"

"My name is WuJian, and I am with the Chinese military. I am a captain." Even his voice was magnetic and appealing.

"Is that very high?"

He smiled. "Some say yes." He then turned to the next person he needed to greet.

I walked away. Then I turned to Yong and asked, "Tell me, who is that man?"

"He's one of the military officials."

I asked with my head tilted to the side, "Tell me something, am I able to bring him onto the set?"

"We can ask the general. I am told he is very lenient," replied Yong.

"Then please ask. It is something I would like."

On the set I met the producer, Jerry. Jerry was someone I had worked with many years before. He greeted me with a gentle hug. "Mary, good to see you again."

"It's been a long time."

"Yes." He smiled. "Weren't you over here once before?"

"Yes, I was."

"I heard it was a hit back in the day," Jerry said. "Maybe it'll bring us some good luck."

"Maybe." I smiled. After a short pause, I said, "Can we go and ask your assistant Yong to get that Captain WuJian to come over and talk?"

Jerry laughed. "Yong was telling me that you were interested in meeting this man. Hey, we'll try, we'll get you whatever you want. You're one of our stars."

I was so thrilled to hear that. "Great! Let's go and do it!"

After we talked to Yong, Jerry and I went to look at the set of the film. It was really nice. Things had come a long way in China since I had last been there.

Things almost seemed like Hollywood. I think the Chinese wanted everything to be an open culture just like all the famous stores and companies that started making things there.

Hollywood was something they took seriously. They tried to make as many movies there as they could. They thought they could lure a bunch of people over and make an English-speaking movie in China. I don't know if they were right or wrong. I was getting paid and I had met someone really handsome.

I had never met someone like WuJian and certainly no one had ever made me feel the way he did. I know you must be asking, "How do you know? You barely spoke to him."

I can tell you that when you know, you know. When I saw him, I said to myself, "I know him." I had to meet him.

People get outraged at the idea that someone could fall in love with someone at first sight, especially if the two people aren't even from the same country or culture. But I had this deep feeling of familiarity and the need to get to know him.

After the first day of shooting Yong came over and said, "Well, the general said WuJian couldn't come today. They are going to let him out tomorrow and he can speak to you then."

"Great! Have him meet me in my dressing room." I was so grateful and excited. I felt like a three-year-old being told she would be rewarded with candy!

"You got it! I'll take care of it right away," Yong said.

"Great!"

I went home to my hotel room that night, laid down on the bed, and smiled. This was the first time in my life I actually was happy about something in a long time.

Don't get me wrong, my kids and grandkids made me smile. But there was never a lasting feeling of something I looked forward to all the time.

The next day couldn't have come fast enough.

I went to the set with my lines memorized and I put on a stellar performance—the performance of a lifetime. Each line was "crystal clear." Each line was passionate. Each line was dedicated. Each line was as if I was in the story.

Jerry came over to me and said excitedly, "Mary, I don't know what you did different today. Whatever you drank, drink it again. Whatever you ate, eat it again. In fact, don't change a thing from what you did last night, because whatever you did, this story, this movie just got a whole lot better."

I laughed and, not wanting to reveal my secret, said, "I don't know what it was but I'll try to do it again."

After that I walked back to my dressing room to adjust my makeup and change. Sitting in one of the chairs was WuJian, dressed in his uniform. I admired his height and charm, his square face and thick eyebrows. His eyes were like he was always smiling, and his nose was cute too, not too big and not too small. His lips were naturally red as if he wore lipstick. Everything about him was perfect. I couldn't study him enough.

Seeing me coming he tried to stand up, but I motioned him to sit. I grabbed a chair and sat down beside him.

The moment I looked him in the eyes I got the feeling of electricity running through my body. My whole body vibrated with warmth. My breathing was faster, and I got a sensation in my stomach that I had never had. It was as if I had butterflies. I said to myself, "What is this crazy feeling?" I mean, who, me? At sixty-seven, *now* I get a feeling like this?

I knew it was because of him. I just didn't want to tell *him* that.

Not yet, anyway.

I calmed myself down because I didn't want to show too much interest in front of WuJian. I simply said, "Thanks for coming."

"My pleasure. I was told I should be here by my commander. I knew it was important that I listen and do what's best for the country."

I wished WuJian would be more passionate, or at least I hoped he would reciprocate the amount of interest I had in him. However, I also understood he was a military man and probably didn't have much freedom. I asked, "How many years have you served in the military, WuJian?"

His eyes lit up. "Ten years!"

"Really?" I asked. "How old are you?"

"I'm twenty-nine."

"Really? Twenty-nine, and you've served ten years in the military?" I raised my eyebrows and challenged him, "How come you're not a general yet?"

He laughed. "In the military in China it's not so easy. Takes a lot of effort. That's how I made captain."

"Tell me, is it Private, Lieutenant, Captain?"

"No," he said, "It's Private, Sergeant, Lieutenant, Captain."

My mouth gaped open. "Wow, so it took you three levels of promotion to get to captain?"

"More actually—there are two levels of Lieutenant!" His eyes were glowing with pride.

I giggled. "You must have done something heroic."

He turned his head away from me briefly and then said humbly, "Well, maybe some people consider heroic what I have done. I don't consider it anything because I'm doing it for the duty of my country."

I asked softly, "Have you ever been in a war?"

"We've been in many wars that no one knows about. Especially not America. There are little wars. Secret ones."

"Can you tell me about it?"

He readjusted in his seat, obviously uncomfortable. "No, I can't."

I didn't want him to feel unpleasant in any way. To me such a handsome young man would be wasted in the military. He could have enjoyed life so much more doing something else. Unless the making of war was his passion. I asked, "Do you enjoy being in the military?"

He thought for a few seconds and said, "That's all I've ever known. My years of service could have been up a few years ago but I decided to stay on. I know the military. I know their process and I know it well. For me, it's comfortable."

I tilted my head and said, "Really? For me being an actress is comfortable. It doesn't mean I enjoy it. Do you enjoy what you do?"

He didn't answer me but kept dogging the question. Eventually I came to realize he didn't like being a military man. It was just something he knew.

I leaned forward. "Tell me how long you have before you have to get back to the military base?"

He shook his head. "I don't know—three or four hours I guess."

"Great! Let's go and get something for dinner."

I had Yong drive us to one of the nicest restaurants in Beijing. He opened the door for us. WuJian and I went in and when we had been seated I said, "Do you get to go to restaurants a lot?"

"No," WuJian said. "I'm sorry I can't do it more."

"Me too," I said, my lips pressing tight. But then I tried to cheer up. "Well then we might as well take advantage while we can. Let's eat."

We ordered the nicest things on the menu. I was paying… well, actually the producer was. I was putting it on his tab! Maybe Jerry would get the bill later and laugh, maybe he wouldn't, but I know one thing. I know that to me it was important to show WuJian a good time.

I wanted to see him again, I knew that right away. So I had to show him a good time. I didn't know what it would take to get him to have a second date, but I thought maybe this would help.

I was quite impressed with WuJian's English. He told me learning English was part of his army training because he was required to understand and speak the language fluently, so that if China and America were ever at war he would be able to listen to the enemy's conversations.

We ate, we laughed, we talked, we ordered some more. We ordered dessert and the time went pleasantly by.

Eventually WuJian looked into my eyes. I saw appreciation. "I really do enjoy talking to you, but I have to get back to the base."

I was so anxious and couldn't help but asking, "Could you see me again?"

"It is possible, but I don't know when. My general makes all my decisions. I can't promise you anything."

I said firmly, "I'm sorry WuJian, but I cannot accept that. Not knowing when is not a good enough answer."

He nodded. "Very well. I will ask my general and get back to your assistant."

"No, you can get back to me directly." I was so afraid to lose touch with WuJian. I had never been so desperate to see a man again. I was always the cool woman who was asked for second dates, not the other way around.

I gave him my telephone number right then and there. WuJian said, "I will call when I know."

We then went our separate ways for the evening.

On our way home, I said to myself, "I have to see him again, I have to." I asked Young for advice about how to make it happen.

He said with reassurance, "We can make that happen for you. Let me talk to the general."

I shook my head. "I gave WuJian my number."

"In China it doesn't work like that, so easily. You have to talk to the general. If the general doesn't approve it, you're not going to be able to do anything."

Reluctantly I said, "Okay."

Eventually I went home and laid down to sleep. It had been one of the best dates of my life and I wasn't sure why. But I knew that I was going to see WuJian again somehow, someway. I knew that I wanted to spend as much time with him as I could.

CHAPTER 6
The Heart Yearns

I never thought I would want to date a military man.

WuJian always seemed so rigid to me, so stuck, so rule based. I was a Hollywood actress who was free, wild, full of life, and full of energy. I went to parties and had cocktails. I went everywhere I wanted, everywhere that I could find a party.

I mean me with a military man? Ha! I never would have thought it, yet alone a foreign one! And even odder, a foreign military man possibly being the love of my life, the love that completed me. This all seemed so impossible.

I didn't believe that one gets to choose the love of their life, their true destiny. I believed it was chosen *for* them. Destiny brings them together, as it chooses.

So when I met WuJian and I saw him and he was so handsome, I couldn't believe that this was the person I wanted to spend my time with. And I'd done this before and it didn't work out. Yet alone a man who was thirty-eight years younger than me.

And yet that's exactly what happened. That's exactly what I wanted to do.

One night after filming I took Yong aside. "It's been a couple of days. WuJian hasn't called me. Why hasn't he called?"

"I told you—it's the general who has to give permission. WuJian must wait for an answer, as must you."

Even though Yong was someone rooted in China, he had been collaborating with American film companies for years. He visited the US frequently and knew Western culture very well. He was always honest and cordial, always spoke the truth. Yong was someone I felt comfortable talking with or sending requests through.

"I don't care what happens, or what it takes. You need to get him here," I insisted.

Yong laughed. "That may work in America where you stamp your feet, or snap your fingers and the man of your dreams just pops up in an instant. This is not some Hollywood snack you want, where 'I want my gourmet coffee and I want it now.' This is something different. China is not a place where you can decide who or what you want, and when you want it. It's a place where it is decided for you and if you don't fit into that system they punish you. It's like a dog on a leash. The rope only goes so far until they pull it back. Same thing here. Maybe you want WuJian to come out to your door every minute, but the military knows everything, and if they don't want him coming around he won't."

"Well then, I'm going to go to the general," I said.

After a short pause, Yong said, "I wouldn't advise it. I don't know if you're going to make it out alive."

"Are you kidding me? I'm a big Hollywood actress! How's it going to look if they arrest me?" I sniffed in disgust at the thought.

"Arrest? Who's talking about arrest? Maybe you'd have an 'accident'; suddenly something happens on the set. The next thing you know the movie doesn't get made or completed or maybe it gets completed without you, if you know what I mean…"

"I don't care. I'm going to meet the general," I said, without thinking.

Yong finally gave up on trying to talk me out of it. "Good luck with it! I don't know if I'm going to drive you there."

I wasn't surprised to hear that. "I don't care. I'll call a taxi."

To me, this is something I had to do, I had to meet WuJian again. Even if nobody was willing to help me I would still do it myself, knowing all of the risks.

I did call a taxi and guess what? I did make it to the military base.

I got out of the car and greeted one of the guards at the gate. The unfriendly guard gave me a dirty look and said, "Why are you here?" I guess they were not expecting to see a foreigner. Or a woman.

I thought it was good to keep up the act. I bowed slightly and put a smile on my face. "I'm here to see the general."

"Which general?" he asked without looking at me. By then other guards approached to see what was going on.

"The general in charge of WuJian."

He examined me up and down carefully while another guard flipped the pages on the directory and said, "It is General Tai Chi."

I knew I was getting closer. I said firmly, "I don't care if it's Tai B, Tai C, Tai D, or Tai E—you're going to get me there."

They were surprised to hear my tone. They could tell I wasn't someone to mess with. Perhaps they thought I was someone with an intimidating background. Whatever the case might be, I finally got to them. One of them said, "Wait a minute."

I waited. Eventually the first guard motioned me forward and said, "We'll open the gate. You can drive on through."

The taxi driver was happy because his bill kept going up because the meter kept running. He didn't care how long we sat there, he was getting paid regardless. I got back in the car and we followed their instructions.

We soon arrived at the main building, a long, two-story structure with the entrance in the middle. That was where we stopped. I paid the driver and got out of the car. I walked through the main entrance into a bedroom-sized lobby. A large picture of Chairman Mao and what seemed like awards lined the walls.

A stern-looking receptionist sat behind a centrally located desk. When she saw me arrive, she said, "Have a seat."

I took a seat away from her and hoped that it wouldn't be too long of a wait. As soon as I sat down, I asked, "When is the general going to see me?"

She didn't answer my question directly. "You're lucky you're here at all. Most people never get this far."

I wasn't sure about being lucky, but I had to do this. I tilted my head. "How many people get to see the general?"

"A dozen people a day make an attempt, thinking they can help him or our general can help them. At the end of the day no one gets through. You, for some reason, he allowed in. I must admit I am curious as to why he allowed you through." She rolled her eyes.

"I don't know why, but I have to see the general." Honestly, I didn't care why the general let me in. I had to see WuJian.

The receptionist went back to her work, saying, "Like I said—wait here."

Eventually the receptionist received the call and promptly led me to the first office on our right. The general opened the door and motioned me in and said, "Come in and have a seat." The receptionist left and I stepped into his office.

It was designed for intimidation.

His office was two-hundred square feet with one small window. On the wall there hung a Chinese flag and some pictures of Chinese officials. He was sitting right under the Chinese flag behind a desk with a serious look on his face, as if to say, "There's no leniency here." He had a round face with a receding hairline. He was obviously fit though. He looked like he was in his forties.

I took the seat directly across from him. As soon as I sat down, I said, "Listen general, I want to see WuJian."

General Tai Chi raised his eyebrows. "Really? Why do you want to see our Captain?"

"I have an interest in this man," I said bluntly.

"What kind of interest? Are you a spy?" He leaned forward. I could smell his sweat.

I would be a fool if I didn't expect him to throw something like that back at me. Luckily, I wasn't afraid. "I'm no spy. I don't even know anything about the United States other than my acting."

"I've checked into you. You are a famous actress over there whose time has seemed to have passed."

I laughed and said, "Well, it may have slowed down but it may not have passed completely. Otherwise, I wouldn't be here on the set, would I?"

"You're very brave for an American woman." He laughed. "Do you know who I am?"

"No," I snapped. "I know you're a general and in China that means a lot of power. In America a general is also brave and prone to show his power, but it doesn't mean much to me."

He leaned forward, his arms resting on the desk and his fists held tight, looking into my eyes. "I can have you executed."

I squinted. "For what?"

"For anything I wish."

"That's really nice, but at the end of the day we both know you're not going to do that. You don't want China to look bad and I really am not a spy and you know it. You just want to think you have power, so let's get this over with. You say how great China is and how much power it has, and I tell you that's nice, I really believe it. I can even record a commercial or two to make others believe it. So, let's speed things up so I can see Captain WuJian."

General Tai Chi nodded. "You are brave once again. You really believe I could not have you executed? That's interesting. I should laugh." And then he did, although I knew that it was fake.

After going back and forth for twenty minutes with this *banter* as I called it, he said, "Very well. I want you to read a commercial script about how China is the greatest country in the world and why everyone should come here."

"Don't you want people to leave? You've got so many people," I said sarcastically.

He smiled and laughed again, this time for real. He said, "You're very funny. Did you do comedy films in your country?"

"I did a few."

"You should do more, ha ha ha."

Twenty-four hours later, a script was delivered to the set. I learned my lines and taped it on the base a few days later, after which one of the general's staff led me to a small meeting room. WuJian stood there, expecting me. Before we sat down next to each other, I said, "It's so nice to see you again."

WuJian reciprocated, trying not to show his emotion. "Likewise." We then sat down at a conference table.

"Why didn't you call me?" I asked while wringing my hands.

"Because they wouldn't let me, and here in the military you have to ask permission for everything," WuJian said softly.

"Do you have to ask for permission to go to the bathroom?" I joked.

He laughed. "Actually, we do."

We both laughed.

"When can you get off the base?"

"I don't know… you tell me. You spoke with the general." I was a little disappointed upon hearing that. WuJian sure didn't have freedom and couldn't make his own decisions. It certainly saddened me.

"I have to speak to him again."

"You should have asked him when you had the opportunity." WuJian sounded a little worried. "I don't think he's going to let you speak to him again."

I smiled my most confident smile. "Oh yes they will. Let me try." I didn't know how but I knew I had to do it, otherwise my efforts would've been in vain.

I left WuJian after our allotted time and walked over to the general's office. As I walked across the reception area, the secretary got up quickly from her chair and said, "You don't have permission to be here."

I kept walking toward the general's door. "I need to ask a question. When can WuJian get off the base?"

"I don't know." She walked over to me, blocking my way.

"Then I'll go and ask the general."

"No, you won't." She rolled her eyes and scowled.

"Yes, I will. If you don't let me I'm not going to leave here today." I crossed my arms.

She pressed a buzzer under her desk because no one had ever done that to her before. Eventually the general let me in. I asked him when WuJian could leave and he said, "Leave? That wasn't part of our deal."

"What else do you want?"

He paused. "I want one more commercial."

"Fine, but then he gets to leave for a visit."

General Tai Chi said, "For how long?"

"For a week." I raised my eyebrows.

"A week? No one leaves the military base that long!" The general gaped at me.

"What's he doing that's so important? Are you at war?"

"No."

"Are you having a military training exercise?"

"No."

"Then tell me why he can't leave for a week other than the fact that you don't want him to?" I leaned forward to emphasize this penetrating question.

He gave me a dirty look that seemed to last an hour. Shaking his head, he said, "Very well. Read the commercial, then he can leave for a week."

The following day I read their commercial on tape, telling everyone how great China was and how everybody was wonderful and the Communist Party was the best thing that ever happened. Yada, yada, yada.

I didn't care much about it. They wanted their thing, and I wanted mine. They got their bargain, I got mine. A deal was a deal, so they let him go.

I arranged for WuJian and me to leave in the next available taxi. I took him back to my apartment and we just sat together on my couch and talked.

Considering how hard it was to get WuJian off of the military base, I thought I would tease him a bit. I had earned it. "Tell me WuJian, have you been on many dates?"

He didn't even need to think on that one. "No, not many. The Chinese government never let—"

Before he could finish his sentence, I interrupted him. "So when are you planning to marry?"

He paused and said, "I don't really think about it. I assumed eventually they will tell me either to get out of the military or get married and remain in the military. They may even help arrange the marriage. That's what happens."

I got up and got a glass of wine. WuJian only wanted water. I sat back down, took a sip of the wine, and frowned. "So let me get this straight. You don't go on a lot of dates, you stay in the military and your job or goal is that the Chinese government is either going to tell you to get married and have kids, so you can stay in the military or just get out?"

He looked at me. "That's pretty much what it is." On some level he was glad I understood the rules.

"Tell me, do you ever think about life, what you *want* to do?" I asked with a frown.

"No, not really. I haven't had time," he said softly. "That's the greatness or goal of the Chinese military. They keep you in line. Keep you focused only on them. If you had time to think, you'd probably want to leave, and if people wanted to leave and actually go against the government they wouldn't have much of an army now, would they? So, I don't think much. I just go and whatever they tell me to do, I do."

"Well, I think that's going to change." I laughed. "Tell me, what do you think of me?"

He stared at me as if I had two heads. "What do you mean?"

I took another sip of wine and said, "Well, how do you see me? Do you like me?"

"I do. You seem pleasant." He smiled. His smile was so charming that it melted my heart every time seeing him so happy. However, I wasn't satisfied with his response about me.

"Pleasant? Is that all I am to you?" I asked.

"Well, we've been on one date to a restaurant, what more should I see you as?"

I nodded. "You're right, that's true. Well, then—we have to change that."

And so we made the most of our week together, followed by a series of weekly dates once he'd returned to the base. Each time I wanted to see WuJian I had to plea to the general. It was such a pain, but I was so pleased to see WuJian each time that it was totally worth it.

The weeks and months seemed to have flown by. I did a little bit on the set each day but the shooting was wrapping up and so I was able to spend more time with WuJian.

I invited him out to a restaurant. Halfway through the meal I said to him, "I think you're my destiny."

He frowned in confusion. "What are you talking about?"

"You see, I've had so many men in my life, so many lovers, and I never felt anything like I do toward you." I reached my hand toward his.

He retracted his hand before I could grasp it. "That's wonderful, but I am a military man in China and you are much older than me," he said cautiously. "I do like you a lot. I find you very beautiful but there's not much more I can do."

After a short pause, I said with sincerity, "Come back to the United States with me."

He frowned. And after a long pause he said, "There's no way the military will let me."

"Aren't you done? Of course you can leave the military. It is your choice," I said firmly.

WuJian seemed so helpless. He froze for several seconds. "What would I do then?"

I nodded reassuringly. "I'm rich. In the United States you can do whatever you want. I'll help you."

"So you want me to leave my family?"

"Tell me, what family and life do you have here? You have the military; do you even know your family?"

"No, but I can know them."

I leaned closer to him. "You are never going to leave the military if I don't ask you now or the government doesn't kick you out. You were never going to know your family. At least in the US you'll see and experience something different. A different life, where you can find your purpose."

At first WuJian didn't know what to say. After what seemed like an hour, he murmured, "I will need a few nights to think about your suggestion."

"Very well. We wrap up shooting in another week. By then you should be in a position to leave. Hopefully you'll be able to make the right decision and come with me. Come and tell me in my apartment in a week if you decide to accept my offer."

He went back to the military base that night. It saddened me to see him leave. Could this be the last time I ever saw him? Would WuJian come to America with me? Was this man my destiny?

I went to bed wondering if the man I finally found, the man of my dreams, would ever agree to come with me.

A week later, WuJian took a taxi to my hotel, as he had agreed. He came up the stairs quietly and knocked on the door. I asked from the other side, "Who is there?"

"Captain WuJian."

With him being so formal I thought it was because he wasn't planning to go with me. I thought for sure he wouldn't go and came there to tell me.

Little did I know how wrong I was! This was the start of the rest of my life.

As we sat on the couch, hand in hand, WuJian told me all that had happened.

The night of our discussion he went back to the military base and thought and thought. He knew everything about the military—even as a child he went to Cadet School. It seemed he was always destined for the military and the military was always destined for him. He did think he should be higher in rank. Maybe not a general, but at least a colonel.

Captain WuJian was very respectable. He went on a lot of military missions and risked his life for his country, but he saw that his country never returned the favor. Perhaps I was right that he should leave the military. Being with me for a few months opened his eyes. He could recognize his rigidity and lack of freedom as a military man. How would he tell his general and superiors? He knew they would not react well at all.

He made an appointment with the general. When it was time for his appointment he knocked on the door with his heart beating fast.

After a few moments the general appeared at the door and said, "Captain WuJian, please come into my office and have a seat."

WuJian did as he was told. "Listen, general, I love the country, I love the army and I love having my service but—"

Before WuJian could finish, the general interrupted with a sigh. "But you want to leave."

WuJian felt like a child whose lie had been detected. He lowered his head and asked, "How did you know?"

"I am not a fool. I've watched you with this woman thirty years your senior and yet there is a spark in your eyes and hers that I can't match. I could force you to be in the military and make up excuses, but at the end of the day I understand what love is. I have a wife and I have a child. I don't need more than that and understand that every person should have the opportunity to find it. You have served our country well and I can't stop you from trying to fulfill your destiny."

General Tai Chi then signed the necessary papers and took out a stamp and stamped them. He said, "I prepared this document when you first started dating this American woman and I never signed it. But now that you have come to me and told me everything that you have, I knew I can't be in your way, so here it is."

He handed WuJian the paper that dismissed him from the military.

It was 1978. The Chinese military needed to appear like communism wasn't the dominant force it was, that there was a balance between communism and the open market, capitalistic society.

After a certain amount of years serving in the army, one did have the potential to be released, and this was done on a case-by-case basis. WuJian's circumstances, because of his relationship with an American movie star, made the general believe it needed to be done.

WuJian gasped upon seeing what the general did. To WuJian, it was amazing to see and amazing to read the dismissal letter with his own eyes. As he walked out of there he couldn't believe they dismissed him from the military so easily. It was as if destiny and fate were telling him, "You know what you must do, now go and do it."

After his story was told, he asked anxiously, "Is your offer still good? Is your offer to take me with you still good?"

"Yes!" I was so thrilled. I couldn't believe what was happening.

"Great! Then that's what I'm going to do. I'm coming with you." WuJian smiled.

I couldn't believe my ears. I gave him a big hug and kiss on the cheek. "Wow! You're really coming with me! Please tell me it's not a dream."

He was shocked by my response. "Yes, I'll come. Is that okay?"

I broke out in laughter. "More than okay. This is the best thing to ever happen to me after giving birth to my children!"

WuJian just looked at me and smiled, and I started to cry. I walked away and wiped my tears because I didn't want him to see me like this.

For his part he thought this was nice. He didn't know if he loved me, but he knew it seemed like destiny was telling him this was what he needed to do.

He needed to go with me to America, to the United States, to Hollywood. He didn't know if he would ever fit in or adjust there, but he did feel that it was meant to be.

We stayed in China for another two months while I helped him get a visitor visa. I broached the topic of WuJian saying farewell to his family, but he dismissed the idea as unnecessary. He said that he would notify his parents once we were in the US, because otherwise his parents wouldn't allow him to leave the country.

I didn't know the details of his relationship with his parents but he told me they weren't close. He seemed to dodge the topic every time I brought up. Part of the reason was his parents put the country first and him second and gave him to the military when WuJian was a very young boy.

Because of the military training, WuJian rarely saw his parents. I didn't want to bring unhappiness to WuJian. I trusted he knew what he was doing. I was just so excited by his decision to come with me.

I was very grateful to the Universe to have brought us together in such an unlikely circumstance. I was curious as to what fate had in store for us.

CHAPTER 7
America Awaits

We took time to go out locally to see the sights, including the Great Wall. WuJian took me to some other historical places as well. We also went shopping to get WuJian new clothes, so he could get rid of his army uniform.

I enjoyed it very much and I think he enjoyed spending time with me too. Each day we grew closer. Each day we talked about things like our hopes, our dreams, and what we really wanted from life.

We made plans to book tickets, to get on the airplane together and fly to Hollywood where I lived.

I didn't think that adjusting to another country could be hard, but I was wrong.

Before we left for America I started telling WuJian all about it— Hollywood and all the rest.

While we were at our final stay at a hotel in Beijing before we embarked on our flight, I said to WuJian, "In America things are not like here in China. People are not so rigid and not so based on 'everything has to be in order.'"

He tilted his head to one side. "What do you mean?"

"For example, you said you had to raise your hand to go to the bathroom." I laughed. "They don't make you do that in Hollywood."

"Oh, that's good," he said with relief. "Do they have cars?"

"Of course," I said proudly. "What do you think this is? We're not a backwards nation. In fact, we are more forward than China. We have very modern buildings, we have the very best restaurants. We have beautiful cars and boats."

"I know what America is. I see it a lot in the newspapers," said WuJian. "But of course I've never been there. So I didn't know how it really is." He was such a child at heart. He never knew the outside world beyond his military base—the one that's so exciting. I felt pity for him that his life had been this way, and I hoped I could open his eyes.

I looked WuJian deep in his eyes and said with loving reassurance, "Well, when you come over you'll see so many things. It really is an amazing place."

His eyes lit up. "I'm looking forward to it."

I smiled. "I know there will be a period of adjustment, but I believe that with my help you will get used to it fast and I think you will be very happy. Do you think you will be happy?"

"I hope so." WuJian smiled.

In my mind I didn't believe that there could be any problems because I thought I had found the love I always wanted, and that it could conquer anything.

Perhaps, looking back, I was being selfish but at the end of the day I was right that there was a love even if it was only from my end. I do think that WuJian loved me too, but I don't know if it was at the same level as me to him.

I don't think WuJian ever gave thought to what he really wanted to do in life before he met me. I guess I had a good influence on him because he talked about how he always wanted to help people but didn't know how. Perhaps that's why he continued to sign up for the military even when he could have left.

I nodded. "You can really do anything you want."

I told him the story of how I became an actress. How my parents worked on the set and how they got their jobs, and I told him about how at a young age I wanted to become an extra in a movie in Hollywood and I worked in those days with memorizing lines.

I told him how, after I became an extra, I gave it my all. WuJian said with amazement, "Perhaps it's like the military in that sense. In the military you must give it your all for whatever role you're assigned to. If you want to move up, you want to show your dedication, commitment and also your excellence. It sounds to me that life in Hollywood is the same. If you want to become a better actress with better roles you need to be not only committed, but you have to be excellent."

"Yes, it is kind of the same in that sense." We both laughed.

I don't know if he ever showed affection to anyone before, but he started to slowly learn how to with me. I can't explain it to you in a way that would do justice but eventually we did learn the art of showing affection to each other.

The time came when we had to get on the plane to America. He had been on military planes many times before, so I didn't think it'd be an issue.

We sat in first class and he sat down on the seat. "Tell me, WuJian, do you want anything?" I said.

"Water is fine."

I laughed and said, "You don't understand. This is first class. On these planes you can have anything you want. Do you want champagne, or some other kind of alcohol? Do you want any kind of food? You name it they will give it to you."

WuJian frowned, tilting his head to the side. "I don't understand."

He was puzzled by how the service worked on an airplane. I explained patiently, "I don't think I explained myself well. This is first class. The tickets are very expensive. These seats come with the ability to have anything you want."

His furrowed brow released and he smiled. "Okay, very well. I will take champagne!"

I said with excitement, "Good choice! I will as well."

He took his first sip of champagne. I watched with delight as he sipped it and smiled. "This is very good!"

It wasn't so much that he was drinking champagne; it was that he was happy. I realized at that moment that all I ever wanted to do was to make him happy. Again, it's not something I could explain to somebody who's rational.

When you look back at our situation and think about what happened, no one with a rational mind would ever say "this was normal."

I never said it was normal, I just said it was real.

As I watched him drink champagne, I explained what else they could bring. He caught on fast and ate well. He ordered steak, caviar, and other gourmet foods that most people only dream about, enjoying each with an ever-broadening smile. I got more and more excited.

I didn't know what was going through his mind. I did ask if he was enjoying it. He did say that he was and that it was really good food.

"Great! With the bed you are able to lie down fully," I pointed out to WuJian when we were halfway through the trip. That was something he had never had in military planes.

At first, he didn't understand how it worked. I explained, "It's like a bed. You can lie down and then you can go to sleep like you're sleeping in your house."

He scratched his head. "But this is a plane."

"Exactly. But look how far back the seat goes." I showed him how I made my seat into a bed.

He couldn't believe it. He laughed. "Wow! This is definitely not the military!"

"No, it's not!"

He laid down and finally relaxed and after a long flight we landed near Hollywood.

The airport in Los Angeles was so busy and bustling that no one paid attention to us. I mean, a sixty-year-old American woman and a twenty-something-year-old Chinese man walking through an airport arm in arm would have probably made many people turn and twist their heads for at least a moment anywhere else in the world.

But here in LA, where anything goes, where Hollywood imaginations come to life, no one really paid attention to us, which was great. Somehow, I was able to duck under the radar.

I knew I couldn't do it forever, so I savored the anonymity while it lasted. WuJian asked, "What hotel will you be dropping me off at, Mary?"

"Hotel? No, no. I have a mansion. You will be coming to stay with me." I winked.

"Okay, then, that's fine." He sounded excited. "When will we be there?"

"Hopefully soon."

The driver came and picked us up and drove us home. When we pulled up with the car to my neighborhood, WuJian looked at one house after another and couldn't believe it. His eyes went wide open. He had never seen houses so big. They looked like military bases.

Each house was built with a unique charming top-of-the-line design, like a piece of art, sitting on a large private lot. The lawns were perfectly manicured, and some properties were fully fenced in. Many houses featured expansive floor to ceiling bay windows overlooking the city or a fancy deck for entertaining or a beautiful home garden. Some houses were secluded and were partially blocked from view, but their beauty shined through. The houses were a breathtaking sight to see. They were vibrant, elegant, and simply gorgeous. They were statements showing how important the people were who populated them. WuJian looked at each and every house we passed with utter amazement.

At first I raised my eyebrows. "Do you know where we are?"
He shook his head. "No."

"This is called Beverly Hills. We are in the most exclusive section in all of California. In all of America actually!"

"Wow!" he exclaimed. "Is every house like this?" He pointed to one spectacular house on our right as we were passing by.

I nodded. "Around here, yes. One is bigger than the next."

"Where is your house?" he asked excitedly.

"Well, it's actually the one after this big one here." I pointed to a house we were passing.

We slowly pulled up to the driveway. There was a giant iron fence, a fence that kept all the paparazzi out and only the important people in. The house was bigger than he had imagined. He couldn't believe the size of it. It was really the size of a military base sitting in ten acres of land.

When we pulled up the gate slowly opened. WuJian asked, "Did you let us in?"

"No, the housekeeper or butler did."

"You have a housekeeper *and* a butler?" His eyes went wide.

"Yes, every day. A lot of other staff as well. I mean who's going to take care of this house? It's not going to be me." I laughed.

"I understand."

When we pulled in, the gate closed behind us. Finally, we pulled up and I paid the driver, who got out and helped WuJian with his suitcases.

Soon an army of housekeepers, butlers, maids and other staff came out to welcome us and take our luggage inside. We didn't bring that much back.

Finally, we stepped into the big hallway and WuJian just looked around, eyes wide open, not able to believe that this was the size of the house that he was actually going to stay in.

I reveled in watching him look so amazed and smile so wide. I said, "You get to stay here for as long as you want."

"Thank you! I appreciate that," said WuJian, who was still trying to wrap his mind around his new reality.

"This is the hallway and on the first floor is the living room, dining room, den, and playrooms. The basement has the wine cellar, the cigar bar, and the spare guest bedrooms. On the upper floor there are seven bedrooms plus an exercise room and my sound studio."

He asked with astonishment, "Tell me, did you always have these many bedrooms?"

"I didn't always live in a house this big. I did live in other nice houses. Smaller, though. This is the nicest one I've had. I've had it for many years. After my divorce I lived in a few apartments but eventually I decided to buy this house. I'm not quite sure why I needed it, after all I was only one person. That is why I have an army of staff. It's not always to do with the things around the house but actually to keep me busy. I don't think having no people in a house this size would be fun. In fact, I'd be miserable."

"Yes, you are right. The amount of people I think you can fit in here is astounding."

"Probably." We both chuckled.

"Go and make yourself at home. It was a long flight. Go and shower, go and do whatever you want, and I'll meet you in the kitchen in two hours."

"That will work."

I summoned my English butler, Nigel. That was his name—I kid you not! Well, that is what I *nicknamed* him. I can't even tell you his actual name after so many years. Anyway, Nigel came and took WuJian and his luggage up to his room. I said, "Nigel, go and be a good lad. Take care of my friend."

That was my way of having fun. I said, "Go serve him and get him whatever he needs. Show him to the shower. Show him how to unpack."

"Very well ma'am, I will show him to his room and show him around."

I also went upstairs to unpack and rest.

I was tired from the long flight, but in my heart I was happy. The man of my dreams was now living with me at my house and would be staying here for as long as we both wished. The future was bright.

Who knew that life began at sixty-seven? I thought life would end at forty, but for me it began in my sixties. It shows you that in Hollywood what you think you know you don't, or what you don't know is what you think you know. I will let you ponder that for a while, while I unpack.

An hour later I went downstairs and sat down for a snack.

"Ma'am, can I get you anything?" asked the chef.

I waved my hand. "No, no. I'm waiting for WuJian."

"Oh, he is in the living room."

My eyes went wide. "He came downstairs already?"

"Yes, about twenty minutes ago."

"I will go and sit with him there, then we'll come into the kitchen together."

"Very well," said the chef.

I left the kitchen and found WuJian looking at the paintings. "I have filled this room and many of the others with art. Do you like it?"

"These must be very expensive. It must be from very famous people," said WuJian.

"Yes, they are actually. Some Chagall's, some Monet's. They've cost me millions."

He looked at me with amazement. "Are they worth it?"

"Well, I think I can sell them for double, so I guess so. If you're asking me whether the paintings themselves are worth it, that is up to as many people as are willing to judge and buy them. After all, that's their only value."

He sat for a moment and took that in.

After a few minutes of talking to WuJian again, I came to realize that he was a very deep man. He was a man that was probably never given a chance to think about much in life. The Chinese government told him exactly what he could and couldn't think, what he could and couldn't do.

I always say that, in the United States, if you give a person just a little bit of room, they can become something amazing. The mind is very powerful and if you put together enough effort and opportunity you can do anything you set yourself to.

Maybe that's a cliché, but I really believe it. I think WuJian just never got the opportunity.

I finally said, after a few minutes of going back and forth about the paintings, "Let's go to the kitchen and get something to eat."

He said, "No problem." We walked to the kitchen together.

As soon as the first phone call came in, my first lie started. The staff member who answered the phone said, "It's your son Bo."

After a short pause, I said, "Oh great, let me talk to him."

I took the phone. After a round of greetings, Bo said, "How was your trip, Ma?"

"Absolutely wonderful! China is amazing."

"Really?" he said. "As good as the last time you were there?"

"Of course! In fact, it's even better."

"Really?" he joked. "Did you bring back any good souvenirs for me?"

"Well, if you call WuJian a souvenir then I guess so." I laughed.

"What is WuJian?" Bo sounded puzzled.

"More like *who's* WuJian."

He suddenly became interested. "Do you want to tell me what you're up to?"

You see, my Bo is very suspicious. He always thought that I was too quick to go headlong into the next thing that blipped on my radar. No matter how much I said I finally was going to settle down a little bit in life he always thought back to the Hollywood part of me, with the parties and running up and down. Running here and there, doing this and doing that. He didn't trust me very much.

As I tried to explain, he got angry, trying to cut me off.

I raised my voice over his. "You don't get it, Bo. This time it's for real. This time I'm actually going to be settling down. I'm not dating anyone else anymore."

Bo said, "Ma, I've heard that before, thirty times over. I heard that with Dad and look how that worked out. Then I heard it with every other man you've gone out with. You kept saying 'this is the one or that's the one. This is the one or that's the one.' After a while, it became like a broken tape recorder, a broken record, or a broken whatever you guys listened to back then. Eventually I just shut it off and stopped listening or if you said, 'this is the one,' I said, 'great Ma, luckily you finally found it.' This time it sounds like you went all the way to China for it!"

"Of course that's not what happened," I said cautiously. "But I don't think people are going to believe me."

"Why is that?"

I didn't want to give too much away. "I guess you're going to have to come and see for yourself."

Bo lived in California and did come by occasionally. "Okay, Ma, if that makes you happy."

I don't think Bo took it seriously. He thought it was another one of these flings that weren't going to work out. And he had no idea how much younger than me WuJian was.

"It was nice talking to you, Bo. Let's catch up later," I said.

"Glad you had a good trip, Ma. Yes—let's do that. Maybe I'll come by later this week."

"Why don't you do that? You'll be in for a surprise."

Bo laughed. "I always am with you. I always am." With that, we both hung up.

I turned to WuJian. "Did you hear the conversation?"

"Only a little bit. I heard the name Bo."

"Yes. Bo is one of my sons. I did tell you I have two."

"Yes, Bo and Bobby."

I will say this—the military was good at one thing. Teaching you to listen. If you're in there long enough you must abide by all their rules. Eventually you do get to listen for a while and you get to see what's going on. You become a very good listener and that probably helped WuJian with the women. Well… especially this woman.

"Bo might stop by later in the week to meet you."

WuJian said, "Okay." He seemed to be at peace with whatever I told him. I couldn't always understand why.

I mean, did he want me for the money? I certainly hoped not.

"When are we going out?" WuJian asked.

"Well, I figured we'd stay in tonight. It was a long trip."

"That's fine with me."

I summoned the chef. "You've met my friend, WuJian. Why don't you please make him whatever he wants."

The chef said, "It would be my pleasure. What would you like, WuJian?"

WuJian shook his head. "I don't know, I haven't had any lamb chops. I heard they're good."

The chef laughed and said, "Lamb chops? Is that everything? How about I make you something both world famous and delicious?"

"No, no. Lamb chops will be good for now."

"Lamb chops it is."

I kind of thought it strange but said, "That works for me as well."

The chef was about to go and make lamb chops when I called him back and said, "I have additional requests."

After I explained them, the chef smiled. "Very good. I'll make you lamb chops and asparagus, roasted potatoes and a bit of wild rice for entrée."

"That sounds wonderful." I smiled back.

Our first night at home had begun.

Half an hour later, the chef appeared in the living room. "Dinner's ready!"

WuJian looked at me and I said, "Well, that means it's ready and we can go and eat. The table will be set."

"Do we have to set it?"

I laughed. "No, silly. That is why we have our housekeepers." I pointed to the dining room table, where one of our housekeepers, Linda, was putting the finishing touches on the table setting. It looked beautiful.

"Do you mind if I sit closer?" WuJian said.

"Of course not. Come closer." I was pleased he made the request.

He took his chair and brought it closer to mine. Meanwhile the butler had brought in an opening of squash soup that looked delicious.

We both ate it and I said, "The chef is amazing as usual!" WuJian couldn't agree with me more.

This happened course after course. We went through three to four with hardly a word. We were both starving! I can't believe how many courses we went through.

The dessert was brought in after nearly two hours of exotic dishes. WuJian seemed a little out of it. He was obviously tired. I said, "We can finish dessert and go to bed."

"I apologize. I am very tired. It seems like the trip was longer than I thought." He tried to keep his head in an upright position.

"Don't worry and don't feel bad. It was a long trip. We will have plenty of time together," I said reassuringly.

Right after a delicious dessert we went off to separate beds. I was so happy to have finally met the man of my dreams.

This was working out better than I had ever expected.

CHAPTER 8
Family Introductions

After my phone call with Bo, I thought of how to properly introduce WuJian to my family. I didn't want to introduce him right away, because I knew they would never understand.

I was afraid they'd think I was crazy.

Was I?

Who would date such a younger man?

And who would think that I was the love of his life?

No one in their right mind would ever do this. Even if I could somehow convince them that I was sane, they would think that WuJian was after my money.

I never knew his intentions, nor at that point did I know if he actually loved me. I just knew I had found the love of my life, even if I didn't understand it. I knew he was the one I'd been searching for all my life. All the acting jobs, money, and fame never brought me happiness. They always led me to more and more sadness, more and more uncertainty, and more and more unease.

With WuJian I felt like I was somebody I'd never been before. I knew that I truly loved him. I can't explain it, but I knew.

Did you ever feel like that in your gut—where you just know beyond the shadow of a doubt, and no matter how many people told you something else, you just kept believing you were right?

The Universe sent me a message: "You are right. It just may take a long time to know it." In this case, going with somebody so much younger than me was the Universe's way of saying, "This is your true love." However, not everyone else would understand it that way, especially not my family.

I thought about it a lot and so I decided to introduce him as a student from another country who was here on a charity mission.

I would explain that when I went overseas I became enamored with the people of China and all their greatness, and wanted to help in any way possible. I had taken this student into my home as a way of doing that.

I didn't think my family would go for the excuse, but I knew I couldn't tell them the truth just yet. Eventually, I would. That was a long way off, and a lot of pain would result from telling the truth too soon.

I called Bobby and Bo and told them I wanted to have a family meeting at my house, their wives and children included. They had some questions. I answered them as generally as I could.

They knew enough about me to know that when I told them that there was going to be a meeting they accepted it for what it was. They said, "Ma is a very strong person. If she wants a meeting then we'll have a meeting."

After my calls, I found WuJian, who sat in the living room reading newspapers. I sat down next to him and said, "I have something to tell you."

He put down the newspapers and looked at me. "Sure. What is it?"

"I want you to meet my family. My two sons are married, and they have children. You'll meet them. It will not be an easy meeting because I don't think they would understand what we are doing here."

"Tell me, Mary. Do *you* know what we're doing here?"

"Honestly? No, I don't." I compressed my lips. "But I know that I find myself very comfortable and enjoy your company immensely."

"I enjoy your company too," WuJian said. It warmed my heart to hear him say it.

I said, "I enjoy your company and you enjoy mine. However, I think to the outside world, especially my family, they wouldn't understand what it is. I hope you understand what I am going to ask of you today. I care for you a lot."

"I care for you as well."

"I hope you understand that no one will necessarily believe what we are doing here. I can't always believe it myself. I'm not sure what this is but our love for each other has the Universe telling us that this is something that's meant to be."

He leaned forward. "I understand, and not everything can be understood in simple ways. We must learn to accept what the Universe tells us. But I understand if everyone else doesn't understand. They are accepted as well."

To me, WuJian's wisdom always surpassed his age. I didn't expect a military man from China would resonate with me so much, but he did. That was another reason why I believed that the Universe put us together.

I looked into WuJian's eyes. "Thank you, WuJian! Therefore, we have to tell my family something else. My family is extremely important to me. My two sons have been my everything. They are an important part of my life. They mean the world to me."

"I understand." WuJian nodded.

"However, I do know that they will not accept what's going on and what we are doing here. I am, therefore, going to ask you to understand the story I'm going to tell them. I'm going to say you are from a country that I fell in love with, and that you are an exchange student who has come here to study, and through this program has agreed to stay at my house. This is something that they may understand or may not understand, but it is believable. They may not understand it and question my validity and sanity. However, people have exchange students all the time and the boys should understand, with the capacity of this house, that I should be no different. Therefore, we will tell them you are a student. I hope you can play the part."

"Play the part? I was always a student. In the military I was a student. I was a student in other places too. I can easily say I am a student here in America. I think they will understand."

I sighed with relief. "I do hope so, because I don't think they are ready for the truth. I know that if I offer limited details there is a greater chance of this succeeding. I don't know if they will believe me, but I may be convincing enough."

"I understand, and whatever makes you happy will make me happy."

When I heard that I had a good feeling inside my heart. It told me that WuJian was a man who truly wanted to do what was best for me, this man who wanted to make me happy.

I thought to myself yet again that WuJian was nothing like the other men I dated, who probably used me for their own attempts of fame. He just wanted to make me happy. That was something I wouldn't trade for anything.

We set up a meeting with my family for the following week. As the week progressed I got more and more nervous. I didn't know how my family would receive WuJian, but I was increasingly fearful that they wouldn't understand, whatever I said it was.

They saw me as a lonely single woman, past her prime, who tried to pass her time by taking acting roles and keeping herself busy and over-worked. If there was a man in my life they didn't want to know it. They assumed I was alone.

When I would present WuJian to them they would see a man who was at my side all the time and living with me. A man obviously much younger than me. Yes, I had a houseful of staff, but I never had anything like this. They would think I had lost my mind, and the thought of that played in my brain over and over again. Each night I stared at the ceiling, wondering what would happen, wondering how I would be perceived.

The day finally came. I went over to WuJian early in the morning and I said, "This is the day my family is coming."

"I remember that. I did not forget."

"Are you ready?" I asked while rubbing the skin on my hands.

"Ready? Meeting your family is a very nice thing. Of course I am ready."

I took a deep breath. "I believe that you are ready, but I don't know if I am." With that, we both gave a chuckle.

I went over to each member of the staff from the maids to the chef to the butlers. I said to each of them I needed their best today. It was important because Bo and Bobby were coming.

They smiled and said they loved my sons and their families.

I said, "I love them too, but I don't know how they'll react today."

They didn't question me. They knew on some level what was happening. They knew there was a younger man in my life, who lived in the house.

You'll be amazed what those closest to you think, but this staff of mine knew not to ask me any more questions other than to agree and say, "Yes, ma'am, we will give it our best."

After that, I went up to my room to prepare. My room was spacious, luxurious and immaculately maintained. Two marble columns held the ceiling high, rising like sentries from the thickly carpeted floor. The room boasted large floor-to-ceiling windows that let in plenty of sunshine. A sliding glass door led to the balcony, which afforded me a bird's eye view of the lush, spectacular hills. The finest quality items that I had chosen to fill the room evoked supreme sophistication and elegance. Two giant walk-in closets, filled to bursting with clothes, were large enough to fit two cars in each. It was a scale and style suited for a Hollywood celebrity and it satisfied my ego. But on that day, I was too pre-occupied to appreciate its beauty.

I tried on numerous dresses. It was not like me to do that, even in Hollywood in those days where everything was style and fashion and media attention and whatever else. I was never one to get involved with any of it.

Back in the day, when I first started acting, I tried on so many different outfits. I thought that was what made me happy, but soon I realized it wasn't, so I became disinterested.

But on that day, I felt like I was reliving the first day of my career. I was going through each and every item in my closets. And let me tell you, my closets were full of the latest designs. I had it all. I tried on so many things.

Finally, I had the bed piled high with rejected clothing. I called one of the maids and said, "You're going to have to hang these all back up."

The maid didn't question me, though I bet you in her heart she was saying, "Did I have to be the one to come in on this day?"

After a while I finally picked a dress that I thought was proper and fitting. I went downstairs to await the introductions.

The bell rang ten minutes later and first it was Bo, who came with his wife and his two girls, Carol and Nancy, three and five, respectively. I loved seeing my grandkids. I always enjoyed being around them.

I smiled and gave each a hug and a kiss. "Hello, girls."

They said, "Hello, Grandma."

I wrapped my arms around them. "It's always a pleasure to see you."

They were quite happy to see me as well.

Bo gave me a hug, and his wife did too. "A pleasure to see you again," I said.

Bo said, "Ma, we don't need formal greetings."

I tried to calm my nerves. "Well, come this way and have a seat in the living room."

Bo frowned. "Ma, is everything okay?"

I waved my hand. "Yes, we are just waiting on your brother."

"Are you sure?"

"Yes, of course."

A few minutes later, Bobby arrived. He had brought his wife and his boys, Larry and Thomas, four and seven. I gave them each a hug and a kiss as well. "Hello, Bobby. Always a pleasure to see you."

Bobby smiled. "Yes, and you as well. Why so formal? Has it been such a long time?"

"Always too long," I joked.

He laughed. "Yes, Ma." He then continued, "Are you okay? I found your call very strange. You didn't give us much detail. Jennifer and I are worried."

I shrugged. "No, everything is fine. Fine. You know me, I'm not much for words. I'm not a phone person."

"Ma, you're an actress. Everything with you is talking."

"Maybe that was true, a long time ago, but I have become less capable over the years. Please, everyone, make yourself comfortable in the living room. I will be there shortly."

A staff member brought Bobby to the living room, where Bo was. As their wives and children said their hellos, the boys moved away to talk.

Never mind how I know what was said.

Bo started. "Have you heard anything other than this call?"

Bobby said, "No, I haven't. Isn't it strange the way Mom's acting? You think she's sick or something?"

Bo raised his eyebrows. "It did cross my mind. I asked her that, but she denied it. She's never one to lie."

"You're right. I guess we'll just have to wait."

Not long after, I entered the room with WuJian. Both of the boys looked at me and then looked at him, and looked at me, and then looked at him.

I pretended to be calm and said, "I don't understand what you're looking at."

Their eyes were wide. "We don't recognize this man. Is he one of your staff?"

"Boys, this is actually why I called you here today. I want to introduce you to WuJian. He is a student from China, a place I fell in love with all over again, just like in my earlier acting days. What a beautiful place it is. As part of my larger duties as an American of note, when I wasn't filming, I looked into the cultural exchange commission. They said they had some student candidates looking for a house overseas while they were abroad for study. I said I was interested in signing up and so they sent me WuJian. I said it was wonderful to have such a young man in my life. I thought he was quite handsome, but I knew he was also smart. Because of how impressed I was by the commission and partly from my love of China and its people, I have accepted him into my house. Without further ado, meet my exchange student."

The boys looked at me and then looked at him, and then looked at me and looked at him. Bo said with astonishment, "Ma, are you sure you want to do this? It's not like you to house an exchange student."

Bobby nodded in agreement. "I don't think this is a good idea. I mean, are you alright with this? It's an extra burden and you've lived alone for so long. I don't mean anything personal against this man standing here, but I'm worried about you taking on such a big responsibility."

I laughed. "Boys, I appreciated your concern. I do. But this is something I've always wanted to do—to give back to the country that I think is so beautiful. I finally had the ability to do so and this is my way of doing it. I definitely have the room. He's not much of a burden on me other than occasionally making myself available to answer his questions about America or provide a little company. He spends a lot of time on his studies. It shouldn't be a problem."

The boys were still a bit shocked. Their wives, although they knew better than to voice their opinions to me, looked just as shocked as their husbands. But knowing how they all knew me and how stubborn I was, they accepted that this was what I wanted.

After a few minutes Bo said, "Okay, Mom, if this is what you want, we wish you luck and hope it works out."

"Boys, you are always welcome to my home and nothing will change that," I said with relief.

They looked at me with smiling eyes. Bobby said, "Okay, Mom, as long as you're happy, of course we're happy. We welcome him and anything we can do to make his life and your life easier of course we want to do."

I smiled. "I appreciate that. I appreciate your understanding of the situation and can't wait for him to become like one of the family. I hope you will treat him that way."

They nodded. Bo said, "Of course we will. Like Bobby said, if this is what makes you happy then this is what makes us happy."

With that we all went to the dining room and had a pleasant meal. We discussed various things. WuJian answered all the questions they had about what he was studying. I'm sure he drew back on his military studies and training and answered accordingly.

As the night wore on, it became apparent it wasn't just me that WuJian was able to charm. His ability to play the student with no romantic interest in me at all was impressive. You would never know this was the man of my dreams. The man I fell in love with. He played the part perfectly, as if he was an actor in his greatest role.

As the night finally came to an end, Bo and Bobby and their families kissed me goodnight, wished me well and shook WuJian's hand as they headed out the door.

After everybody left, I turned to WuJian and said, "You are an amazing actor, did you know that?"

He laughed and said, "Perhaps all the military training finally paid off. I had to cultivate certain acting abilities when I was just beginning in the military and they've stayed with me all my life."

I gave him a big hug. "You really mean a lot to me. I hope you know that."

"I do, and you are starting to mean much to me as well."

With that, we both went off to sleep.

I felt as if I got a step closer to WuJian that night. For now, I could keep the story of a foreign student. I would have to pass that on to my friends. That would be the next step in my journey, and the next step in the process of what I hoped was eternal happiness.

CHAPTER 9
Friendships Tested

I had gotten through introducing WuJian to my family. That was a great relief to me. I didn't know if they would be receptive, but for now it seemed they would be on board with my new arrangement.

We got to spend a lot of time together. We ended up spending more and more time each day, walking in the park, talking about life, going to the movies and going out to eat, things that a husband and wife or people truly in love would do.

However, this all came with a price.

I had over the years made friends whom I stayed in touch with. I wasn't one to make many friends. I didn't stay in touch with a lot of people. I didn't trust a lot of people.

After the divorce, I didn't always assume people had the best intentions with me, and when you become rich and successful you never know if people are actually interested in you for what you have to offer in life, or if it is your money, your connections to Hollywood, or that they want to be able to say they know a famous actress.

You never know what angle they are taking, so when someone comes to me that I don't recognize, I simply say, "What is it that you want?" Perhaps this comes across as rude, but I know deep in my heart if I don't do this, I wouldn't be able to go on.

Every day, I would get more and more requests for my time, and nothing would ever get done, and I would never enjoy life.

As I spent more time with WuJian, there were a few friends whom I did keep up with. One of them was named Glenda. She was one of my oldest friends. I met her on the set of one of my movies. The story is kind of funny.

You see, back in the day—and I know I told you this many pages ago—you needed to memorize your lines and had someone memorize them also in case you forgot. They would quickly whisper them to you on set. In fact, as I'm sure you recall, that's how I had my first big breakthrough.

Glenda was the one who helped me when I first made it big. She was a few years younger than me when we first met. Glenda was a typical Irish girl with deep blue eyes and a few freckles. She was a young person who was eager to get started in Hollywood any way she could. She started by literally serving coffee to the actors and actresses.

She would bring them a cup and then an actor would say, "I need another" and she would say, "Coming right up!" It was as if she was a butler on a stage. I had felt sorry for her at first, but she always said it with a smile.

The person whom I'd used as a personal assistant on many films decided to move on to other things. One day I said, "Glenda, come here."

She nodded. "Sure. Can I get you a little water or some coffee?"

"No, I don't need either of those. I want to ask you something. Do you want to come work for me?"

A look of puzzlement crossed her face. "What do you mean?"

I said, "Well, my old person that memorized my lines decided to move on to other things. Do you want to work for me?"

She was surprised and delighted at the same time. "What do I have to do?"

"Well, all you have to do is memorize lines and in case I forget, just whisper them to me, that way you can rehearse with me as well."

"Sure, I'd love us to do that. Will I lose this job?"

I laughed. "I don't think so. Let me talk to the boss."

I went over to the director of the movie I was filming at the time and said, "I want Glenda to come work for me, because my old line person is gone and I need someone to help me."

The director looked at me for a few moments. "Do you really need a line person?"

"I don't know if I *need* one, but by myself it is going to take a long time, and each time that happens it's going to cost you more and more production time, which means more and more money that's not in your pocket."

Having studied the logic of my response, the director quickly realized that it was in his best interest to have Glenda work for me, so he said, "Fine, Mary, whatever you want."

I called Glenda back over after the director left. "Glenda, the director is on board. You're going to work for me."

Her response was, "Great! I'm so excited! I can't wait to start."

I laughed. "Great, because here's the script to start working on immediately. Get to it!"

She was a bit taken aback but eventually got used to my style. As the years went on, after she also moved on to other things, we kept in touch.

When I got married she was not only at my wedding—she was my maid of honor. When she got married I was the same for her. Through my divorce and the death of her husband we always kept in touch. We would go out at least once a week and talk often on the phone.

One day she called me and said, "Let's do lunch."

"I can't," I replied.

"Why?"

"Because I have an exchange student living in my house whom I have to help on the side."

I decided to use the same excuse I had on my family. I couldn't take the chance something could go wrong if I changed the story.

"That's very nice, but can't you find some time where we can just do lunch, or at least get a coffee?"

"No. I'm really busy right now."

The next week the same thing happened. And the week after that. After four weeks of my making excuses not to see her, she decided she'd had enough.

I was reading in my room when the butler appeared in the doorway.

"Miss Glenda wants to see you, ma'am," he said. "She's waiting in the living room."

"Do you know why she's here? Did she say anything?"

"No, ma'am. She simply said she wished to see you. What shall I tell her?"

I thought for a moment and decided I could no longer hide the fact WuJian was very important in my life. However, I would still stick to the same story no matter what.

I slowly made my way down the stairs, getting more and more nervous with each step. I knew that I had the right to fall in love and be with whomever I wanted. However, I also knew that, just like my family, my friends would never understand.

I made my way to the living room. I gave Glenda a big hug and said, "It's so great to see you!"

"It's great to see you too. I don't understand why you've been avoiding me."

"I've not been avoiding you. Like I said, I've been busy."

Glenda looked at me and frowned. "I realize you're busy; you always have been. But even when you had the busiest acting jobs, you always made time for at least an hour a week for a coffee. You've been unresponsive to me for four weeks, each time saying the same thing. Tell me something. What is really going on here? Do you not want to have any friends? Is it me? Did I do something wrong? If I did, I'm sorry, I don't know what I've done."

I looked at her and felt bad. I knew in my heart if I allowed this to continue, I would probably lose her as my friend. I thought for what seemed a long while. I wanted to tell her so badly, "Glenda, there's a man I met, I am so in love but yet I can't tell anyone because he is so much younger than me. You would never understand."

However, I bit my lip and said, "I told you WuJian is here because he's a student from China and adjusting to this country is not something easy. However, as you know I have fallen in love with the people over there. I really did want to help and so I brought this man back as part of a student exchange program. It takes a lot for someone to adjust to a foreign country."

I paused and said, "I know you've been outside the United States on at least one occasion. I remember you telling me, Glenda, how hard it was and how painful it was to adjust to a foreign language and culture. You didn't understand the signs, you couldn't read, and the people there— some spoke English, some didn't. It was hit or miss. You tapped one person on the shoulder, they said, 'yes ma'am', you tapped the next one and they spoke a language you didn't know—it might as well be gibberish. Therefore, I know that you understand how hard it would be for someone to get accustomed to this country and why it is important that I spend much time with him."

Glenda looked me with sympathy and understanding as I continued. "I realized this could take away from time we spend on our friendship. I apologize for that. And within a week or two I will be fine and be able to be back to normal. In fact, why don't we make a date in two weeks from now to do lunch? You pick the time and place."

Glenda nodded. "Two weeks from today. I'll pick the place on the day."

I smiled. "Perfect."

Glenda smiled back, gave me a hug and said, "Okay, Mary. As long as you're okay."

"Of course I am. I'm fine. Nothing has really changed. I'm not sick. None of my family members are sick. It's not a mental breakdown. Everything is great."

She laughed and said, "As long as it's not a mental breakdown then I guess we are okay."

I laughed, because deep inside I knew that perhaps someone would think I really did have a mental breakdown if they knew the truth. This was my way of dealing with the fear.

Glenda and I then sat down on the couch for two hours and had a conversation over sandwiches and tea. I guess in a weird way we did have that lunch, although we didn't have it in a restaurant. I guess at the end of that day you could say it was our typical Friendship Day.

I am amazed at how time seems to stand still when you're in love. Four weeks had passed, but it felt like only a day. I don't know if you've ever felt the same.

When you're in love everything else seems to be put to the side; all friends, all family, all things that aren't completely necessary. I don't know if that's the way love should be, but that's how it was for me.

In fact, the more I reflect on it the more I think that love shouldn't be an independent thing. It should be a part of a bigger thing. Therefore, I wish that I understood and recognized time and friends a little bit more in those early weeks.

However, I was getting older, and perhaps things that now made me the happiest and brought the most joy were things that were aligned with my purpose the most. I don't say this to you to justify it, I say this to you because that is actually what happened.

For now, my secret was safe. Glenda hadn't guessed it. There would come a time and a place where everyone would find out, including my best friend. It was strange to spend time with her, knowing I was hiding something so important.

Again, I didn't wish to do this. I felt I had no choice. My friendship was indeed very important and testing it in this way wouldn't be worth it to me. I guess you could say I wanted the best of both worlds.

I wanted to be able to have WuJian and his love to myself, but I also wanted to be able to keep my friends and family just the way things were. I'm not saying they were ever perfect, but they were certainly better than what would have been had I lost them.

Eventually, the time and place would come when all of this would be flushed out.

That moment wasn't now.

I walked Glenda to the door, laughing all the way. Both of us agreed it was amazing to catch up and in two more weeks we'd do our lunch date again.

"Glenda, it was as if we never lost touch. Four weeks flew by like a day."

"You're right. It's amazing. When you really are a good friend, it's hard to not catch up and be happy."

I smiled. "I agree. See you soon."

Our friendship had been tested, but not in a way that she thought or the way I thought. I dealt with it the same as I did with my family. I didn't have to deal with other friends in the same way. I didn't look to initiate anything about this with them. However, if it did come up I would stick to the story.

As I went upstairs, I saw WuJian. "How are you?"

"Great," he said. "How was your lunch date with your friend?"

"Amazing. I decided to stay with the exchange student story."

He nodded. "That's okay. I understand completely."

I gave him a hug and a kiss. "How am I so lucky to have met a man like you?"

He smiled. "I am lucky too to have met you. Would you like to go eat dinner?"

"Sure."

And that was how it ended for that day.

CHAPTER 10
Love Tested

Although it had been a few months after my friends, relatives and children were all introduced to WuJian, they seemed to have fallen for the story I gave them.

Occasionally, they would ask when he would be going back to China. I would brush it off and dismiss it with a wave of my hand or a tone of my voice that said I wasn't sure and didn't want to discuss it.

I told them he enjoyed America so much he wanted to stay and finish his studies. I said I worked with the Chinese government and the US government to be able to do that.

No one really understood exchange students very well. That was to my advantage, because I was able to pull off this lie without many issues. No one understood you needed visas that probably only lasted a semester or a year at best.

After a few months of this routine, people seemed to be used to him, and I think we were used to each other. I didn't know what prompted it or what really started it, but one night as I lay alone, still in a different bedroom, I asked myself, "Does WuJian really love me?"

Why isn't he in the same bed as you yet? I thought about it and said, "Well, I don't think we were prepared."

Again, this wasn't to anyone special—just thoughts in my head. Yes, we had been together on a romantic emotional level like lovers, but I don't think it went deeper than that.

I didn't know if it was age or just neither of us were willing to speak, but the arrangement of staying in the same room and sleeping together never came up. I know that may be strange to others and you might be asking, how could you live for a few months under the same roof, have an intimate relationship and yet never sleep in the same bedroom?

I realized that was part of what probably started to go on in my head. I never expressed my thoughts directly to WuJian. I simply dismissed them as no more than being over-worried and protective.

My husband and I dated for what seemed like forever. He would stay over with me and I would stay over by him, not thinking anything of it at the time. Perhaps I should have seen that as an issue. Perhaps that is why I didn't care what was happening with WuJian.

Men would come and go, but staying over, sleeping in the same bed overnight for long periods of time didn't mean much. They never led to long-term relationships, and the only time they did was with my husband and that ended in divorce.

I didn't believe that was the key to a successful relationship. These thoughts continued to gnaw at me day after day, time after time. Soon it wasn't only at night, but even if we were sitting and dining together.

I knew WuJian was bored, so I decided to get him small acting jobs to keep him busy. It was my way of saying that I enjoyed spending time with him, but I realized if we spent every minute of every day together, eventually one of us would get sick of the other.

At first he took small jobs as an extra in movies and TV; whatever was needed. I had a lot of connections in Hollywood and I was able to utilize them to the fullest.

However, soon it became apparent that he wanted more. One night he came home and looked a little depressed. His face was long, and his body slumped downward. I asked, "What's wrong WuJian, my dear?"

He sighed, "I'll tell you. I didn't realize that being an extra required so little effort. I thank you so much for all the parts you've gotten me, and I'm of course eternally grateful for them. However, I don't believe they take the mental exercise I need to be able to keep me going."

"Believe me," I said. "I understand."

I explained to him how I started with memorizing lines for others. Eventually, it led to extra jobs and more acting jobs and finally significant acting jobs. However, I could totally understand and relate that being an extra wasn't very exciting, very enjoyable - very anything, for that matter.

He obviously didn't have to worry about money—I took care of everything. That wasn't the issue. The issue was more him being fulfilled in life. His happiness became my happiness, so when I saw that he wanted to be more than an extra, I totally understood.

I called one of my producer friends and said, "Listen, you cast my friend WuJian in two of your films."

The producer said, "Yes, I remember him well, Mary. He was quite nice."

I said, "I need more for him. He has tremendous acting potential. You have to give him a starring role in your next film."

The producer laughed and said, "Mary, I love you. You're a dear friend, but a *starring* role? I don't believe he's ready."

"Well, then," I said, backing off but not giving in, "he can certainly handle more than being an extra. Give him a line or two at least."

He thought about it for a few moments and finally said, "Okay, Mary. You have a deal. I will give him a small part in the next film I do."

Later that night, as we were talking, I said, "WuJian, I spoke to a producer who had cast you in two of the movies he had previously done." I mentioned the movies by name.

His eyes lit up. "Yes, I remember. I did enjoy working on those sets."

"Okay. I got you a speaking part and I don't know if it will be a lot of lines, but it is a start for you."

He smiled broadly. "I am tremendously thankful. I do believe this can help me a lot."

We ate, we kissed, we had fun, and we watched a movie and went off to our separate beds.

While I laid down in the bedroom the thoughts came creeping back. *Why is it he is so insistent on having more than an extra acting role?*

It wasn't as if he needed the money. I took care of everything for him. *Perhaps it is because he's only using me to get better paying acting jobs, so he can be on his own. When he is big enough he'll dismiss me and throw me to the wind like all the other men in Hollywood.*

I lay there thinking that thought for many hours that night. This was unusual because, like I said, these small thoughts that occurred to me at night were eventually gone by day. They were just that, small thoughts, which usually dismissed themselves quickly. But on this particular night, the thought persisted. When I finally got up I was extremely tired, as I had barely slept.

The thought continued to stay with me as I went down to eat. The chef had prepared an amazing breakfast, yet I had no appetite.

WuJian came down a little later and started to eat. He looked at my plate and then looked at me and said, "Mary, what's the problem? Is there something I can do to help?"

I put on a smile. "There's no problem. Everything is fine."

I knew that he could tell by my eyes that was not the case. I watched him fidget in his chair. He wasn't sure if he should press me further. After a moment he said, "I can be of help, I'm sure I can. Please tell me what's wrong."

"Let me ask you a question. I know this is not the case, but I have to ask because it is in my heart. Do you love me?"

He looked me in the eyes for a long time and said, "Yes, I do."

"Do you really?"

He stared at me and said, "Where is this coming from? Why are you asking me this now? If I didn't, I would have returned to China many months ago."

I sighed and said, "I know. Well, perhaps there is a silly thought in my head that I can't get rid of."

"What is it?"

I paused. "Are you using me for my Hollywood connections?"

He looked up at me and didn't know how to react. He froze for what seemed like an hour. I thought about the way his face looked and the disappointment in his eyes. I asked myself, *Does he not want to react because he knows the truth and I finally confronted him about it, or does he not want to act because it's completely untrue and therefore he thinks that I don't trust him any longer?*

I waited for what seemed like forever. I tried to hide how nervous I was.

Finally, he looked me in the eyes. "Mary, I have to be honest. I understand completely why you would think that."

After a short pause, he continued. "I mean, after all, I have asked you for more acting roles. However, I want to tell you that anything I have shown you is loyalty and even beyond loyalty. As you may know, based on my military background, I would never do anything to jeopardize a comrade, a colleague or especially a general. And you are far beyond any general in my estimation." He had a look of great pride in his eyes.

Taking my hand, he lowered his voice to a whisper. "I know that this case is not the same. I feel for you as though you are the closest person I know. I have feelings for you that I have not had for many others ever. I can't dismiss the fact that you distrust me, but I must ask that you turn those thoughts from your mind. I realized that this could be something that put up a block in our relationship. However, I believe that we can get through it."

He leaned forward, tilting his head. "I hope you understand and believe me when I tell you that I don't have any intention of using you for anything. Acting jobs are an enjoyable passion and hobby. If you wish for me to stop them, I will do so. However, I must tell you there is a lot of benefit to it because it does fulfill me."

I had thought about what he said for a few minutes, because I wasn't sure how to react. He was so genuine and so innocent, he made me want to hug him.

On the other hand, was this also a ruse?

A ruse to get me to leave him alone?

What if I should call his bluff?

I should say stop acting. Well, he'll be miserable and if so, will eventually leave me anyway, in which case I gain nothing. At least now I have his company. Even if it's not real, it looks like it's real.

You see, to me it seemed that way. At least I could have someone like WuJian in my life. I had not had anyone that I had ever truly loved, so what was the risk?

With all these conflicting thoughts in my head, I decided that the status quo was the best way forward to see what happens. I nodded and simply said to WuJian, "I truly believe you. I believe that acting is something you enjoy. I'd never want to stand in the way of your happiness, because to tell you the truth your happiness has become my happiness. I need you to understand you are so important in my life, and if acting is what makes you happy I understand. I believe you would never want to harm me or hurt me, that you do truly love me."

We continued to eat breakfast, both of us with happiness in our hearts. However, my happiness was also conflicted, conflicted by the fact that I didn't truly trust him. I was on one hand happy with WuJian's confession but on the other I was so afraid to lose him.

As much as I wanted to believe him, I also believed the reality of the story that was right before my eyes—the reality of an older woman with a younger man. Most people looking at it would say it was a Hollywood story in itself—a younger man looking for an older wealthy woman to take care of him. It was like one of those Hollywood stories that they tell all the time.

I continued to be around him, just like always. I didn't know if the thought got worse or better over time. Eventually, I learned to live with this conflicting thought. As much as WuJian tried to prove his loyalty, it was hard because at the end of the day I never truly knew what his interest in me was.

He never said anything that would conflict with anything previously said or done, but the confirmation that he truly loved me and wanted to be with me. He never did or said anything otherwise. Even when I got older and I got sick, he never mentioned anything other than the fact that he was there for me.

It was something I always appreciated until my dying day. It was something that I took with me wherever I went, and it was something that gave me hope every day of my life.

CHAPTER 11
Continued Distrust

I got WuJian about twenty different acting roles within a single month's time. Even for the most powerful people in Hollywood, this was unprecedented. Many actors appear in major movies that take months to film. That makes a lot of sense. Even small roles take what seems like a month with all the shooting, reshooting, retakes and other things that come up in the production of a typical movie.

However, to be in twenty different films in various roles and different opportunities was unheard of. I gave WuJian all these opportunities, because I really believed that this was what he wanted.

He wanted to become an actor and put his effort into something. He thanked me each time I got him a role. He gave me a kiss on the cheek and said, "I really do appreciate it." This scenario played out over and over again.

As he began to accumulate roles, people noticed his ability. He would be a man who worked in a store one day and be an army general another. Then, on another day, he would be leading a group of people up a hill telling stories. The next week, he'd be a restaurant owner.

All the variation increased his skills. Eventually, producers noticed him and wanted to cast him in more featured roles. As his popularity grew, so did his following. Audiences began to recognize him. His popularity increased.

He had to first block his phone number and then change it. I laughed. "Now, that's how you know you're becoming a star, when you're able to block your phone and be able to tell others that you don't want to know who they are. That's when you've made it." Then we both laughed.

However, with each role he landed, with each success he had, that feeling of distrust in me grew. On the one hand I believed that he truly loved me, but on the other, that feeling of distrust and doubt kept getting worse and worse. I didn't know what to do.

I saw friends and I couldn't tell them the truth because of what I had told them previously. I finally decided to go to a therapist and tell her what was going on.

The therapist was non-judgmental. She didn't care about the age difference between us, didn't care whether the love was real or not. Her entire job was to help me and put me on the path to being healthy.

After our second session, my therapist, Barbara, said, "Let me ask you a question. If you believe that WuJian has your best interests at heart, why do you keep doubting yourself?"

"Isn't it obvious? To me he is someone who could be an opportunist who used me for my Hollywood connections. I had gone over to China to do acting jobs, so wouldn't it be logical that he saw me and wanted to use me?"

"I don't know whether that is true or not, but I do know this. You're not happy and this feeling is ruining you. The way I see it, you only have two alternatives—you can either learn to trust him and quell your doubts or send him away. Send him packing. Wherever he goes with his life, it will no longer be your concern. I do believe that this is something you emotionally don't want. You truly love him, and you wish that he felt the same, except you don't know if he does."

She paused and then added, "Let's focus on the first one. If you let him stay, you have to make peace with the situation, realize that he does have your best interest at heart and dismiss this feeling of doubt. I know it will not be easy, but if you build yourself up with some exercises, you can do it. First thing you must say is that every night that he comes home to you, you are someone he still cares for.

The second thing is, you must increase your relationship. It's not for me to say how to proceed, but I do have some suggestions. For one, stop sleeping in separate rooms. I don't understand this dynamic, considering how long he's been here. More importantly, the more we talk, the more I realize that this is not a dynamic that you can handle. This is not an emotional level that you accept, and this is not a level that you want. You really seem to want you two to be close on all levels. Therefore, if you really do want to act like someone who's living together, act like someone who's living together. Sleep in the same bed. I think this will help you, because it will test the relationship. I don't mean to cause harm, but I do believe if you really want to get this relationship going in the right direction you need to take it a step further. This would seem like the most obvious choice."

I sat and listened to Barbara and understood what she said. Part of me wished I had done this months ago. However, there was another part of me that said, "Oh, no, what if it's true that this will push us further apart." I didn't want to understand whatever this was. I still didn't have the proper name for it because I didn't know what we were.

Were we girlfriend and boyfriend?

Were we lovers?

Were we just two people who enjoyed each other's company?

What were we?

That question remained with me for a very long time. I didn't know the answer. However, I did know that by sharing the same bedroom we had a chance of growing closer.

After the session ended I went home, more determined than ever to be able to discuss this and be able to move forward with the plan. I got cold feet as the night wore on, but I knew that I had to move forward.

WuJian tended to come home later those days because his roles were continuing to grow. I of all people knew and appreciated how long the days on set could be.

When he did come home, I was waiting for him on the couch. He came over and gave me a kiss. "Hello, Mary!"

"Hi! How was your day?" I asked, trying to hide my nervousness.

He raised his eyebrows. "It was wonderful. I had the best director. He kept pointing and making sure I was in the right place to have a strong focus in the scene. This particular role is quite unique for me. I play a young widower who is looking to once again find true love. I'm not the main character, but an important one. I can't say I completely understand it."

I looked at him and smiled. "WuJian, I have been in so many roles, there are still so many things I didn't understand, but to me it sounds normal. And exciting!"

We laughed.

And then I turned serious and said to him, "I need to ask you something."

He was a bit surprised by my change of tone. "Sure, Mary."

"Let me ask you, do you think that sleeping in separate bedrooms is a normal arrangement for us?"

He probably didn't know what was coming. He froze and thought about it for a moment and then replied, "I don't know what normal is."

To break the ice, I laughed. "I hope you're meaning that in a good way."

"Of course. My whole life before America was lived in a non-normal way." WuJian laughed.

I knew that he wasn't playing with me and that he meant what he said, so I took a deep breath and said, "I have to ask you something. I need you to move in with me."

"I already am."

"Yes. In the house. That's not what I mean. I want you to move into my bedroom with me." I said this slowly, making sure my intention was very clear.

He looked me in the eyes and spoke slowly, as if to confirm I knew what I was talking about. "Hmm… Is that a step you want to take?"

"Yes. Very much so."

He sat in quiet contemplation for a moment. His face was so serious. His eyes began to move back and forth as he thought, and I was nervous as to what he had to say. After what seemed like forever, he nodded. "Yes, I agree. That makes a lot of sense."

I felt like I was a sixteen-year-old again, hearing my first crush say, "I love you too!" I couldn't help but give WuJian a big hug. "I appreciate that!" It wasn't that I was begging or anything, but to hear WuJian agree to the arrangement was important to me. It was like I was living out a fairy tale.

However, I wanted to be totally honest. "You do know this comes with a risk?"

He frowned. "I don't understand. What risk?"

"Well, as people get closer, sometimes they grow apart. I'm not sure if you understand what that means, but when a person gets too close to someone, they tend to learn a lot about them. Sometimes that drives them further apart."

He laughed. "I don't worry about that. I feel I know you very well on a very deep level. It is as if I knew you my whole life. If going to the bedroom together is the next logical step, I think that is what we should do." With that I smiled and gave him another hug.

We agreed that that night he would move his things into my bedroom. I was excited and nervous at the same time.

Who knew what might become of it?

Who knew if all of it would ultimately work out?

I called to one of the maids and said, "WuJian will be moving his things into my bedroom. You need to be able to place it and find space for it in an organized way."

"Of course, madam, right away."

WuJian smiled and said, "I look forward to this. I think you and I are a normal couple living in a non-normal situation."

"I think you are right. I don't think everyone else would call us normal, but for us it's normal."

We sat down to eat dinner and enjoy each other's company.

Our first night was one of trepidation. I walked into the bedroom and got ready for bed. He did the same.

He smiled. "Well, what is your normal night routine?"

"I don't know. I rarely watch TV. I read, try to do something to make me a little bit more relaxed."

"I do the same. I usually read because it's easier for me. It tends to put my brain in a more relaxed state."

"Very good. That's what we shall do." I nodded with a smile.

Both of us took out the books we were reading, dimmed our lights and read. When I was finally ready to sleep, I looked over at him, he looked over at me and we gave each other a kiss and said good night.

This was the first time we had slept in the same bedroom since WuJian arrived from China. It was a big step in our relationship. I could never say for sure that it allowed us to get closer and that I never had doubts. But it did make me feel a lot more comfortable with our current situation.

CHAPTER 12
The Lie Begins to Unravel

As with any good lie, the key is to keep consistent over time.

Friends, family and even colleagues began to believe WuJian was here as a student. However, cracks began to form in our story.

One day a Chinese exchange student from the same town as WuJian happened to cross paths with my son Bo.

When Bo phoned me about it, I said, "Oh, you met another student?"

"Yes, his name was Wei, and I asked him 'do you know WuJian? He's from your town.' And he said he didn't. In fact, he said the only WuJian he remembered was someone whom he had trained with briefly in the military."

I immediately laughed and said, "Ah, WuJian is like Smith, such a popular name, nobody really knows who anybody is over there. It's such a big country. Such a giant population."

Bo wasn't sure if I was telling the truth, but he seemed to buy it temporarily. With that, we continued our conversation as if nothing happened and hung up.

When we hung up, I had an uneasy feeling in my stomach. I could hear my own heartbeat and my hands got sweaty as if I was preparing for a fight or flight crisis. I went over to WuJian. "Do you know a man named Wei from your hometown?"

"Yes, we were briefly together in an army training unit," he said. "Why do you ask?"

"Because Bo somehow came across him. What are the odds of that happening? But he did. And of course, Bo being Bo, he asked this Wei if he knew you, and he said he did and that he briefly trained with you. That created some confusion and Bo called me up." I told him what I'd said about the commonness of the name. "I don't know if we can keep this up for much longer," I added.

WuJian looked at me, eyes wide open. "Well, what do you wish to do? Do you wish to tell them the truth?"

I quickly dismissed it. "I don't think I'm ready for that. I don't need the world to judge me on who and who I shouldn't love, who and who I shouldn't date, and who and who I shouldn't be with."

He laughed. "Mary, I'm happy to do the ruse we are doing if that makes you happy. Ultimately, your happiness is my happiness. However, I do think as we get more and more cracks on the wall, it'll become harder and harder to do this. But I'll keep telling people that I am an exchange student here honing my acting skills while finishing up my studies."

I was relieved to hear it. I said, "Thank you, WuJian, my love. It is very important for me that we keep it up. Please be consistent with what you are telling people. When the time is right the world will know our love. However, for now, please don't tell the truth."

I knew that the fire had been temporarily extinguished.

But I was nervous. I was scared. I felt I couldn't keep this up forever.

What should we do?

What should *I* do?

Maybe my kids would just make fun of me. Maybe they would disown me. Maybe they would think I'd gone crazy. I knew that the world would judge me, which would bother me a lot. At the end of the day I had to let go of this incident and pretend that nothing had happened.

The next stumble in our story came when one of the actors on set recognized WuJian from China.

Sam had been to China briefly, helping out on the set doing little odd things while we were filming and happened to have seen WuJian with me a few times.

He saw WuJian on set and asked him, innocently enough, "WuJian, is that really you?"

Sam had long wavy hair, and it was hard for people not to recognize him, even if you had seen him only a few times in your life. WuJian recognized him right away.

First WuJian was surprised to see Sam. Then he said cordially, "Yes, it is me."

Sam was shocked. A Chinese military man he saw almost a year ago in China turning up on a Hollywood set? He couldn't believe it. "Are you really the one I met in China?"

WuJian, not really understanding why and how to keep up the lie, said, "Yes, of course, I'm the guy you met there."

"Wow! You've come a long way. Look at you now!"

"Yes, you as well. You have become a stagehand and an actor. I'm sure you will rise continually. I'm happy for you."

"What do you do these days?"

"Well, I'm an exchange student and am also honing my acting skills."

Sam seemed a bit suspicious. He rolled his eyes and asked, "Who are you staying with?"

Without much thinking, WuJian replied, "I'm living with Mary."

"Mary Maddin? Of course. Makes sense. I saw you often with her in China. Did you marry her while we were overseas? Wow, she's an older broad. You're into her?" Sam grinned.

Confused, WuJian asked politely, "Into her? I don't understand."

"Are you living with her like a boyfriend–girlfriend type of thing? What's the deal?" Sam winked.

When WuJian realized he could be caught in his lie, he lost his composure and quickly tried to cover. "Oh, no, no. She had pity on me when I was in China when I expressed my interest in wanting to become an actor and she agreed to take me over here and teach me."

Sam laughed. "Oh, teach you a couple things, huh?"

"I don't understand what you mean, but yes, she is going to teach me a few things."

With that, Sam burst out into laughter, because he thought one thing and WuJian definitely thought another. WuJian thought he properly put out the fire while Sam thought that he confirmed that WuJian was living off me.

At the end of the day WuJian came home as usual and told me what had happened. He termed it a "funny story."

I didn't find it funny at all. I almost jumped off the couch.

At that point, WuJian turned serious. He could tell I wasn't happy. He was a little intimidated by my dramatic response. He whispered, "Yes, I said I was living with you."

"Tell me exactly how you said it." I moved closer to him.

"All I said was we're living together and that you brought me here out of pity. I was going to be an actor and you wanted to help me. He made fun and some sort of reference to you 'teaching me things' that I didn't understand."

I completely understood where the stagehand was coming from, as if my fears were coming true. He was judging us without knowing the facts. Imagine had he really known the facts, what kind of judgment he would have.

I frowned and said, "WuJian, he was joking about a sexual relationship. He thought we were intimate lovers and that I was using you."

WuJian stopped for a minute. "Is that really what he meant?"

"Yes, he was trying to make a joke, but it wasn't very funny."

"Oh, I didn't mean to tell him that. The impression I gave was that you were helping me, similar to our story."

"I know, but he's probably going to talk. You know Hollywood—once people hear a rumor about something they continually investigate. Soon the paparazzi will be here trying to snuff us out. I don't know what to do."

WuJian's head went down as if he wanted to bury his face. "I'm so sorry. I didn't mean to cause any problems."

I held onto his hands and said, "It's not your fault, it's the world's fault. People judge too harshly, people don't understand things, they judge, they make fun, they insult."

WuJian kept apologizing and feeling very, very sorry for what he had done. He didn't mean to make any problems for us.

I wasn't sure how to proceed.

Luckily, that day I had a therapy session. I arrived at the therapist's office early. I couldn't wait for my session to start. When it was my time, I sat on the chair nervously. I said to Barbara, "I have a big problem. I think my lie is being unraveled."

Barbara leaned forward with a frown. "What do you mean?"

"First my son Bo ran into an exchange student who happened to know WuJian and remembered that he was in the military. He kept thinking it was funny that he was here. Secondly, WuJian ran into an old stagehand that was on one of the sets while we were in China. The stagehand remembered him and asked him where he was living. When he said he was living with me, he started to make fun of us, thinking we had an intimate relationship."

Barbara listened carefully. She was silent for a moment and then said, "Mary, is this fearful feeling that you're having because you know it's the truth?"

"Well, it's probably that, but also because I'm afraid of the way the world will think of us. I mean, think about the stagehand. He barely even knew of the situation and completely made fun of us. Imagine if people get word of the real situation?"

Barbara said, "Well, perhaps this is the Universe's way of telling you that it's time to reveal the truth. There's no way you can keep this going forever. I mean, look at the situation. Two coincidences in the span of a week. That is pretty funny for our person from China and our older actress from California. Somehow two completely unrelated people happen to know you or WuJian or both. Perhaps you should listen to the Universe."

I sighed and said, "I understand that, but I'm just not ready for it. I can't handle being judged, even if WuJian somehow could. To me, there is still an option to keep this going for as long as possible. If people bought the lie, even for a little bit, it'd be revealed slowly over time. At least maybe that way I will be old enough and ready to accept the situation. There is no way anything good comes out of me telling the truth right now."

Barbara sat quietly while I continued to talk. Her job wasn't about giving me lessons instantly; it was about letting me get out my thoughts properly and then being able to put my concerns into a possible working solution.

The session ended. I thanked her and left. I didn't have much more clarity other than I wasn't ready to tell the world the truth.

When I arrived home, WuJian asked, "How was your session?"

"Actually, it was good to get everything off my chest. I don't know if I have any ideas, but I do know that it was extremely important for me to go."

WuJian frowned. "Mary, we can't keep this going forever. We can if you want to, but I don't think it would properly work. At the end of the day, we both need each other, we both need to be happy. If we live a life of secret, it will ruin us all."

"I know you're right and in my heart I know it's true. We will have to come up with a plan of how to tell the world the truth. It will have to be something we worked on slowly as I am really not ready."

We continued to talk and formulate a plan. The next step would be to start with my family, then our friends, and then the greater population.

It would be a relief for us to not to have to tell everyone the lie, make up stories and excuses and constantly come up with ideas. It would be good to get this off our chests.

Especially mine.

CHAPTER 13
Living the High Life

I would be remiss if I didn't tell you how we lived. After all, I was a Hollywood actress, and WuJian has started to see success.

I didn't need his money, nor did I take any of it. I didn't want anyone to think that I needed him for anything other than his love.

I know that we didn't reveal our story to everyone yet, and the truth and meaning behind it. However, I want to tell you a little bit more about how we lived and how we enjoyed each other's company. This is not to show off in any way, but to simply describe how we were living at this time.

For me, the life of abundance was something I had become used to. As you know, I didn't always have this wealth, but I did acquire it, and once acquired it was hard to give up. I loved my maids, butlers, and chef. I viewed them as people in my life who helped me with what I needed. The chef, for example, cooked healthy meals or occasional snacks I probably shouldn't have eaten. But I did so enjoy them!

I also viewed the chef as someone I could talk to, someone I could speak to about different things. If I had a bad day or a bad acting job, I would run it by him. He was someone I could bounce ideas off of. It's like when you're in a bar. You have a bartender standing behind there, so you pick his or her brain. Isn't that what you would do?

You would simply go over to the bartender and say, "Bartender, pour me a drink."

Then the bartender would say, "What do you want?"

You would say, "I need a double today."

The bartender would say, "Wow, is it that bad?"

"Yes it is…"

Same thing with the chef. He would make something nice and I would eat it. As I sat down, I often invited him to join me. He was happy to oblige.

When we sat down, we would have a discussion. I'd tell him about how I didn't like the director or fellow actor I was working with, or maybe my agent didn't give me a role I really desired.

I would also invite the maids, if they were finished making my room, to come have a drink with me. I'm not sure what they thought of all this. Perhaps they thought I was nuts, perhaps they thought I didn't understand what I was doing, or that I was desperate for people's company because I lacked it in my life.

I'm not sure, but I never asked, and it didn't matter to me because at the end of the day, I just enjoyed having their company and being able to say something to someone who somehow might understand. I suppose on some level the same thing was true with WuJian.

I did enjoy his company. I enjoyed his love, but I also enjoyed his companionship. He provided so much more than my staff ever could. I was able to speak openly about different things with him. It didn't matter that he enjoyed things that I had not benefited from— his happiness became my happiness.

If he wished the chef to cook him a specific meal, different than mine, I said, "Go ahead." If we wanted to go somewhere or he needed to do something by himself, I said, "No problem."

I never thought twice about any of this. It never entered my mind that, "My gosh he was using me for my money."

I know I said that it entered my mind that he was using me for my connections and that is true. But for my money, it was something I had in abundance anyway… it wasn't as if it was going to be used for anything else.

To me, the most important thing was that he was happy. If using these things made him happy, then so be it.

We would often go to a tennis club I'd joined. WuJian had never joined one before, and I was happy to give him a new experience.

I laughed the first time we drove there. "Oh, WuJian, have you ever played tennis before?"

"No! Actually, I've never even held a racket."

We both laughed at that.

We arrived at the tennis club that day and Steve, who was the manager there, said, "Mary, good to see you again!" Steve was tall and muscular, always well dressed in sports outfits. He was a very friendly fellow who I had known for many years. He always greeted people with the biggest smile and a sincere wish to help.

"Good to see you too. I brought someone new. His name is WuJian. He's an acting student of mine."

"Oh, that's nice. Any friend of Mary's is a friend of mine." He walked over and shook WuJian's hand.

"Yes, he is a great friend," I said.

Steve said, "No problem. What can we do to help him?"

WuJian and I just looked at each other. I said, "Well, Steve, WuJian has never actually picked up a racket."

"Wow. Okay, we have a newbie."

"Yes."

WuJian pointed at himself. "Yes, whatever a newbie is, that is me." We all laughed.

"Okay. I'll get you all set up," Steve said.

WuJian was outfitted with a racket, proper attire and was assigned the club's best coach. I went to play with my usual partner while WuJian had his first lesson.

At the end of the lesson we both came together. "How was your lesson, WuJian?" I asked.

"Tennis is an interesting game. It requires a lot of exercise but also a lot of discipline. The discipline part I certainly enjoyed from my days in the army, and the tennis part was actually more fun than I anticipated."

I was glad to hear it. "WuJian, would you like to join and become a member?"

His eyes beamed with delight. "Certainly. If my schedule will allow it, then I certainly would make time. Anything else that involves going with you, I'll try that as well."

I was able to fully integrate WuJian into the world of tennis. This wasn't the only world that I integrated him into. I integrated him into the golf club as well. You see, when I had a lot of down time between acting roles, I tried to keep busy.

I know I said I had a lot of men in my life and they certainly kept me busy. At the end of the day, there was more to my life than that. I hosted charitable events and raised money for charitable causes, but I also involved myself in things like tennis and golf.

WuJian had seen golf in China, where it was becoming popular. However, it was reserved for high dictators, wealthy businessmen, and the upper class of society. WuJian had risen in the military but he wasn't a typical high-ranking official to be considered for such things. Therefore, he didn't get a chance to ever play golf. For me, I was happy to show him how.

We went to the golf store and picked out a proper set of clubs, got on proper attire and I took him to the driving range.

At first, his first few shots off the tee resembled more of a ball falling in a baseball field than it did a golf shot. The ball seemed to go high but not far, or far but not high.

I laughed and said, "You'll get the hang of it."

WuJian got frustrated at times, something I had not seen too much in him. I said, "Why are you getting frustrated? Tennis was new for you and you seemed to enjoy it so much more."

He sniffed, "It's not that. It's that I remember seeing in China all the high dictators and high officials hitting shots so well, and I said someday I would like to do that as well. Here I have the opportunity to do so as much as I want, and yet I seem to not be able to do it. It is quite frustrating that I can't make it happen."

"WuJian, that's a lesson in life, because at the end of the day, we all have challenges. This one is trivial. However, I do believe with practice you'll get it."

Again, I arranged for a coach. He was eager to start his studies. It seems to me that golf was more for him than tennis. I didn't challenge him and simply watched with enjoyment as he seemed to get the hang of it.

Slowly but surely, he became better and better until his tee shots became those of an amazing pro. He hit far and wide with accuracy. It was an amazing thing to behold.

"WuJian, you've come so far."

"Yes! It's as if I envisioned it in my dreams. I finally have gotten to play this, and I owe you for it and thank you very much!" WuJian looked me in the eyes with deep appreciation.

I gave him a kiss. "It is the least I can do for the happiness you're bringing me."

He smiled and went back to practicing.

At the end of the night, we went home, and we sat and had dinner. We enjoyed each other's company, and we went to bed together. It was definitely enjoyable.

Sports weren't the only thing I enjoyed doing with WuJian. We loved to find new restaurants, wine bars, wine tastings… You name it, we probably tried it.

In fact, WuJian said one night that he had seen a commercial about a cooking class that was held near us. To be honest, I don't do much cooking. When I was younger, my parents did the cooking and when I got good acting jobs I could afford to eat out. Eventually, I hired my chef.

Once the chef was hired, I no longer even considered cooking my meals. But when WuJian asked me to go, I said, "Sure!"

We enrolled in the class, which was full of couples, so we fit right in, to a point. After all, because of our age gap we were probably the oddest couple there.

It seemed to me that the other couples had more in common with each other. However, we didn't care. We simply focused on the teacher and the task at hand.

She said, "Today folks, we're going to be cooking lamb chops a la carte."

I didn't understand what that meant, but I figured it was something I'd probably had on one of my menus.

WuJian listened eagerly as the teacher spoke. He followed each step diligently. I wasn't as graceful and certainly not as careful.

If she said one ounce of sugar, I probably poured four. If she said to dice the onions, I sliced them. I didn't pay too much attention, other than to the most general steps.

As we were pulling our trays out of the oven, I laughed. Mine resembled mush, and WuJian's look like something that came from a five-star restaurant.

The teacher walked by and looked down at our plates. She turned to WuJian. "My gosh, you have a future in cooking. Very well done!"

WuJian smiled. "Thank you!"

The teacher then looked at my plate and shook her head. "Well ma'am, at least we have openings for next week's class."

We all had a good hearty laugh about it. At the end of the day, we both got to take home what we'd made.

I joked and said to WuJian, "I think I'm going to share yours. I'm not sure if you want to eat mine."

He laughed and said, "Well, we could try it. I do think that we might need some medication after."

It was these types of things that we enjoyed; they enhanced each other's company and enhanced the value of our relationship. I do feel that we would have had a deep relationship, no matter what. It was a love that was destined to be. As we grew, each thing we did together seemed to make more sense.

In fact, we did similar things that a normal couple would do. We went to the movies, we walked in the mall and park, and we did simple things, like reading together or gardening. It was a sight to behold for me to look into someone's eyes and adore him so much. I had never felt this way about any man before. I knew I never would again.

I mean, going to the movies for fun was something I never considered. After all, I'm an actress—to me the movies are no big deal. I knew what went on behind them. How they were made. I couldn't watch them without pulling them apart, over-analyzing them. If I liked a story I certainly would watch it with more attention, but it still had never been fun.

However, it wasn't about the movies, it was about the fact that I had this man in my life whose company I so enjoyed. For me that was the biggest change. A life well-lived, with fine things was certainly well worth it when you had the man of your dreams at your side.

CHAPTER 14
The Love is Tested Through and Through

I had always known that WuJian was handsome. It was apparent from the moment we met. While I did fall in love with his many qualities, I would be lying if I said it wasn't true that he's extremely handsome and beautiful to look at.

I had seen other women looking at him. It wasn't a surprise to me in any way. After all, a handsome man does generate a certain amount of attention.

However, I wasn't prepared for someone to make advances toward him. I perhaps should have known that this would happen eventually. After all, someone looking at us from the outside wouldn't see us as a couple, because we had continued telling people that he was an exchange student here to study and finish his degree.

Of course that would open him up to the advances of other women.

Who was I to stand in his way?

After all, I was just doing him a favor as an older woman hosting him in my house. I should have expected this. However, when it actually occurred I wasn't prepared. I was certainly not emotionally prepared, so I had a feeling of jealousy in the pit of my stomach that I couldn't explain.

Let me tell you what happened.

It was a normal day on set. I decided to surprise WuJian and visit him. I had often done this to make him happy and also because I enjoyed it. I would go down to the set, see him performing and I would feel so satisfied. I felt a certain pride that I was able to bring this talented man into the world of film.

As I entered the sound stage I saw that WuJian's co-star was extremely beautiful. Ironically, she wasn't the one who was interested in him. I'm sure she found him attractive or else the acting wouldn't have worked as well as it was.

Perhaps she had other men in her life, or perhaps she didn't want a man in her life at that moment. I have been in both places.

I had been in places where I had so many men, so many dates, I didn't know what to do with them all. I had also been in places where I was so busy with my work that a man in my life would complicate things, and I didn't want that. So, I could relate.

However, there was another woman, just a bit player, really, who was extremely cute, perhaps some would say pretty, who did find him attractive.

How did I know this you ask?

Because I found her flirting with him at every opportunity that day. And I did think that WuJian appreciated the interest. I'm not sure if he took it as such, but it seemed to me that he was very interested in the fact that she was interested in him.

I didn't know what to do with this. I watched in horror as this woman would touch his hand and laugh at silly things he said. "Oh WuJian, that was such a funny line. Oh WuJian, you're such a great actor. Oh WuJian, I really *love* what you're wearing today. It is really stylish."

I couldn't believe this girl made such remarks, especially in front of me. I wanted to go over to her and say, "Do you know who he is? Do you know he is taken?"

However, I knew I couldn't say that because of the situation we had created for ourselves. I started to think out loud and blame myself.

When WuJian came home that night, I was very cold to him. He wasn't used to this behavior, and it shocked him.

"Mary, what's the problem? I was so appreciative that you came to the set today," he said.

"Nothing at all, WuJian. Nothing at all. Just thinking about some things." I shook my head and tried to brush it off.

After a half hour of silence, he realized it wasn't me just thinking about things. There was more to the story.

"Mary, there is something obviously wrong here; you're never this quiet this long. Please, please tell me what's wrong so I can help."

I shook my head and sighed. "You would never understand."

"Try me, perhaps I would."

"WuJian, let me tell you something. I don't really know if you realize this, but you're an extremely handsome man. I've occasionally told you this, but probably never enough. That being said, I expected others to find you attractive. However, I wasn't prepared for this in the least. Your fellow actor, Priscilla, I think likes you very much. I think it is more than just a simple friendship she's interested in. I think there is a romantic interest as well."

He laughed. "Don't be silly. She has no interest in me. She flirts with everyone like that."

"No, I've seen that look in a woman's eyes before; I have had it myself. It's the look of 'I am attracted to you. I wish to get to know you better.' I have put that move on many men in my time for many different reasons. Some I actually had a physical interest in, some it was emotional, some I just wanted to be with to keep me company for those moments. Believe me when I tell you that if a woman is giving you those eyes, putting her hand on your hand, laughing and giggling and throwing her hair, that is a clear sign that she's interested in you."

WuJian thought for a moment. It was clear he didn't realize the extent of the pain caused to me. "You know, Mary, I never thought of it that way. I am not sure if this is the first time a woman has behaved this way around me... perhaps yes, perhaps no. I don't know. I do know that many women laugh at me but that's because I always found myself to be a funny person in my own quirky way. I think maybe she might be interested in me, so I will set the record straight right away."

"How could you do that? What could you tell her? Anything you tell her will compromise our story. We can't have our story compromised just yet. I don't think it's the right time to tell anyone."

"I understand what you're saying. However, I will think of something to show that I'm not interested in her, because if I don't it will continue to happen. If it doesn't happen with this one, it'll happen with the next one. They will keep happening until I find a way to make it clear that I have no interest."

I laughed and said, "Well, I don't know what to tell you, but I do know as a handsome man you'll probably experience this plenty."

WuJian laughed. "Don't worry about it, it will be taken care of."

The next day on the set, from what he told me, WuJian went over to Priscilla and said, "Can I talk to you for a moment?"

Priscilla's face lit up. "Sure."

WuJian rephrased, "Can I talk to you alone for a moment?"

She got even more excited.

Perhaps to her this was the big opportunity she'd waited for to be able to finally go and have a real conversation with him.

When they actually were to the side WuJian said, "Priscilla, I think you're a really great girl. I think you're cute, you're pretty and you're funny, and I appreciate that you're actually laughing at my jokes." Priscilla blushed as WuJian was speaking.

He paused and then continued, "However, I want to tell you there is someone else in my life. I can't reveal who because I want to keep it private, but I will tell you that there is someone very special in my life whom I love dearly. At this time, I am not sure if I'm being presumptuous in that there was some level of interest, but I do appreciate it and I want to put it down before it gets more and more and then someone gets hurt."

Priscilla was quiet and didn't know how to respond. She looked down as if she was searching for something important.

After a short while she looked up at WuJian and said cheeringly, "No, sweetie, I really do find you handsome of course. Let me tell you the truth. Matt, the costume designer… I have had my eye on him for a while. He's the man I'm after. Don't you worry about it WuJian, we're good."

WuJian smiled and said, "Are you sure? Are we okay here? I don't want to mess things up between us. After all, we are acting in this movie together and I'm sure we'll see each other again in other roles."

Priscilla waved her hand and said, "Of course, sweetie. Don't worry about it, yes, of course."

And with that WuJian gave her a quick hug and said, "Great! I appreciate that," and walked away.

WuJian probably didn't take seriously the parting reaction from Priscilla. Her eyes looked down to the floor and an overall sadness came over her.

I have been there myself when a man has rejected my advances. Not that it happened very often I must say, but the few times that it did certainly bothered me for more than a day, more than a week, sometimes more than a month. I'm not sure the longest that I've taken to get over a man, but in those rare occasions when I was rejected it was very painful.

My suspicion was confirmed when WuJian came home and told me what happened.

He said with a big grin, "Mary, you have nothing to worry about. I pulled Priscilla to the side and had a conversation. In that conversation Priscilla insisted that she was into another man."

"WuJian, tell me. How did she react when you spoke to her?"

WuJian's face twisted into a scowl, "I don't understand the question."

"What was her face like? Was she up, down, where was she looking?"

"Oh, mostly down at the floor, no big deal."

"Oh, you're wrong. It's a very big deal. You see, she's trying to avoid eye contact to avoid the pain. It wasn't that it was an awkward conversation she didn't want to have, but a conversation she was hoping would go one way, but it went another."

"So you mean to tell me, Mary, that she really was upset and *was* into me? That I have disappointed her?"

"Exactly, WuJian. That's exactly what I'm saying. You have tremendously disappointed this woman. However, I do think being the big star you are and the fact that she's still an up and coming actress, she has no bearing on this situation. It's simply a matter of getting through the work. I've been there myself, many times. Don't worry about it. This is a lesson that will happen more and more, as you get better and better and bigger and bigger. It's something I'll have to get used to as well. Having such a handsome man in my life is something I don't take for granted. I will never do that again and I'll treasure you always."

CHAPTER 15
The Children Must Know the Truth

It had been a year of acting out our ruse as the host and the exchange student. Having my children over occasionally, Bo, Bobby and their families, things seem to get more and more awkward.

After the incident with Bo and Sam, it seemed that there were more and more cracks forming around our story.

Perhaps one time I held WuJian's hand too close, having been so used to it. Perhaps it was a hug that was too long. Perhaps it was a look in each other's eyes that went too deep. Bobby and Bo, and their wives as well I'm sure, were getting very interested in what was going on.

The final straw came when Bobby came over to our house for dinner one day. As he walked in, he said, "Ma, is WuJian home?"

"No, he's out. He's rehearsing a play."

Bobby sighed. "Great. Actually, I wanted to talk to you alone and haven't found the time. Please, let's sit down."

That was an unusual move for Bobby. He never told me to sit down. Usually if he had some issue he would talk about it right then and there. We would either resolve it or not. We had never had the simple insistence of sitting down.

I motioned him into the living room and asked, "Is something the matter?"

"Yes. I want to have a conversation. It's easier if you sit down." He looked at me so strangely, like I was some kind of alien.

I tried to distract him. "Very well then. Can I get you a drink or anything?"

"No, Mom, I'm fine. Let's just sit down and have a conversation."

With that, and the nerves in my stomach aflutter, we sat down.

"Listen, Ma. I've been wondering about something for a while and haven't had the perfect opportunity, or the right way to tell you this. It is not only me; it's my wife as well who has these thoughts. You are a lonely woman, a divorcee and someone who has had many men in her life," Bobby said.

"Yes?" I scowled.

"I'm not here to judge. I'm not here to say anything other than the fact that I think there is something more to the relationship you and this exchange student WuJian have than you are letting on."

I frowned. "What do you mean?"

"Ma, I've seen you hold his hand more than once. I've seen you looking into his eyes in that way only a lover can. It's not easy for me to speak these words. I feel kind of nauseous about it. However, I must admit what I see. I'm not the only one who notices." Bobby paused for a moment as if he needed to summon up more courage for what was coming next.

He took a deep breath and continued. "I have to ask you. Ma, are you and WuJian dating or more? Please don't give me the excuse that this is an exchange student you've picked up, because in all the years I've known you, I've never seen you once have an exchange student in your house. In fact, the only sleepover I can remember was a friend of yours who happened to be a male colleague who was in town for a meeting. I don't know when the last time was you had a man over, especially someone as young as WuJian."

He stopped and gazed me as if he was trying to find answers from my subtle reactions to what he had been saying. After a few seconds he continued softly, "If you are dating just let us know and let's get on with it. Whether it's judged good or bad doesn't matter. It's the fact that we need to know the truth."

I looked away the whole time he spoke, thinking of how I should respond. Once he finished, I looked at my son, knowing I had to make a decision. To continue to deny the truth, insisting that WuJian was an exchange student, I don't think he would honestly believe me. It would cause tension. There would be an increasing level of mistrust.

On the other hand, if I told him the truth there was no way he would be okay with it. He would simply judge us for what was going on at the moment and look at it as an older woman trying to be fleeced by a younger man for her money.

I looked at Bobby and said to myself that I had to make a wise decision right then and there. I took a deep breath and finally said, "Bobby, you're right. I have to tell you the truth. Perhaps it started as a student from overseas relationship, but it has certainly become more."

I paused and watched Bobby's mouth slightly open from the shock. I then softly continued, "Yes, we are dating and yes, I do have feelings for him. I don't think you could ever understand because you and your wife have this perfect marriage. Well, even if it's not perfect, it is what others consider normal. People within each other's age brackets is what people expect to happen in marriages. Someone like me, an older woman, is interested in a younger man? People automatically assume that the man is after it for one reason and the woman for another. The woman is after this relationship for companionship, while the man is into it for either money or something else."

Bobby nodded. I continued, "In our case, it is easy to judge that WuJian would be after my money, perhaps my Hollywood connections. In fact, don't think for a moment I have not had those thoughts myself. I have often thought about how WuJian could be after my money. I quickly dismissed that, but I never gave up on the fact that he could be after my connections. In fact, the fact that he is doing so well as an actor… I like to think that can be attributed to me. After all, I had started him in bit parts and moved him up; used all of my producer and director connections to continue getting him bigger parts."

Bobby stared at me silently for a moment. "Listen, Ma, you know your happiness is the most important thing in the world to me. I am not here to judge you. I'm not here to make you feel bad or sad, but I will say that, well, perhaps I and even Bo, our spouses, yes, we may say something behind your back, being brutally honest occasionally, but it'll be in your best interest. I don't think the world will judge you the same. In fact, I know they won't. Hollywood is a bunch of liars and fakes, if I'm being honest. I mean, let's be honest. I've watched you in the industry for so long. There is so much out there that is full of garbage, two-faced, people spreading the worst gossip about you—are you ready for that? Are you ready? Is this what you want in a relationship? I'm not asking if you love him, I'm asking simply if you can handle what's about to come."

I thought about it for a moment and said, "Bobby, I've been thinking about this for a long time. Let the world think what they want. I can't control this anymore. I found someone I can be happy with. I found someone that's extremely important to me. If we stop to think about it, eventually we all have one life to live. If we stop and judge what others are thinking of us we'll be finished. It took me a long time to come to peace with that. When I first started in Hollywood my entire focus was on how to please others. Even though I tried to blaze my own path, at the end of the day in order to succeed I had to give in and kiss butt, speak nice to this one or that one while I wanted to throw up. This is the way of Hollywood, where I finally came to the conclusion I don't need their respect, I don't need their money, I don't need their connections. It's simply a matter of what makes me happy."

I heaved a sigh of relief, because I didn't need to hide anymore from my son. I continued, "Being with WuJian this past year has opened my eyes. He's made me feel young and invigorated like I've never felt before. It has made me think about the fact that I finally found true love. I can't help it if the world wants to judge us. Let them. I know that for you and Bo, it will not be as easy. People will judge you because you have a mother like that. I realize that. If that is something you can't accept, and you want to sever our relationship to some degree I understand. I'm not asking for you to take this journey with me if you don't want to. My house is open all the time. But if you guys are upset enough that you want to keep your distance, I completely respect that need."

Bobby gave me a hug and said, "Ma, I understand. I'm never going to disrespect or disown you, you have to disown me first." He smiled.

I was appreciative of the fact that he was able to understand this at such a deep level. I didn't know if the rest of the family would be as forgiving.

After our conversation I had asked Bobby not to tell his brother or his wife, leaving it up to me. I called another assembly where I had Bo with his wife and family over and Bobby with his.

Finally, after a beautiful dinner and dessert, I called my sons and their wives into the living room and said, "Have a seat."

They looked at each other with confusion and worry, knowing that we didn't really sit when talking about our issues; we actually stood and spoke. However, after insisting they take a seat, everyone did.

I realized very quickly it would be hard to tell them. I brought WuJian into the room and I said, "I want to properly introduce you to WuJian."

They all laughed and Bo said, "We know WuJian, it's no big deal."

This time I shook my head. "No, you don't know WuJian; not really. You know him as an exchange student from China who is over here staying at my house. What you don't know is that he and I have been dating for over a year. We are in love with each other and enjoy each other's company."

The room fell silent. Dead silent. If there was a pin to drop on the floor I would have heard it. The silence was suffocating.

Bobby, who of course already knew, looked at everyone else's faces for their reactions.

Bo looked up and down several times. I saw in his eyes the anger, the betrayal, the feeling of confusion.

Finally, he said, "You know, Ma, it's funny. I had a feeling something else was going on. I didn't know *what* exactly. It had at some point crossed my mind that you two were in love or dating. I quickly dismissed it, saying how foolish that would be… my older mother and a much younger man. But now that I know the truth, it doesn't seem foolish at all. This may seem unusual, but I'm very happy for you because you have found happiness. If this is what you truly want, you feel that this is the man for you, then I want you to be with him."

I looked up at Bo. "Son, I appreciate that so much, you have no idea. Your blessing means a lot to me."

The two wives came over and gave me a hug as well. Soon all the grandkids were called back and each gave me a hug as well.

We brought WuJian into the mix and soon it was one big family hug. It was an amazing sight to see everyone laughing and smiling with him.

At the end of the day, my children had come around and accepted WuJian. This was very important to me. I don't know if the world would be as forgiving as Bobby and Bo and their families, but for now I had my kids on my side.

That was one big step in the right direction.

CHAPTER 16
A World Revealed

After I had told the truth to my children, it wasn't my intention to tell anyone else right away. I was content with the fact that WuJian and I were now a couple in their eyes. That was enough for me for now.

However, I wasn't so sure that WuJian felt the same.

One night as we're sitting down to dinner, he said to me, "Mary, let me ask you a question. Are you sad that we can't go out in public holding hands like a normal couple would?"

I raised my eyebrows and said, "What do you mean?"

"Well, I know that we are in Hollywood and everything is fake, everything is stories, everything is unreal. However, just once I would like to walk down the street with you, holding hands, without anyone caring. I know that Bo and Bobby and their families appreciate us. I know how special this relationship that you and I have is. However, just once I would like to be a normal couple, not thinking about things."

I was grateful that WuJian had such a question. It touched my heart that he was so loving and wanted to display affection in public. How I would love to hold hands with him too in public, not caring about anyone gossiping! However, I knew that it wasn't time yet and I didn't want to risk being judged.

I sighed. "WuJian, my dear, the problem is not that we can't hold hands, it's the fact that the world will never understand what we are doing here. If you look around history most people that are out of the norm are always judged harshly, especially in Hollywood where it's so easy to do so. I too would love nothing more than to hold your hand in public, as we do at home. I realize though that there is a world out there that never has our best interests in mind. Perhaps I am jaded.

Perhaps I am formed by the world and the Hollywood that I've seen. Hollywood is a tough place. It is not easy for someone like me to be with someone like you. I mean, like I've said, so many women look at you in such a beautiful and loving way. I too look at you this way. We also know that I can have you to myself. However, I understand your feelings, but I do think we should wait just a little bit longer."

WuJian said he understood and went back to his meal in silence.

He was a good man to always agree with me. Maybe that's why, one day soon after, as we were walking, perhaps without thinking I grabbed his hand. Perhaps it was subconscious. Perhaps it was the Universe's way of telling me that it was time to bring the truth out into the open.

You see, even an old actress like me who occasionally still appeared in films had to deal with the paparazzi now and again. I called them the pariahs of Hollywood, who never had your best intentions in mind.

They say a picture's worth a thousand words. I say a picture's worth a thousand bucks. Every picture they snapped, their bank accounts got bigger. No matter who or what context, or what the cost to the subject of the photo. As long as they got the shot.

I had seen occasional paparazzi following me before; they never bothered me because there was never any reason. Even when I was out with WuJian, and we would occasionally laugh, there was no physical relationship to demonstrate there was anything more. If the world wanted to speculate, let them go ahead, I always told myself. But the reality was there was nothing more to it.

I don't know if I read every newspaper article or watched every celebrity news show on TV, or was aware of everything that's out there in Hollywood. The occasional snippets of us out in public were uneventful in terms of revealing our relationship and didn't make much news.

However, this one time when I grabbed WuJian's hand it was our "luck," or shall I say, "the Universe's way of telling us something," that a paparazzi caught the act and snapped away at us.

The next day I saw the local Hollywood tabloid. It said, "Mary Maddin, the famous actress, was caught holding hands with a much younger man. Is this the new norm? Is sixty-nine the new thirty?"

I don't know how many copies were sold and I'm not sure how many people read the story online. Once it was out there, we knew what was going to happen.

The next day I got calls from our children, each one half excited, half scared, saying, "Oh my gosh, Mom, I was at the newsstand, did you see what they wrote in there? The cover in a small right column had a picture of you and WuJian!"

"Well, I guess my actress status is not high enough these days to command a full front page." I laughed. It was my defense mechanism.

I went to visit WuJian on one of his sets that day, and people were staring at me as if I were naked or something, but I didn't care. I pulled him aside. "WuJian, I have to tell you something."

"Sure, Mary, what's the matter?"

"There's a magazine out there written by the Hollywood press. It's called *The Hollywood Extras*," I said. "Are you familiar with it?"

"No, not really." WuJian shoot his head.

"Okay then, I will pick up a copy. They caught us in a moment of weakness holding hands and walking together. A member of the paparazzi was there and snapped a photo. He presented it, I guess, to any newspaper who would pay for it, and sure enough *The Hollywood Extras* wrote the check."

"Wow," WuJian's eyes widened. "They get you at every moment, don't they?"

"Yes, this is the price you have to pay to be in Hollywood and be making a lot of money. I suppose someone can go and be a garbage man and have a simple life, but if you are more than that this is the price to pay."

WuJian understood. "Well, I guess we'll just have to be more careful next time."

I said, "Yes, perhaps this is something we have to do or perhaps this is the Universe's way of telling us we have to come into the open and be who we are."

He smiled and said, "Mary, I have supported you and your desires from day one. If you wish to open our relationship to the world I'm okay with that. However, if you wish to keep it a secret, while being disappointed, I understand that as well. As long as I get to have you by my side, I'm okay with this."

I smiled from ear to ear and said, "I feel the same."

Then I actually gave him a long passionate kiss on the lips, wrapping my arms around his neck.

There was more than one person inside the studio where we were standing when I did that. Obviously, I had made the decision that the relationship needed to become public no matter what would happen.

A couple hours later, I got a call from my agent, Mike. "Mary, I don't know if you saw the tabloid *The Hollywood Extras*, but it seems to me that they have a picture of you holding hands with WuJian. Rumor has it from somebody I know on the same set of the current movie WuJian's shooting you gave him a big kiss on his lips. Is there something you want to tell me that I don't know about before it goes everywhere?"

I was surprised that the news went out so fast, but I was prepared. "Sure. Would you like to meet for a cup of coffee?"

"Yeah, let's do it in thirty minutes."

We met at our local coffee spot—the one he and I used to spend hours talking about my old acting roles in. It was still around after all this time. Back in the day, we would discuss various scripts. Today, we were about to discuss something completely different.

After we ordered our coffee and sat down at a table in the corner, Mike said, "Mary, tell me what's going on in your life. I know we don't talk as much. I thought perhaps it's because you don't have the roles you want or don't want the roles like you used to. I'm getting older and don't take as many clients, but really, what's going on? Tell me as a friend, as someone who's been there for you and with you all this time."

"Look, I'm not going to hide it anymore, Mike. I'm going to tell you the truth. I've been in a relationship with WuJian for more than a year."

He looked at me with a grin. "Very interesting. I didn't know Asians were your type." He gave a laugh.

I smiled. "So that's what you picked up on?"

"I'm kidding. Look," he frowned and said, "the world's going to judge it because it's a younger guy. I get it, *a much* younger guy. I really get it. But, are you really happy with him? Do you think he's using you?"

"I've never been happier. Mike, to be honest, it's the happiest I've been in all my life. You know my story. You know how many men I've been with, you know I got divorced. Listen, my two children are the most important things in my life, but WuJian comes a close second. To have someone who actually really loves you the way you love them is rare. Don't think for a moment I haven't thought the same things you're probably thinking. You're probably thinking right now that this guy's using me for my money, or for sure to get into Hollywood. After all, you of all people know how hard it is to break into the business. So, I'm sure you're thinking that right now as we speak."

He nodded. "If you only knew." Mike was someone I could be open with. I didn't need to pretend to be sophisticated, which was why I liked him. I felt safe to tell him things.

I took a sip of coffee and said, "Listen, if someone makes you happy, wouldn't you just want to be with them and not think about anything else and just keep it that way? Keep it simple? I mean, overthinking it—money this, Hollywood that, connection this—it can drive you crazy. I finally just gave in and said it's much more worth it for me to be happy for five minutes than to be miserable for twenty years."

I paused. Mike nodded in understanding. "I mean, what was my option here? I'll tell you—I was going to live out my life, alone and bored. Reading a book, hoping it actually changes my mind and changes the scenery in my head for five minutes… Of course I have my kids, but at the end of the day coming home to a big house full of servants, chef, butlers, whatever it is, you name it, just staring at the ceiling, watching TV till I pass out is no kind of life."

Mike leaned forward. "I get it. I just want you to be prepared for what's going to come down. I mean, you know how it is in Hollywood. If you tie your shoe the wrong way, it's a story. Imagine you, nearly seventy, dating a thirty-something and calling it a relationship. Especially this up and coming foreign actor? You don't think people are going to think what I'm thinking?"

I let out a deep sigh. "I already know that. Why do you think I hid it for so long? It took a lot to bring out the relationship to where it is now. You know how hard it was to tell my children? I finally decided that was the right move in my life at the time. I'm not sure why the Universe said that this was the time to bring it into the world, but it was. In one moment of weakness, I held his hands, and the rest is history. With that, I decided to kiss him on the set. I'm not going to deny it. In fact, it was the best thing I ever did. That kiss was probably the best I've had with him yet."

Mike rested his hands on the table. "I hope it's worth it. Listen Mary, don't worry about the rumors. You're a great actress and if anything, your reputation will probably get stronger. People love tabloids, people love scandals, people love things that go viral. This is going to take it to the roof. WuJian can market this for millions. I mean, look at some of the deals these reality stars are inking. And this is not even a reality show—it's real reality!"

I put down my coffee. "Hey, more power to him if you can! In fact, if you help WuJian I'd appreciate it."

"I'm done with representing people. You know I'm not taking on new clients."

"Really? Who's representing him with all these roles he's getting?"

Mike looked surprised. "You are. That was the favor you did him. I mean, you called the producers, you did all the work. That's how it works. Sure, sure—Hollywood actors still need to be represented, but I don't have the strength for it anymore. I don't need the money, I'm set. For me it's just a matter of keeping me busy and I am already busy."

I frowned. "Mike, you owe me. I was your biggest star for how many years? Let's be honest—all the other stars you signed were because you had me as a client, so you owe me. Big time. Come on, let's capitalize on this for him. I have no interest in it for myself, but I think he deserves it. He's earned it."

Mike leaned back a little as if being startled. "Earned it? What's he earned? He isn't even a good actor. But come on, we did it for you."

"It doesn't matter how he did it. The fact is that he did it. I want you to take care of him. Make him a VIP client of yours from now on. Go out and really represent him. Get him the big roles."

He sighed. "All right, all right. I hope you know what you're getting in to, because if I get him the big roles he's going to be busy. Yeah, he's local now, but maybe he has to travel, you don't know. May not be home till late at night, every night. You sure you want this? I mean, if he's the man in your life, don't you want him to be home and around? Keep it like this, it'll be easy."

I nodded and said, "I thought about that many times, but the reality is if I do that then I'm ruining him. I'm not doing him a service. There's no reason for him to hamper his life, just because I need him in mine. He'll be there for me if I need him, I know that. Go represent him."

Mike thought about it for a moment. "If not for all the years we've had in our relationship there's no way I'd be doing this for you. But, because it's you, I'm going to make a few calls, get a few scripts together, start working the usual way. You know the deal—you might want to prepare him when he comes home for how it's going to work."

With that, I said goodbye to Mike, gave him a hug and said, "I really appreciate this one."

Mike winked. "Mary, you owe me. At least you could read the couple of scripts I sent you."

I laughed. "You got it, Mike. Deal!"

We parted ways and I went home.

An hour or two later, WuJian came through the door, smiling. He said, "It was a really terrific day on the set; we got so much done."

"WuJian, I need to talk to you. I hope it's okay, but I asked Mike to represent you full time."

"Oh, hasn't he done that already?" WuJian's eyes opened wide.

"Sort of, but not in the way that you deserve. There are big parts you could probably get with Mike doing his thing that'll build you years of experience and connections."

I sighed and continued, "With me doing the connecting, they needed to take it with a grain of salt, and especially now they might not even listen. With the tabloids out there, there's no way they're going to be thinking that you're a great actor on your own and deserve the part. They will always be thinking that I am your lover, companion, girlfriend or whatever they want to call me, just trying to get a gig for her boyfriend. I can't have that anymore because no one's going to take it seriously. We need a real agent who presents your work in the proper way it deserves. And so, I asked Mike to do that. I hope it was okay. It wasn't a big deal to ask him, but again I didn't ask you first and I'm sorry for that."

WuJian laughed. "It's okay. I always thought Mike represented me anyway. So, this little transition is not a big deal."

We both laughed and gave each other a hug. I felt that we had each other's back, that we wanted the other to feel happy and would like to do anything we could to achieve it. For me, it was very fulfilling to watch WuJian grow in his acting abilities and I would spare nothing to help him on his path.

CHAPTER 17
The World Indeed Judges

Two weeks later Mike and WuJian met in Mike's office to finalize how they were going to work their relationship. The standard agent fee was ten percent and Mike insisted on doing no different.

He told WuJian, "Listen, if I'm going to represent you right, I'm going to represent you the way I always represented everyone, including Mary. We have a ten percent agreement on everything from royalties to upfront fees and anything else in between, you got it?"

WuJian nodded. "Yep, I got it."

"Okay, I'm going to give you three scripts I think might be good for you to start with. They're prime roles. You're going to have some heavy competition for them. You're going to have to reach for those directors, but I think you've got a shot at it. Hope it make sense?"

"Yep, I get it."

Mike handed him some scripts. "Go home, have a read of them, then see what happens."

WuJian came home and showed me the scripts.

I was so excited because I thought they were really perfect for him. They fit in terms of style and background and the role he would play in each just made so much sense.

I beamed with excitement. "WuJian, you have to get one of these roles, if not all of them. I really think you have a shot at all of them!"

He laughed, gave me a hug and said, "You know, Mary, I also thought that. The more I read, the more I'm into the scripts. I don't like to take roles where I'm not into the story. Perhaps that's cliché or perhaps that's experienced actors trying to throw their muscle around, but for me it has to be something I really feel passionate about. If I can get into a role then I really could perform well. If I can't get into a role, it's like forcing it and I can't force it well. But these three scripts that Mike gave me are amazing. I hope I can get them."

WuJian went back to Mike and gave him the green light to represent him in getting however many auditions he could manage. Mike didn't disappoint—he got WuJian appointments with the producers or directors of all three scripts. It was an amazing feat that only Mike and his connections in Hollywood could pull off.

WuJian had the first audition a few days later. When he went in he felt like everyone was staring at him as if he had four arms or something. He thought he was just paranoid. But, the reality was that people *were* staring at him.

How could they not? I thought when I heard about it. He was so handsome.

But the reality was that they weren't staring at him because of his looks. They were looking at him as the guy who was dating a seventy-year-old lady.

WuJian did well during the first read-through and then they had him read a couple of other sections of the script.

The director looked at him with a sigh. "You know, WuJian, you really are perfect for this role. You've got the acting chops, the lady-killer looks… But I don't know what the world's going to feel if I cast you."

"What are you talking about… how the world feels… who cares?" WuJian waved his hand.

"No, no kid, you don't get it. How the world's going to feel about who you're dating."

WuJian clenched his jaw and lashed out, "What's anyone's business about whom I'm dating?"

The reply was instant.

The director scowled and raised his voice, "Don't you get it? Everything about a movie and its promotion relies on the main actors. If the main actors have issues people won't really love, then you have nothing. We can't do that, and I don't know if you can afford it. However, we will think it over and get back to you."

Same thing in a weird way happened on the second and third auditions, completely different directors, completely different producers, with the same result. The directors gave some sort of garbled speech about how they had to think about their reputation in film production and marketing. The whole thing didn't make an ounce of sense.

WuJian came home from all three readings frustrated, confused and upset. He sank into the living room couch like a rock, staring blankly into space, lost in his own deep thought.

I knew that something wasn't right. I walked over to him and sat down next to him. "What happened?"

He smoldered with resentment. "The auditions went great, but I'm not hearing a word."

"What are you talking about?" I bewildered with a frown. "These are big decisions. They take time. It's only been a couple of days."

"It's not that. They all looked at me. I'm telling you, they all stared at me. Even on the jobs I'm already working on. They all think I'm weird—the directors, the producers, the costume designers, the movie hands, my co-stars, everybody."

My heart sunk, and my body chilled. It was as if someone dumped a bucket of ice-cold water on me. I was so disappointed with how the world reacted.

After collecting myself for a few seconds, I said, "The world has no right to judge you, WuJian. It has no right to judge *us*. I told you we'd moved beyond that when I kissed you on set. That day was my way of saying to the world to hell with them. We have a right to do what we want to be happy."

WuJian actually tried to squeeze out a smile. "I agree with you more than ever. However, I do see that the world is not a great place, like you said. They do judge us at every corner, and every nook, and cranny."

He went upstairs to the bedroom to watch some TV, trying to numb himself.

I quickly phoned Mike and said, "I think we've got a problem."

"Why?"

"The auditions all went well, but he kept saying the same thing. He kept saying people were staring at him and they weren't going to take him because it could hurt their reputation."

Mike thought for a moment and said, "Listen, Mary, as far as the reputation aspect, I don't know… people are weird. They get these crazy ideas in their head and then they just do whatever they want. I've seen more than one occasion when one of my clients had a commitment for a role, but something happens and it all falls through. It's a complicated business. Tons of variables. If you think they're going to go against you only because of the relationship you have with WuJian, I can't see it, I just can't. Like I said, perhaps I misjudged how stupid people are, but I don't think it's going to happen."

I just simply listened and said, "Mike, it doesn't make any sense."

"Look. Let's see what happens with these producers. I'll follow up with them in the morning. I got two more scripts that came in recently. The roles are not as well defined and they are newer producers but I think you might consider these. Let me send them over tomorrow, all right? I know you wanted to be able to tell WuJian about this, but listen, just tell him you're going to read the scripts as well and afterward you say you're interested in the story, all right?"

I hung up the phone and went upstairs to WuJian, I put my hand over his shoulder. "WuJian, I spoke to Mike. He said don't get discouraged. He's got two more possible scripts for you to read; newer producers that could probably help you better."

WuJian let out a deep sigh. "That's not the point, Mary. It's just going to keep happening. Even if it's new producers, old producers, young directors, new directors it doesn't matter; everyone is going to judge us."

I really wanted to cheer him up. WuJian's life was just blossoming and he had a promising career ahead of him. This wasn't the end of the world. Suddenly an idea hit me. It made me feel warm and my eyes glowed. I said to WuJian, "I don't think so. In fact, I want to ramp it up. Let's go for some ice cream."

"Sure, if that'll make you feel better," WuJian said reluctantly.

"No, it's to make *you* feel better."

We got in the car and went for a drive. We pulled up to our local ice cream spot, which had a beautiful outdoor patio area surrounded by several expensive stores.

After we ordered I took the ice cream in one hand and his arm in the other. We walked side by side, arm in arm like the young couples did. The paparazzi snapped their photos and writers put their pens to their pads, but I didn't care. It was more important to me that the world started to realize that this was something that was here to stay. It wasn't a fleeting fling that was going to be here today and gone the next. For me it was all about simply making a point.

I took his arm and held it entirely. In fact, we even shared each other's ice cream. And then shared a passionate kiss. To me, it was more about showing the genuine relationship with somebody than having the world judge us.

If they wanted to judge us, let them go right ahead. I'd like to see their reactions. In that moment, I simply didn't care how they would react.

WuJian smiled after another long kiss and said, "Okay, Mary. I appreciate this. I appreciate everything you're doing. I'll read the two new scripts Mike will give me tomorrow."

"Great! Let's go home and we'll read the scripts together tomorrow tonight. I don't want to waste any time. If those other three producers don't appreciate who you are or what you bring to the table, then let's move on."

The next morning the major newspapers had a giant picture in their gossip sections of me and WuJian holding arms, saying, "This is the new norm folks. Get used to it in Hollywood."

I paused with my breakfast, laughing. "Ha. Maybe it *is* the norm; maybe I'm a trendsetter."

WuJian sat next me, eating his breakfast. I showed him the pile of papers. "WuJian, we're trendsetters!"

He shrugged. "Oh boy… more of that, huh?"

"You have to look at it positively. It's great exposure for us."

He laughed and said, "I don't know about that, but okay."

That night after work, WuJian and I read the next two scripts. Mike was right; these Hollywood producers were so much younger and the material not as strong.

When WuJian had his audition for one of them a few days later, the producer said to him with a smile, "Listen, you've got talent. I saw you in some other films. I really think you're going to do great. As far as the other producers, the hell with them—they don't deserve what you've got. I'm telling you, I'll take care of you."

WuJian grinned ear to ear and said, "Sure."

The second producer had a similar reaction, saying, "WuJian, you'll be great exposure for us. Excuse the script—I know it's a little weak—I know you'll help to make it better and give us so much more exposure than we would have otherwise had."

WuJian came home almost bouncing. "I think I got the parts, Mary. I think I got the parts!"

"Which parts?" His happiness was infectious—I felt my heart opening with his news.

"The two newest ones." He was glowing like a ray of sunshine.

WuJian called Mike and said, "Mike, I think the second new audition went as well as the first."

Mike laughed and said, "I already got feedback from the two new producers. They want you, kid. They want you in *both* films. I'll have to figure out the start dates and how to make it work, but let me tell you, you're back on, baby. This is great news. Forget the world and how they judge you. I'm telling you that exposure is everything. They think logically, these new kids. Those other three producers think like they want to make the perfect Oscar film every time. Let me tell you, it doesn't work like that. Dollars and cents drive marketing and it's all about the viral actors you cast. Believe me—these newbies are going to do everything in their power to get you out there."

WuJian was very excited to hear that and his eyes beamed with joy. "Thanks, Mike," he said.

I yelled into the phone, "Please negotiate a great deal!"

Mike yelled back, laughing, "Of course—that's what I'm here for!"

WuJian hung up the phone and we gave each other a big hug. I said to him, "See, I told you—this is going to work out great."

We smiled and went off to bed in a very joyful mood.

CHAPTER 18
A Health Scare

I was never one to go to doctors, even when I was young. Occasionally, I had a fall on the set or a cut that needed some stitches, but the reality was, I felt invincible to everything.

I didn't believe in doctors, especially in Western medicine. WuJian fully supported this, coming from the East. He supported alternative medicine as a way of healing and dealing with the sick.

If I had a cold, he would bring me certain herbs and teas. I would drink what he mixed up for me and magically I would feel better. It was an amazing thing. The more that happened the more I said Western doctors are full of it.

For five years I canceled my visits and even occasionally canceled semiannual appointments. My children were worried and always prompted me to keep my appointments, saying, "Ma, are you sure you want to do this? It's very important to keep your health. How long is a checkup? Probably an hour of your time. It's not a big deal. Why don't you just go get checked out, get the confirmation that everything's fine, and then just move on with your life? It's not a big deal… you have time."

I'd always dismissed them with a wave of my hand and said, "I know what I'm doing. Believe me, WuJian got me on this regimen of herbs and vitamins and all this stuff. I'm telling you, I'm the healthiest I've ever been in fifty-five years."

They looked at me, wide eyed. "Fifty-five years, huh? So you're going back to your teenage years?"

I beamed with delight and replied, "Yep, that's me! Forever young!"

However, on a random Wednesday, everything changed.

I will never forget it.

WuJian had gone off to the set. I was in between jobs, as in those days I wasn't taking very many new ones—I was very selective, and enjoyed my down time.

As I was walking to my favorite coffee shop, I suddenly felt faint. I felt woozy as if the ground and everything on it was being tilted to the side and I lost my balance. My vision blurred and went pitch-black as if the world was closing in on me. It was a scary feeling— like I had been taken over by something evil.

I said to myself, "Woah. I better sit down."

Luckily, there was a park bench for buses right where I was walking when the incident happened. I quickly grabbed the bench and sat down, took a deep breath and tried to recover as fast as I could.

There was an older man sitting next to me. He frowned. "Ma'am, are you all right?"

I summoned my energy and replied faintly, "I'll be fine. I just need to sit a minute. Got the wind knocked out of me."

"That doesn't look like the wind, lady. Get it checked out. Believe me—and I speak from experience—it starts out as something small, but it can get a lot bigger a lot faster. You don't want to deal with that. Why don't you go get it checked right away?"

After a few deep breaths to calm myself, I finally looked up at the guy and said, "I appreciate the advice."

The bus came, and the man got on. I stayed there for another few minutes and then got up. I slowly walked into the coffee shop, dismissing the episode as not having eaten properly that morning.

I got myself a cup of coffee and something to eat and sat down again. After I ate, I felt better and said, "I'm fine" and walked back to my car and got home without further incident.

However, thoughts of what had happened started gnawing at me, saying, *My kids were telling me to get my health checked out and the stranger said that too, maybe it was a sign that I should.*

When WuJian got home I told him what happened, thinking he would easily wave his hand, dismiss it, and give me some vitamins or herbs. I figured this would be a very short conversation.

However, I was surprised when he said to me with furrowed eyebrows, "Mary, listen, I'm a realist. I believe in Eastern medicine and it really can heal people. However, I'm not a fool. There's something more here that we're not noticing. You should get it checked out. I love you very much and want you in my life for as many years as I can have you. If you don't get it checked out, then we'll never know."

Surprised by his reaction, I readily agreed to go. I asked, "Would you accompany me?" And he of course said he would.

We made an appointment at a time that was mutually convenient, time in between publicity appearances and shoots so there was a day off and he was able to go. I went to the doctor's office feeling quite nervous, not sure why. My hands were sweating, and my body tended to shake.

I told everyone, "I am healthy as a woman half my age, I don't understand why I'm feeling so nervous." I attributed the fainting spell to something just simple as not having eaten properly. So why was I so nervous?

WuJian held my hand tight and said, "It's okay to be nervous. Listen, doctors' offices aren't a fun place. I remember in China, we were once told in the army we had to go visit the doctor to get a physical. I hated that physical even though I was perfectly fine. Having a doctor snip, snap, prod, whatever else it is they do is not fun. No one wants that. I totally understand."

I smiled. "I appreciate that." He always knew how to warm my heart.

The nurse came in and made us fill out some forms and was very pleasant and polite. Eventually, after waiting for what seemed like forever, my name was called.

I walked into the doctor's office. I asked WuJian to wait in the hallway as it wasn't fair for him to see me poked and prodded, nor did I want to have to explain for the millionth time what our relationship was. The doctor came in. He was a middle-aged man, very strong in appearance, very professional-looking. His name was Doctor Earl.

He shook my hand. "Mary, I haven't seen you in a while!"

"I know, Dr. Earl, it has been a while."

"Well, you've been skipping out on your physicals. So, since you're here, I am guessing something's wrong. How are you feeling?"

I sighed and said, "Well, I should have come for physical, and that was my fault. However, I don't know what I have, actually. I was walking to get coffee the other morning and I felt very faint and dizzy. I sat down at a local bus stop, rested, went to the coffee shop, sat down some more and got something to eat. After that, I don't know what happened, but I seem to be fine now. However, everyone says I should check it out, so that's why I'm here."

He nodded his head. "Well, I actually think it's good you checked it out. I will be happy to do blood work, give you a thorough physical, and I want you to go for a CAT scan. It is not to scare you in any way; it's just to simply rule out some common possibilities in a woman your age."

I wasn't thrilled to hear that news, nor do I think anyone else would be either. However, I knew that I had no other choice. Therefore I replied, "Well, Doc, if that's what you think is going to help the situation, then fine, let's get it done."

He had a nurse do the blood work, then he gave me a physical checkup and said, "Everything seems to be okay. Your blood pressure and heart seem fine. However, like I said, I do want to rule everything out so let's schedule that CAT scan as soon as you can."

I went over to one of the nurses who helped me schedule the CAT scan for the following week.

After the doctor's visit, I was extremely nervous for the entire week. WuJian would come back to me immediately after his acting jobs, my sons would come visit me more than they usually did. They acted so concerned, it was as if I was already dead to them.

I'm not that sick, what are they thinking?

Do they think I'm nearly gone?

I would get angrier at each visit. It wasn't them I was angry at, but me and my life. I still had so much to do, so much to live for. Finally, I had someone to live with, someone else to live for, and here they were taking that away from me.

The day of the CAT scan finally arrived. I went in quite nervous, more nervous than I was when I went to the doctor. I wished that there was a hole on the floor that I could jump in and disappear. The technician was extremely friendly and knowledgeable, extremely slow and methodical, walking me through every step—why he was putting me in the machine the way he was, why he was holding me in the position he was, the way the machine worked…

I thanked and complimented him. "Your patience with me is truly appreciated. I'm not really one to go to doctors and certainly not someone who readily agrees to CAT scans. The fact that you've allowed me to do this in such a safe, considerate way is really appreciated."

He smiled and said, "It's my job and I truly try to take care of every patient; every patient has a unique story and no situation is the same."

We got the CAT scan done. I asked the technician, "So, what do you think?"

"Well, I can't tell, nor am I allowed to. Dr. Earl will have to review the results. I'm truly sorry. I know that this can be a frightening experience. I'm told that Dr. Earl is quick to review, quick to get back to his patients. It should help immensely. We're going to process this, upload it and send it to the doctor right away." I thanked him and went home.

WuJian came home that night and wanted to make sure I was okay. He had insisted on going with me to the CAT scan, but I dismissed it, saying he was on set filming, which was more important.

And I knew from firsthand experience how directors and producers are so touchy that if you miss a call time, they go really bananas on you. It wasn't worth stressing him out because you had a reputation in Hollywood once you angered the people in charge.

Once a producer spreads the word that an actor is difficult to work with, people will begin to consider that when considering them for a role. If it was between you and another actor and the other actor was easy to work with, they would take that one. It wasn't worth taking a chance on something like this, especially because I felt fine.

I had one of my maids with me when I went for the CAT scan, just to make sure everything was okay. I had a driver drive us there and back. I couldn't sleep that night after the CAT scan. I tossed and turned and kept thinking, *Is this what's going to happen to me? Is this my end?*

I was really, really nervous.

The next day, I got a phone call that Dr. Earl wished to see me.

"Why can't he tell me over the phone?" I asked.

They said, "Well, it's not our practice. Come in this afternoon and he'll discuss the results with you."

Reluctantly, I went in. I made it at a time when WuJian could come with me, which really helped me for moral support. When we were at Dr. Earl's office, I took a deep breath and said, "Okay, doctor, lay it on me, how bad?"

Dr. Earl leaned forward. "Well, I think you're okay. There are some arteries that concern me as the blood flow in the brain could be blocked, but I think they're okay for now. That being said, I do want to start prescribing a certain blood thinner, not in large doses. Don't get worried, it doesn't have crazy side effects, especially in such low doses, but I do want to be prepared. We must evaluate you more often. I think we're going to have to do monthly checkups, Mary. I know you don't love doctors. Or maybe it's just me… did I do anything to you?" and he laughed.

I'd never seen him laugh before, I knew that he was friendly and courteous. I felt more comfortable with his laugh, and I replied with a smile, "No, Doc, it's just doctors in general, but if monthly checkups are what you want then that's what we need to do."

"That's good to hear. I'll give the prescription to the nurse; she'll take care of you."

And so I started a regimen of taking a medication that I had never taken before. I was already taking daily vitamins, so I just added the blood thinner to my daily regimen.

WuJian was happy that I was okay and that with this medicine I should be fine. He did say to me that keeping those appointments regularly was extremely important and that he expected me to do so.

If he had to take off from an acting job in order to do it, he would. I waved my hand and said, "Nonsense. Not necessary. I can take care of myself. Don't worry, I will make the appointments and keep them."

We looked at each other, thankful it was nothing more than a scare. However, plotting the way forward was something we would have to be very careful with.

CHAPTER 19
WuJian's Independence

WuJian's prominence as an actor had grown over the years, and it kept growing. Award ceremonies were the norm, as were late nights out and lots of press attention.

While we kept going at this rate, scripts kept coming in… so many we couldn't keep up. Mike would filter them all and send only over the good ones. Mike considered us family and met with us regularly.

One night we were out to dinner at a high-end restaurant. The place was bustling with important people having joyful conversations while eating their meal. We were sitting at a table in a corner. After we ate, Mike turned to WuJian and said, "Kid you are doing something really right. I don't know what you're doing but you're doing great. All I know is keep it up, you are so in demand that I only send you a third of the scripts. There are so many I don't know what to do with them."

WuJian should have been delighted, but instead he seemed emotionless and said to Mike, "I appreciate that, but I must confess something. Just for once I would like to be able to make a decision on the scripts that I take. Please send me all of them."

Mike shook his head in disbelief. "Okay kid, I don't have a problem with that, but I try to do it for your benefit. There are so many duds out there, you don't know what it's like."

Mike then turned to me. "Mary, do you remember the time we did *The Grass is Green on the Other Side?*"

I immediately burst out laughing. "Yeah, that was the worst movie I have ever been a part of. I can't believe what happened with that. I mean, who thinks about dancing penguins and clowns all in one movie? I don't even remember the ending… I tried to blank it out of my head. It was so awful." Mike and I both chuckled.

WuJian also smiled and laughed a little bit. "At the end of the day it's my life and my decision. I'd like to see my own scripts please."

"Listen, there were fifty that came through just the other day, I'm trying to filter them out in your best interest. However, if you really want to see all the scripts I have no problem doing that. I just want to make sure you are going to be okay with the amount of time it will take you."

WuJian said firmly, "Yeah, I actually am. It's my life and I don't mean any offense. I appreciate everything you both have done for me. Honestly. Mary, I really do love you and appreciate you. And Mike, I appreciate what you are doing for me—you have helped me so much with my career. However, I do want to be able to choose things that I wish to work on."

"All right, kid, I'll start forwarding them to you. Let's first go over the few I picked out, so you can at least get started."

"I have no problem with that."

We talked, laughed, and went through the scripts. When it was done Mike went home. WuJian and I were in our car.

I frowned. "WuJian, I didn't want to upset you so I didn't say anything at dinner. But I do think Mike has your best interests at heart when he screens the scripts."

"Well, I'm being honest. I appreciate his intentions, but just for once I would like to do this."

He paused briefly and continued. "I appreciate what you and Mike have done for me, but again, it's my own life. I do believe that choosing the scripts is something I want to do because acting is my life. For that matter, I would like to have a say in other things too. Perhaps where we go out to eat as an example. We go out and eat often and do other social things and I never get to choose."

"I'm sorry. I didn't realize that bothers you so much." I gave him a hug and said, "Of course I was happy to do that. The only reason I didn't let you is I didn't think you need to labor on it. I thought that it would be better for me to make suggestions. I always ran it by you to see if it's something you wanted to do. If you had no interest in going to a particular place and you said no of course we wouldn't go. It was never my intention to hurt you or get you upset."

He gave me a broad smile. "Of course. I knew it was never your intention. However, again, just once I would like to make my own decisions."

"I have no problem with that."

We pulled into the driveway and went into the house. After we sat in the living room for a few minutes, WuJian went upstairs but soon he came back into the room and frowned. "One more thing while we are on the topic of independence. The clothing you chose really bothers me. I may not be the most fashionable person but bearing in mind based on what I see going on in Hollywood I see new trends. I can decide if a trend is good or bad. I certainly have an opinion when asking for something in terms of clothing, but to me it's really important that I'm able to actually do this for myself—going to a store, picking out some clothing, then running it by you. Again, I know I'm not some Hollywood A type, at least not yet, but I do know what's fashionable and I think I will do a great job at it."

I scanned him up and down. "WuJian, you look good in anything to me, so I'm not concerned. If you want to go pick clothing out you are more than welcome to. You have earned it. After all, it's you who has to wear it and not me." We both laughed.

WuJian was certainly craving a bigger sense of independence.

Every movie that was successful boosted his ego a little bit more and made him feel special. I don't regret that for a moment.

I appreciated knowing my parents did the same for me. They resisted the urge to have me go to Hollywood and I was very against the idea that they would do that and in fact fought with them greatly. And, as you know, that's how I became an actress in the first place. I did it despite them, not because of them. For me being an actress is the only thing I wanted to do, and their disagreement really felt bad.

This was a similar situation. It was important to him to have his independence and I respected that.

I moved closer to WuJian and said, "Listen, I know one more thing. I know where you're coming from. When I was a child it wasn't easy for me. My mom always wanted for me to follow in her footsteps to be a fashion designer, and not work in Hollywood at all. My father had the same idea. Being in Hollywood wasn't the place for me. In the end I did it anyway. I persisted, I pursued it, I succeeded. It's the same for you. You need to persist, to overcome so much to be able to get to where you want to go. I totally admire that and completely respect it. I love you and only wish you the best. If you think gaining your independence is really important then that is what we're going to do from now on." WuJian nodded with a big grin on his face.

I was very grateful that he was being completely honest with me in sharing how he felt and clear about what he would like to do.

CHAPTER 20
Love Rekindled

When two people have very busy lives in Hollywood, the results usually don't end well. There is a reason why there are so many marriage break-ups, infidelity, and the like in Hollywood. I had seen my fair share of it and totally understood it.

When you are busy working on sets 24/7 sometimes it can get very grinding. Exhaustion creeps in. Top that off with the fact that you are invited to constant parties and award shows and the like, and the person has a big ego with little attitude to deal with it.

Why do you think therapists are so in demand in Hollywood?

I mean, even the person who is the least crazy uses a therapist once every several months, just to keep them sane. Well, for me it was not about sanity—it was the matter of keeping my relationship with WuJian alive.

You see, with each successful film making him more in demand, WuJian was home less and less. I think it really started to affect our relationship. We would simply look at each other, exhausted, and go to bed. There is no romantic level of anything anymore; there is simply how are you, how was your day, and off to bed.

That might have been good enough for a week or two, a month or two or more even, but eventually we got tired of it.

One night after a rare dinner together I turned to WuJian and said, "Listen WuJian, we need to go on a vacation. I don't care if it's Mexico, Japan, or Australia. You pick the place."

Just like the previous times I had asked, he brushed it off by saying that he was too busy with the shooting and we should plan for something later.

I said it to WuJian again and again day after day until finally, he said, "My shooting is wrapping up in about a month's time, I think we can do it after that."

I scowled, "I don't know if I can wait a month, it's getting too grinding for me."

"Let me talk to the director and find out the exact timetable they have in mind. You know he's always going over the things that didn't work out as planned, but at least I can get a timetable."

The next day, WuJian went to the director. "Tell me, when do you think the shoot's going to wrap up?"

The director replied, "I don't know the exact date. I'm hoping three weeks, but you never know. It may take a month."

"Let's try and make it in three weeks. I need a vacation. All these back to back movies are getting to be too much for me."

"I understand kid. Let's get you some rest. Finish this scene off and I'll let you get a break."

That night WuJian came home and told me, "Mary, they expect the film to finish in three weeks."

I was completely frustrated, but accepted that the movie needed to be finished. All this momentum in his life was too much to bear. Not wanting him to think me overbearing, I put on a happy face and gave him a hug, a kiss and said I understood.

WuJian knew I wasn't happy. However, he felt good about the fact that I accepted it. Once more I kept myself busy with different things.

One of the things I kept myself busy with was planning our vacation. Planning vacations was important to me because it kept me thinking about the future, kept me thinking about how we would go as a couple somewhere, not care what anybody thought and be able to go anywhere we wanted.

I had been to Italy more than once, and I so enjoyed Venice. It was so pretty with the boats and the gondolas in the water. I told

WuJian that that's the place I wanted to go. He said, "There's no problem, Mary. Wherever you go is where I will want to go."

I waved my hand. "No, your independence doesn't—"

Seeing me so serious he laughed and interrupted me. "No, actually Italy was on my bucket list. I've always wanted to go."

I went to a travel agency, started asking for brochures. I bought a book on Italy in the local bookstore, and Italy became my passion. The food of Italy, the wine of Italy, desserts of Italy, anything Italy, because I was so looking forward to that vacation.

The three weeks thankfully went by fast. And then WuJian said with dismay that the filming didn't look like it was going to wrap up.

I felt like the bubble burst inside of me. A feeling of emptiness creeped in, but I tried not to show it. "Well, I didn't book the tickets yet. How much longer?"

"Hopefully very soon. I'm really sorry."

"It's okay."

I turned around and went to the garbage can, giving it a good slam; I was so upset.

Finally, WuJian came home a week later almost bursting into a happy cry. "Baby, it's done, it's over. I finished the film. Let's go, let's pack our bags tonight."

I laughed. "It's not so easy as that, but I will get us the next available plane tickets."

The next morning, I went down to the travel agency and got the whole itinerary sorted out. It was a full two-week excursion. It was beautiful. First class flights, first class hotels, amazing restaurants, gondola rides every day; it was the vacation of a lifetime.

I told WuJian all about the plans. He took a deep breath and said, "It sounds relaxing. There were too many shoots going on. I do need a break, some down time."

We packed our bags and the next day we were off. A car drove us to the airport. We settled into our seats on the plane, held each other's hands and gave each other a kiss. We had fine champagne and a beautiful flight. It was really flying in a lot of luxury, so enjoyable, so very, very good.

Finally, we landed. There was a limo to pick us up and when we arrived at the hotel a concierge offered us drinks. The hotel was the best money could buy.

We had a beautiful room that overlooked the water with the gondolas. I can't tell you how fabulous the scenery was; I wouldn't do it justice.

I had never been so happy. This was finally what I had dreamed of, a vacation with the person I loved. A few days later, I turned to WuJian and said that the only thing that would make this better is if we became a true couple.

WuJian shook his head and said, "I don't understand. We are a couple. I know we haven't talked about the future, but anything you want to do I am game for."

My eyes were beaming with joy. "Let's get married!"

WuJian's eyes widened. "Let's get married? Are you sure, Mary?"

I hugged him tight while he did the same. I said softly, "Yes, it's something I want to do. I feel like this is what our destiny is."

WuJian held me even closer. "Mary, are you sure you're not doing this because you are on vacation in a very beautiful place? When we get back to the United States will you be very disappointed we did this?"

I slowly released myself from his hug and looked deep into his eyes. "No, this is something I've wanted to do."

We found a local priest in a beautiful old church and we got married. WuJian wasn't Catholic but the priest was more than willing to accept us. We had an official wedding ceremony with very few people in attendance—just some local workers and some other people. I invited one of the restaurant owners who became familiar with us while on vacation. It was a simple ceremony, perfectly matched with the fact that our union was simply based on love.

I supposed that was our destiny all along. After being together for seven years we finally got married and our honeymoon came early. We really did enjoy each other's company and had an amazing time.

As the two weeks wound down, I was so sad to leave. I didn't want to go. One morning as I lay on the comfortable bed in our hotel room, I said, "WuJian we can't leave, we just can't. I want to stay here forever!"

WuJian had just gotten out of shower. "Part of me agree with you, Mary, but next week I have a shoot. While I do appreciate this time away, I do think you need to be there for your children. They adore you and appreciate you and your grand kids love you as well. It wouldn't be right if we simply didn't go back to the United States."

I thought about it for a moment and about how well he had expressed himself. I was very proud and impressed.

"WuJian, you have your priorities correct. I am extremely impressed with what you have done and what you have become."

He smiled and said, "No, I learned this from you, the family, the ones you have and the ones you trust. You will always be somebody in my life that I completely trust."

"You are the same to me." I gave him a long hug.

Finally, we both looked at each other and agreed to make the most of our last two days in Italy. When it was finally over, I was deeply sad at the fact that I had to leave such a beautiful country. Its beautiful restaurants and its beautiful scenery kept me going as never before and invigorated me, as if I were young again, with a brand-new start in life.

I couldn't imagine having a better vacation. In fact, I don't think that I have had a vacation like that in my entire life.

I have been to many places in the world—money and fame does that for you. You can go anywhere at any time and not think about the price. However, I don't think I really enjoyed it to the fullest.

Each time it was with a man I didn't love, or it was long and miserable. Now I finally had a vacation with the man I loved, in a place I loved, and a situation that just made sense. For us it was just right.

I knew that I would have to tell my children some day what we did in Italy, but for now we could keep to the simple fact that we were living together as a couple on a continual basis without having to reveal the details. I knew that I would have to tell them about our marriage and perhaps they would understand.

CHAPTER 21
A Sudden Return to China

I didn't know much about WuJian's family. He didn't talk about them. One day out of blue, I simply asked, "What was life like in China?"

WuJian sighed. "Well, I was in the military for the most of it but growing up I never had a very loving father and mother."

"Did you have any siblings?"

He looked down. "No."

I knew that he probably would have liked to have had a brother or sister, which was something that the government did allow and strongly encouraged at that time. WuJian told me that his parents put the country first and him second. They even turned their only child over to the military to serve the country they so loved. WuJian clenched his jaw and his body went tense every time I mentioned his parents, so I figured it wasn't a good topic. I didn't mention it again and moved on.

One day, we were sitting home at dinner, and he got a phone call. He went to the other room and spoke in Chinese, a language I didn't understand.

I had picked up a few words and phrases over the course of our relationship and the few trips overseas I had made there. But I didn't understand most of the conversation. At times it tended to get very heated, sometimes it seemed as if he was being told something he didn't want to do or hear.

When it was finally over, he hung up the phone and shook his head side to side as if to say *this is not happening*.

He sat back down at the dinner table, profound sadness engraved in his face. He said, "Mary, I have to tell you something."

I used a low voice, trying to comfort him. "Sure. Is everything okay?"

"No, it is not. My mother is sick. I didn't have the best relationship with her, therefore I don't want to go home right away. However, my father insists. Being the only son, it is my duty to honor that relationship. I understand if you have things in the United States keeping you here, but I must return home for now. I don't envision this to be a long-term situation; but I must go home for at least a little bit."

I was deeply saddened by the news he told me. On one hand, I was saddened that his mother was ill. On the other, I was saddened even more that he had such a bad relationship with her.

I couldn't imagine what it would be like if Bo and Bobby felt so ill toward me. I didn't know what caused such a bad relationship, but I had a feeling. The feeling was simply the fact that WuJian, as a boy, didn't want to go into the army and that his parents forced him to do so, thinking it was the proper way to honor their country.

They say when you force a child to do something against their will, they come to resent it and eventually resent you for doing it. I never asked him again about it or confirmed my theory. It was something I always suspected even when I got sick and older later.

I gave him a big hug. "WuJian, we are a team now. If you need to go home and deal with your issues, then I'll also do the same. I'll accompany you. Of course I will. Your pain is my pain, just like your happiness is my happiness. The same way I have happiness when you succeed in a role or get honored or anything else that goes on. It is the same pain that I feel when such things happen. I do suggest though you call Mike because you're in the middle of a shoot. Suddenly leaving in the middle of a shoot is problematic but you do have a very valid excuse. I don't know what they will say. It depends on where they are at with filming, what adjustments to the schedule they can make. You must call Mike as soon as you can. I would suggest doing so right now."

WuJian held onto my hand. "I appreciate your willingness to go back with me. I welcome that. I will go call Mike now." He got up from the seat and picked up the phone.

"Mike, I have some bad news. I need to leave for China to attend to my sick mother for a little bit. I don't know how long I will take. I know we're in the middle of a shoot, what do I do?"

Mike sighed. "Ah, man, this happened to me a few times in my career. It doesn't always end well. I'm going to be honest with you— the producer might be pretty pissed off. But you know what? You have to do what you got to do. You only got one mother in this world. You got one shot at this. If your mother dies without you by her side, you would regret it for the rest of your life."

Little did Mike know WuJian probably didn't feel that way at all.

"Listen, Mike, I appreciate that. You want me to tell the producer or do you want to handle it?"

"It always looks worse if I'm the one doing it, as if you need an intermediary. You go do it yourself tomorrow. Bust your butt during filming and afterwards pull him aside. That's my suggestion to you— tell the truth like it is. Tell him you don't know how long but you don't expect it to be that much."

WuJian thanked Mike for his advice, hung up the phone, and told me what he said.

"WuJian, I don't know if I've ever done that in my career. I'm trying to think of a situation, but I don't think I ever did." I then nodded in sympathy and said, "However, I do think you've got to tell the producer what's going on. And I think Mike is right, that if you tell him yourself, it's going to come across much better than if he did it for you."

With that, we went to sleep.

The next morning, WuJian was up bright and early. He ran up to the set, gave his best performance and then at the end of it, when they yelled cut for the day, he went over to the director. "I've got to talk to the producer."

"I don't know if he's around."

WuJian shook his head. "It's important."

"Is everything all right?"

"No. I've got to talk to him about taking a leave of absence. I have a very sick mother to attend to who is in China."

The director shook his head. "Are you kidding me? We've got another three weeks of this film, and you're in every scene."

"I realize that, but I can't wait. If she dies, I don't think I'll forgive myself."

The director stared at him and just shook his head. "Okay… so maybe you can bring her here. Or you can visit her after the shoot."

"My understanding is she's too sick to travel."

The director's tone softened. "I feel for you, man. I lost my own mother two years ago, and it's a pain. You do what you got to do. Here's the producer's phone number. Why don't you give him a call? This isn't a decision I want to make."

WuJian hadn't reached the level where he had the producer on speed dial—he usually went through the director or Mike for things. Having gotten the producer's number, he decided to take the plunge and make the call.

He was very nervous, but he had to do it. While his phone was dialing the producer WuJian's hands went sweaty. He wasn't sure how the producer would judge him. When the call got through he said with a shaky voice, "Hi, is this Mr. Johnston?"

"Yeah, who is this?"

WuJian took a deep breath to calm himself down. "My name is WuJian."

After a short pause, the producer said, "Oh, WuJian, what's going on, my favorite actor! I'm telling you this film is going to be a multi-million-dollar baby, it's coming along great! You're the star! You do this the way you have been, and you'll do many more."

WuJian had to step in before Mr. Johnston was too carried away. "Mr. Johnston, that's why I'm calling you. Unfortunately, I got a call from China that my mother is very ill. I have to rush home. I can't finish the next three weeks on the set. I don't know if she'll pass away before that. I'm truly sorry. I don't have an official timetable of course. However, you have my word that I will come back as soon as the situation allows me to. I'll come back and finish the film. I completely understand if you want to cast it with someone else."

The producer went silent.

WuJian didn't think that was a good sign. I mean, most producers were busy talking about their own egos, and all their accomplishments. This producer staying on the phone quietly wasn't a good sign.

"Mr. WuJian, I get it. I recently lost my father and I regretted not being there in his final days. I looked at the coffin and said all the things I should have said but never got the chance. I don't know what's going to happen with the studio. I'll talk to them, but either way you go and do what you have to. I'll let you know what they say. Like you said, there's a couple of options here. We could recast it with someone else completely from scratch, or just wait and pick up where you left off when you come back. Though, I don't think the latter is a good idea. We could just kill you off at this point or we could rewrite the whole script. None of those options are good, but I'll let you know which one the studio wants."

WuJian thanked him for being so understanding and hung up.

When he came home that night, WuJian told me what had happened, adding, "If they decide to kill me off or recast me I'll have to move on to another script when I get back."

I looked at him with pride. "WuJian, you did the right thing. Don't feel guilty for a second. Your parents come first."

We booked first-class tickets to leave for China the next night.

We flew to China and all along the way I kept wondering to myself what was going to happen when I got there.

How could I best support WuJian in his hour of need?

He was there for me so many times, willing to do anything for me, for my happiness. How could I do the same for him now? It would be so hard to do that.

I was very nervous, as if I were to perform an important test. I turned to WuJian. "Listen, you don't need me as your third wheel. Wherever you need me to be in terms of anything at all you let me know. I'm here to help. View me as someone who wants to support you in every way possible. I know going home is probably not easy. You don't know the last time you saw your parents, let alone the fact that you're going to see your mother in this state. I'm sure there are issues well beyond our relationship time period. They must go back a long way. I could tell just by the way you would describe the situation."

WuJian leaned in closer and put his arm around me. "Don't worry too much, Mary. It's not worth it. My parents and I never got along too well. They insisted I do things that I never liked. It's not your fault, it's no one's fault, it's just a reality of life. However, if they had not done that, I suppose I wouldn't be the man today standing in front of you, sitting next to you actually. I suppose I have that to thank them for. I do believe at the end of the day that perhaps she's going to pass on to the next world soon. This might be my father's way of trying to get us somewhat closer in a relationship that never was. I don't know. I don't know what I'll find there. How sick is my mother? Does she have a simple cold and they're trying to trick me? Or is it she is really sick, on her death bed? Either way I expect to find out and get the answers we need. Having agreed to come on this plane and fly all the way to China is something I really appreciate your doing with me."

We leaned into each other, holding hands for a little bit, just staring into the ceiling. There was no particular thought in mind for each of us, other than all the random, rushing thoughts running through our heads.

For me, it was simply about how I could help WuJian.

What does he think?

What's his family like?

What's life in China like?

There were so many unanswered questions. There wasn't much I could do other than to go with him and support him in any way I could.

CHAPTER 22
Life in China

The plane touched down after what seemed like forever. Los Angeles to China was a long flight, about fourteen hours.

Finally, it touched down in Beijing, pulled up on the runway, and we got off the plane. There was a man awaiting, a simple man, a short man with a very, very serious expression on his face. The corners of his mouth were pulled down and his stare was kind of blank, lacking focus. He looked a bit like WuJian. However, I dared not ask if that was his father without being told.

He greeted us with a slight gesture of his arm. As we got close enough, WuJian greeted him back the same way. I nodded and said hello. He held out his right hand. I didn't know if I was supposed to take it in my own and shake it; however, instinctively I did.

The man then said something to WuJian. WuJian smiled and said something back. He then turned to me and said, "Mary, this is my father. His name is WuXiao. He doesn't speak much English. He can only speak a few words such as hello and goodbye. I suppose I'll be your intermediary to translate between the two of you."

"Okay. Please tell him it's really nice to finally meet him and a pleasure to introduce myself." I smiled.

WuJian's father smiled and nodded. I said to WuJian, "Are you going to tell him we are married?"

He immediately scowled. "None of his business. He wasn't there for me enough growing up, he doesn't need to know the happiness I have now. I told you, I'll do what I need to do and no more."

Afterward the man walked with our luggage toward where the gate was. He said something in Chinese. WuJian grabbed his hand and said something back.

We silently followed his father into a taxi.

The drive home had the two of them talking in Chinese, which I didn't understand. WuJian would occasionally translate the important things. For the most part it seemed like an endless conversation on a loop.

Finally, when we pulled up to the house, WuJian opened the door for me and I got out. His father motioned for the two of us to follow him. We walked into the house. He motioned to a bedroom where WuJian's mother lay.

We walked into the bedroom. The bedroom was so small, with only a queen-sized bed WuJian's mother was lying on and a dresser and nightstand. WuJian's mother had shoulder-length hair, but it seemed she wasn't able to comb her hair for a few days since it was all over the place. Her face was worn and wrinkled with no glow. Her lips were dry and pale. Her eyes were half open.

She was covered with a towel on her forehead and she had frequent coughs. I whispered, "WuJian, did your father say how sick she really was?"

"No, he just said that she's been like this for days. The doctors are not sure what's wrong."

"Are they good doctors?"

"They have called in Western doctors, which is rare for them. Therefore, I know this is serious."

When WuJian's mother spotted WuJian her eyes lit up suddenly. She gave him a hug as he walked to her and she said a bunch of things again in Chinese that I didn't understand. I bowed my head at the head of the bed. WuJian's mother waved at me as a way to acknowledge my presence. Then she spoke with WuJian for a few minutes.

Afterward, WuJian turned to me and explained, "My mother wishes to thank you for how hospitable you have been to me in the United States. She wishes to express her deep thanks, how you have taken care of me, helped me with whatever I needed. She knows that you are an actress and appreciates the fact you have gotten me acting jobs. She really does regret the fact that she can't travel, or at the very least travel someplace closer to us."

I let out a deep sigh. "Please tell her that wasn't necessary, she's ill, she deserves to rest and doesn't need to be jumping on planes simply to please others."

I believed that response was greatly appreciated by his mother because she tried to get up and bow to me, to which I said, "Please don't, it's not necessary."

Finally, she motioned me closer and gave me a hug. After that, his father pushed us both out, saying his wife needed her rest.

"Do you still not know how sick she is?" I asked.

"No. I can't figure it out. I don't know if this is something that's serious or not. I will go and speak with the family doctor in a little bit."

WuJian showed me to a guest room and looked me in the eyes. "While we are here, we unfortunately will have to stay in separate rooms. I do know that this bothered you in the United States and I apologize for that. However, I don't think my parents and the customs are ready for us to do otherwise."

I nodded. "I understand. Don't worry yourself with these little things. In the grand scheme of things us sleeping in separate rooms is the least of your problems. You go tend to your mother and call the doctor and please keep me posted. And anything I can do, please let me know."

WuJian called the doctor. The call lasted nearly twenty minutes. After that, he opened the door to my room and spoke. "My mother has a severe case of pneumonia, her lungs are filling up. The doctor doesn't know how to drain it properly and suggests that we need to go to a more mainstream Chinese hospital." He lowered his head, sighed and continued. "Unfortunately, my parents don't want to go, stating that alternative medicine's the only way to reduce it. I have tried to argue with my parents, stating that the doctor himself has given up on this course of treatment, but it was in vain."

WuJian's eyes shifted to the side and I saw a thin layer of tears being held back. He said, "I asked my father 'what do you want to do?'. His response was, 'at the end of the day if the Universe wants your mother out of here she won't be here. It's not as if it has anything against us, it's simply the fact that this is the way it is.'"

WuJian said to his father, "Then I can't stay here forever. While I appreciate seeing mother, I will continue to tend to her. However, I do believe after three weeks I will have to go home. I don't think I can stay here if you refuse to get additional help. It's as if you're making her deathbed and just simply do not care."

His father was silent, neither agreeing or disagreeing.

"Then what happened?" I asked.

WuJian moved closer to me. "He did not move from his position. So I said again that after three weeks with no change, I would be flying home. The home we have there is our home, it's not the home I have here. This is a home I tried to leave many times, a home I finally left properly, a home that I no longer have an interest in…"

WuJian tended to his mother for the next three weeks. He was attentive as only a devoted son could be. However, the situation didn't improve. It didn't get worse but it didn't improve.

When the three weeks were finally coming to an end, WuJian walked into the room where his parents were and simply said, "I have tried to be respectful. I have tried to serve you properly. I've tried to make you proud. However, I must protest the fact that you refused to get additional medication, refused to go to additional doctors who may help you. There are doctors even within Chinese borders and you don't have to leave the country. However, you insist on being only in one place. I can't handle your situation. This is not a normal situation you are living, you need to know that. You need to know that you need to go to real doctors. However, your refusal has left me no choice but to leave tomorrow."

His parents gave WuJian a look as I watched. They then simply turned their heads and refused to acknowledge anything that was said.

It was as if they were telling WuJian, you do what you have to, and we'll do what we have to as well. It was very depressing and disheartening for me to watch.

There were two people who could solve this problem, help themselves and have his mother live, and they refused to do so because they were stubborn. At least, they were stubborn in my eyes. I do understand how the culture of eastern Asia used alternative medicine; however, at some point you have to be realistic, and be able to combine treatments to your advantage.

The next day came. WuJian and I packed our suitcases. We were going with extremely heavy hearts.

WuJian seemed to take it better. Perhaps he was internalizing the fact that his parents were never there for him in the first place and that they didn't listen to him even now.

That being said, WuJian and I went back to the United States and we moved on, burying ourselves in our work I suppose—in our life—and just burying the fact that his mother was very sick.

CHAPTER 23
Hollywood Honors Come to Me

Having been in a relationship with WuJian for nearly nine years, I had felt so invigorated, like a young child again. It was as if I was in a teenage love romance that would never end. I felt more bounce in my step.

However, the reality was that I was an aging actress who had been in many films; some acclaimed, some did very well at the box office and some flopped. It was the flops that Mike and I would laugh about all the time.

However, one day I got a call from Mike out of the blue.

"Mike, how are you?"

"Good, Mary. It's been a while, I know. I'm sorry we only got a few scripts that made sense, but you know me—I like to filter them for you. There's one or two I'm going to send you this week."

"There's no rush."

Mike swiftly changed the topic. "But I did get a very interesting call; it was from the Academy. They want to honor you with a Lifetime Achievement Award."

"Me? I haven't done enough." I gasped.

"Nonsense. You've been in enough acclaimed films that this is warranted. I didn't know how you'd feel about it. So many actresses at your age say that's a very big accomplishment, although some see their youth going away and are very miserable about it. I didn't know which way that wind blows with you, so I figured I'd give you a call before the talks progressed."

I was amazed. I never expected to be nominated for a Lifetime Achievement Award. But on the other hand, I would welcome any awards.

"Well, the truth is, I mean, dating a younger man, I feel pretty young. But a Lifetime Achievement Award would be nice because it is something that I have put all my effort into. Strange how Hollywood has been to me. They have treated me fairly, given me riches, given me fame, and given me WuJian. I couldn't have had any of those without them, so I suppose it is fair that I return the favor. Tell them yes and I'll see them there."

"The Academy will be thrilled. It's going to be a blast; there are so many parties after it. You go out with the who's who of Hollywood. You know the drill."

I laughed. "I know the drill more than you think, Mike. I've been to so many of those parties. I hated them all. But, hey, like I said, it's my turn to return the favor." Then we both laughed.

When WuJian came home from the set that day, I said, "I got an interesting call from Mike today."

"Oh really, what was it?" His eyes were wide open from anticipation.

"They wanted to honor me with the Lifetime Achievement Award for all my efforts in Hollywood."

He smiled. "Mary, you should accept it, it's a great honor! I mean, look—everybody accepting that award was an extremely powerful person who had acted in many great films. You have done the same and should be treated no different. You deserve this. I'm happy for you!"

I grinned. "I'm happy for it too. It's a shame that it's a Lifetime Achievement Award; it means that you've been in Hollywood way too long. The years of your life have gone too fast."

"Don't be silly. There's so much more to life and so much more to do. However, the fact they recognize your acting ability is something worth being grateful for."

I smiled and began to celebrate. We began to plan what gown I should wear and where I'd get my hair and makeup done. After all, the red carpet was its own entertainment: you had reporters, bloggers, and international media commenting on everything, from what you wore to how your hair was, what shoes you wore, to what jewelry you wore. I mean, the list goes on and on.

I insisted on him being by my side. He said he was happy to do so and rented a beautiful tux.

As the days slowly continued toward the ceremony, Mike would call me with updates saying they need you here, they need you there, you're invited to this party or that party, make sure you smile and rub elbows with this person and that person.

Finally, after one of those long sessions with Mike, I said, "Mike, you do know that after all these years I don't care, right?"

He laughed. "I know that, but your husband does, and that's important. So why don't you do it for him?"

I wasn't sure if Mike was serious but either way the thought did cross my mind, and if this could help WuJian in any way, I would do it fully and smiling all the way.

And so I made sure to rent the perfect gown, have my hair and makeup done by the best, and have my shoes shining so I walk the red carpet as never before.

WuJian came down from our house toward the limo on that day, where I was waiting for him, in his beautiful tux. He had looked so handsome, so dapper. I had not seen him like this for the longest that I could remember. It was as if he painted a ray of sunshine all over him. He truly looked like an amazing young buck that I could totally appreciate. I was so thankful that I was able to be in a relationship with him.

"WuJian, you look amazing!" I tilted my head and winked at him as he grabbed a seat in the limo.

He studied me up and down. "No, you look more beautiful than I look amazing!"

As he leaned in to give me a kiss, I moved away slightly. "Careful, my makeup could run."

He laughed. "Fine, we'll save that for later."

We both settled into the limousine and headed for the red carpet. The red carpet at the Academy Awards was an affair that I tried to explain to him, that it would be unlike anything he'd ever seen. Although he had been to many premieres and other red carpet affairs, this would outdo them all. There would be cameras going off like never before, an endless stream of interviewers and yelling fans, and the lights would be blinding.

When we arrived within three blocks of the Beverly Hilton, where the award ceremony would be held, it was already lined with limousines. Each car was shiny and fabulous, carrying important celebrities. But stuck in this mess wasn't fun, and it took forever to just move one inch. I had plenty of patience having done this more than once. WuJian seemed to lose interest after a little bit and said, "Can't we just walk?"

"Easy for you! You're in regular shoes, I'm in six-inch heels. Try walking three blocks like that."

"Okay, I understand."

We finally made it close enough where the limo driver stopped and opened the door for us. We slowly got out.

The minute we got out it was like a flash mob war went on: cameras everywhere, flashbulbs going off, reporters wanting interviews. We were surrounded by media, camera guys, and fans. Again, it was hard to move an inch. Everyone wanted to capture photos of us, interview us, or greet us. It was as if we were the most important people on earth. The amount of attention was hard to bear.

WuJian was so taken aback he didn't know what to do. He looked like a lost puppy. I laughed. "I told you this, right?"

"I understood it, but until you see you don't realize..." He shrugged.

I nodded. "Listen, this is Hollywood, this is really Hollywood. You think filming a movie is Hollywood; this is the real Hollywood." We both chuckled.

We did our fair share of interviews as we walked along the red carpet. It was like making pit stops. Every few feet there was a television station or radio show that wanted me to have an interview with them. We did as many as we could.

Finally, it was time for the awards.

We walked into the auditorium and took our seats. Someone from the event staff came over and said to me, "Mrs. Maddin, you are going to go at the end, right before the best picture. The Lifetime Achievement Award is a big honor. Right before the commercial break you'll go behind the set. We'll make sure your hair and makeup are perfect and we'll help with any lines you want to go over."

I nodded. "Thank you very much. I'll see you there."

I had prepared a short speech thanking some of the most important people in my life. I didn't think that a long-winded speech about some political issue or some religious institution was what I needed. It wasn't my style anyway, and anyone who knew me would think I was out of my mind.

The award ceremony continued on. It was actually quite enjoyable. Near the second to last commercial, sure enough one of the event staff came over and motioned for me to come.

During the commercial break I went backstage and the staff made sure my hair and makeup were perfect. Finally it was my turn to wait backstage until my name was called. A prominent actor and actress went up and did a speech. After a short intro, they played a video clip of some of my films, plays and other things that I've done. And finally, my name was called.

I walked out on stage as inspirational music played, amazed at how people were looking at me. A sea of flashbulbs went off as I gracefully walked to the podium. I was no stranger to award ceremonies and I actually liked the fact that all eyes were on you and all ears were waiting to hear what you got to say.

I felt extremely proud and humbled at the same time—proud of what I've accomplished in my acting career, and humbled by the fact that the Academy wanted to honor me of all people, given all the greats that had come before me.

"I'm here having a trail blazed before me by many, many actresses and actors; I am honored to be among these amazing actors and actresses," I said. "There have been so many people in my illustrious career to thank that I don't know where to begin. I will say I thank my parents for pushing me not to go into Hollywood, so that I could do just the opposite."

The audience chuckled. That was my opening joke.

It's always smart to have one.

After that, I said, "I want to thank my agent, Mike; he's been with me so long. I'm not sure whose hair is grayer, his or mine. I want to thank my kids, Bo and Bobby and their families for giving me so much joy and so much enjoyment every day. I could never thank them enough. Finally, I want to thank the man in my life, for those of you who don't know, his name is WuJian. The way we met is a story in itself. The fact that he's in my life now means more than anything to me in the world. I thank the Academy for all their efforts and for accepting and honoring me. Thank you!"

After the speech and hearing the loud applause and cheering, I simply went away, and the ceremony went to commercial.

I went backstage. The few Hollywood actors and actresses who were still there gave me a hug and congratulated me. A staff member gave me an acceptance gift bag that I could take with me, and I moved on.

After that, I met Mike on my way back to my seat. Seeing me approaching, a smile cracked on his face, and he said, "Great acceptance speech, Mary! Glad that you managed to fit me in there. I don't think my hair is *that* gray!" We both laughed.

"Mike, listen, after all these years you think I wouldn't thank you?" I winked.

"You know, I wasn't sure, because you only have such a short while on stage for your speech. Every awardee only had a short window up there, so I wasn't sure if you would squeeze me in or not."

I laughed. "Of course I would! Couldn't have done anything without you!"

Finally, I made my way back to my seat. WuJian smiled. He held my hand and gave me a hug and kiss and said, "You were great up there! I was really inspired by your speech!"

"Thanks so much! It means a lot to me."

After the award ceremony ended, we slowly made our way out.

The limos were piled up. They called you in shifts because there were too many to count.

Finally, our limo pulled up and I said, "Which party would you like to go to? There are ten that I'm invited to in the next hour alone."

WuJian's eyes lit up as if he were a child who had just been told he could get anything he liked for Christmas. "Tell me, which one will have a good drink?"

I laughed. "Probably all of them. The one I remember that had the best drinks was the Walka party. Walka is a fashion line and always wanted my business."

"Let's do that!"

We went to that party and had a couple of drinks. It had been a while since I drank some good hard liquor, but it felt great to have a scotch on the rocks. WuJian did the same and so we felt a little bit more buzzed than we would have liked, but we did enjoy the party.

We danced, we ate, and we had fun. I don't remember ever having had so much fun at one of those Hollywood parties, and I had probably been to hundreds. Again, perhaps that was because WuJian was now in my life. That was something I truly appreciated.

With him by my side I didn't feel alone, nor did I feel miserable or like a failure. In fact, I felt empowered at the fact that I was given this amazing award, with this amazing man in my life.

We got home that night and we both admitted that it was an amazing event, amazing evening, and amazing time all around.

CHAPTER 24
Hard Decisions

Once you're in Hollywood for too long, you get the drive to have a family, to realize your place in this world. That was probably why I got married the first time; it was definitely not why I married the second time.

The first time it was to be with a man and do what everyone else did and actually have children. Once I had a family, however, my marriage didn't work.

With WuJian, however, he was entering the prime of his life.

Did he want a family?

Was that something he wanted?

Where did he stand on all these things?

At this point, I had married a man I truly loved but I didn't know where he stood on many things.

One night as we went out to dinner at a quiet restaurant in the corner place where no one was bothering us, I whispered, "I have to ask you something."

"Anything." He beamed as usual.

"Do you want kids?"

He looked at me as if I had two heads. After a few moments he said, "I don't understand the question."

"Do you want kids of your own?"

"Well, I kind of view your grandkids as kids."

"I understand and appreciate that, but they're not your kids. Do you want your own?"

He thought about it for a few seconds. "Well, I never thought of it too much. I never thought about it in my life after the situation of my own family life. I thought it best to live as a bachelor until I met you. Once I met you, perhaps my life changed. But I realized obviously that the way our relationship works that's not something that could be in our life. If having kids meant giving you up, I will not do so."

I held his hand tight and said, "I appreciate that. I love you, but I would never want to do anything to make you miserable. I do want you to be honest and open with me because that's the type of relationship I think we have. I need you to understand that having children is a big step in one's life; it's a legacy to give. While I might not be the perfect mother or was the perfect mother, I certainly don't regret for a moment having kids in my life and what they mean to me. I don't want you to miss out on that experience because of my age."

"Thank you for being so concerned about me. But believe me, if that was my major concern, we wouldn't be in a relationship anymore. I would have run away from you a long time ago." He laughed.

I knew that he was serious about the matter and I appreciated his response. I said, "Okay, but if anything changes please do let me know."

It was thoughts like this that occurred to me many times. I thought that I was doing a favor for WuJian to change his life, but I didn't know how much. I didn't know how much he valued our relationship.

Did he value it as much as I did?

Did he regret being with me?

Did he want a family of his own?

Those questions were always gnawing at me, even when I was able to dismiss them for a short period of time.

After a little bit, we decided to get our first pet. Well, our first that didn't live in a cage or a bowl. I always loved fish, and I had a parrot as well. I figured that it may compensate for the lack of children in the house.

WuJian asked me, "What do you want?"

"A dog, but not too vicious. I don't like big, vicious dogs."

"No problem. How about a Pomeranian?"

I said, "Sure. I don't know what that is, but it sounds exotic!" I trusted WuJian enough to get any type of dog he wanted.

I was never much of a dog person growing up, even though so many people in Hollywood seemed to walk a dog as a fashion statement. People loved to see what their dogs were wearing! I suppose the paparazzi would shoot pictures of just the dog alone, let alone the owners. I thought it would be fun for WuJian and I to have a dog.

We went to the pet store and asked for a Pomeranian. The clerk asked, "You sure you want that?"

I raised my eyebrows and asked, "Why? Are they vicious?"

"No, they are actually pretty cute to me, but they kind of act like divas."

WuJian made a joke, saying, "Of course this is perfect for Mary, it's just like her!"

We both laughed, and I said, "Yes, the Pomeranian would be perfect."

"Okay, ma'am, I'll get you whatever else you need," she said. "Leash, toys, foods, you name it, and you'll get it."

We slowly made our way out of the pet store and brought home our first pet. It was a strange sight to see myself and WuJian taking turns walking the dog.

I suppose in some way it became our child, for it gave us the emotional attachment that both of us needed at the time. Bo and Bobby's families came to love our Pomeranian as well. It was a female that we named Angie.

We loved Angie. She became a part of our family. We would take her for walks, had fun in the yard and had fun around the house.

Angie was a very playful dog who knew her place and never got too angry. She understood why we needed her. It was as if the Universe told us that this was the pet we needed at that time. Angie was amazing. I don't regret getting her for a second.

I think WuJian enjoyed her presence too, because he would give her hugs, even occasional kisses, to my chagrin.

We did never have kids together. I don't think WuJian suffered for it. He seemed to be at peace with his decision, having made it a long time before.

I was tremendously thankful for that.

CHAPTER 25
Additional Riches

I had made a fortune in Hollywood; millions and millions of dollars per film, and I had made a lot of them. With Mike's help, I had hired the savviest investment advisers possible. They made me a fortune over time, never mind how the markets fared. They went up, they went down; it didn't matter. Things got worse, things got better, I felt for people less fortunate, but on the other side of it I truly was making millions per film.

I gave freely to charity. I never understood why people would hoard money and never give it away. Money wasn't meant for their exclusivity alone. Money was meant to help others. At some point, you don't need all the money in the world.

How much could you buy already?

How many cars?

How many yachts?

Did those things make you happy?

Seeing someone down on their luck and turning them back from the edge of ruin is worth way more than all that hoarded wealth.

I knew Hollywood gave all kinds of donations. I saw actors and actresses being honored all the time for their generosity. But for me, it was simply about being able to help people.

Don't get me wrong; I enjoyed the shiny things we had, the vacations we took, the cars we owned, the house we lived in, but beyond that there came a point where I had more than I needed.

However, as luck would have it, one day I got a call from one of my attorneys. He said, "Mary, there was an uncle of yours apparently that you were not that familiar with."

"Okay…" I tilted my head not knowing where this was going.

"He was in the textile business and seems to have made a mint. He had one son who he had disowned years ago but even that son he left some money. However, the rest of it he left to you."

"Me? Why me?" I found that hard to believe.

"Apparently he liked your films and the work you did, and he felt you made him happy when he watched them, knowing somebody in his family had succeeded besides him. With that, he left you fifty million dollars and some items of considerable value, to use at your discretion."

I exclaimed, "Fifty million! Wow! Apparently there is excellent money in textiles."

I made arrangements to fly to Texas to sign the will and the executive order of the estate. WuJian stayed behind to be able to finish filming what he needed to.

On my way to Texas, I gave some thought to if I had met this uncle. I didn't remember ever meeting him. Perhaps I did once when I was a child, but other than that, I don't remember. When I arrived, the house didn't seem that familiar to me.

I arrived later at the lawyer's office and asked for the details.

"Well, you get the estate, which you can sell if you wish. You'll also get the fifty million in cash, as well as some cars and valuables. It's up to you how you wish to proceed. You can have the cash wired and the assets sold to pay the taxes. Whatever you wish to do, we are open to it. We have taken care of everything to this point and our fee is already paid, so it doesn't matter to us."

"That's interesting." I said.

I thought about it for a moment. I thought about giving it all to charity, but then another thought occurred to me—if this uncle wanted me to have it then I should use it in some other way. I could give to charity from my own funds. So, that's exactly what I did.

I walked around and drove back to the estate. I looked around trying to find anything I could remember. I didn't find much other than a beautiful house well taken care of, except for one room.

I came into this room, which looked like some sort of den, and saw pictures of me and all the different films that I had done. Early in my career, later in my career, even very recent—all framed beautifully and meticulously hung in neat rows.

I thought about what the attorney said. "He liked the way you acted."

It was very fitting, therefore, that all of the pictures he had were of me acting in various roles. It was simply a sight to behold; it was like a walk down memory lane to see all these people I had portrayed and to go back to all the films that I had done.

I didn't know there was a silent fan who I had never met, or only met when I was very young. I was appreciative of the fact that he thought I did a great job.

"I appreciate all this," I said to the lawyer. "The only thing I don't want you to sell off are those pictures. Please have them boxed up and shipped to me."

"No problem. We'll do that right away, ma'am."

"Thank you. I appreciate it."

It was truly a walk down memory lane to see all these things. However, it did get me thinking of the fact that I didn't have a proper will. I certainly didn't have one that included WuJian.

When I got home I went to one of our attorneys, who specialized in wills and trusts. I told him the problem.

I frowned and said, "I have a dilemma; I have children who I obviously want to leave things to. However, I have this amazing man in my life who I want to leave even more to if it were up to me."

The man said, "In my experience, ma'am, if you leave too much to the lover, or whoever this man is, the kids will end up challenging the will, thinking you've gone insane. It really isn't worth the headache of the legal process that follows. I have been through too many of those situations to count. At the end of the day, what you need to do is come up with a reasonable estimate of what's fair and what's not fair. Can I provide that action plan for you now?"

I thought about it for a minute and said, "That makes plenty of sense. One thing I could do is either split the money now, or, if not, I could somehow arrange a separate trust for WuJian that no one had to know about."

We talked about the pros and cons of each of the possible actions and came up with a plan that would satisfy everyone. No one would be poor, the charity would get their amount, and everybody would be happy. At least, I hoped so.

One thing I learned about money is, if you want one hundred dollars to make you feel good, try to get two hundred; after you get the two hundred try to get four hundred and so on; you could double it to infinity. But that being said, I knew in my heart that I was doing right by everyone. That was what was most important to me.

So, I left the lawyer's office that day after I had signed the papers. I took a copy of them with me and hid them in a safe. No one needed to know, neither WuJian nor my children. They didn't need to know about the visit or about the contents of the papers.

To me, this was simply about doing the right thing and being able to, after my passing, leave a legacy that helped everybody, and that's what I did.

CHAPTER 26
The Slow Decline

I had been on the blood thinner medication for a few years. I felt fine. Young at heart. However, my body betrayed me, and I didn't even know it.

I did start seeing the doctor more regularly as prescribed. I went once a month and he was very patient. Each time he would do simple blood work, take my blood pressure—you name it, he ran the full gamut.

I learned to bite my tongue at some of the tests even though I thought they were completely unnecessary. I told myself to be super healthy and completely comply. However, that being said I was realistic. I knew that because of my age I should get it all checked out.

Once, after I checked out, Doctor Earl looked at me and said, "Mary, you're on a blood thinner, that's working. However, I'm seeing signs of an aging disease of your heart. I'm not thrilled with what's going on there. We may need to do a more robust blood test. We have to monitor it from week to week. I know this is a pain because you've been coming monthly and even that was difficult; however, I do think it's important."

I pouted. "Are you kidding me? My heart? My heart feels fine! It's beating strong and even every minute."

"If it was only beating every minute you'd be dead." He laughed and said, "The point is that there's something wrong that we don't like. You can get a second opinion if you wish and I would totally respect that. However, we think that this is the best course forward."

"No problem, doctor." I walked out of the office feeling disappointed.

When I got home, I sat down and shook my head.

Can you believe this doctor?

He wants me to come in once a week now?

What disrespect!

I go there once a month, I take his blood thinner medication, I do everything he asks, and this is how he treats me?

I can't believe it... what nerve!

In my heart I knew Doctor Earl was very experienced and respected, but I did want to get a second opinion.

I called some friends, and even called my agent and said, "Mike, can you recommend me another doctor?"

"Is everything all right? What's the matter with Doctor Earl?"

"Nothing. But now he's telling me my heart has a problem. I've had enough of this guy," I said with disappointment.

"Mary, those things tend to be serious. You should really take his advice. If you want a good cardiologist, I'm happy to recommend one."

He gave me the information. I made an appointment and went through a whole battery of tests—cardiograms, blood work, you name it, I did it all.

Finally, the cardiologist came back and said, "Well, I don't know if I would have suggested once a week, but I can certainly conclude that there's an issue. I don't know if it requires surgery or just monitoring. It's very hard to tell. I'm sure it's unnerving what I'm telling you, but at the end of the day, if you want to live you've got to attend to this."

"Fine, doctor. Thank you!" I walked out feeling as if I was struck by lightning.

I knew that the first doctor's diagnosis had been confirmed. It was devastating to me to know this, because I didn't think that there would be another health issue after the last one.

I thought that with the proper regimen and the proper medication I would be able to outlive everyone. Heck, I thought I could outlive WuJian!

At that point, I decided I would have to tell WuJian what was going on. Until then, I didn't want to worry him.

He came home that night from one of his filming sessions. I pulled him into our bedroom and said, "WuJian, I have to tell you something. I was at the doctor a few days ago for my routine physical. I don't want to worry you, but they found something. In order to get it set straight, I went to get a second opinion, and they concluded that my heart has issues. They don't know the extent of it, nor do they know if I'll require surgery."

He furrowed his eyebrows, looked deep in my eyes and said, "I'm sorry. I'm really sorry. Is there anything I can do to help?"

"No, just being there for me is good enough. However, we will have to monitor this closely. I need to go to the doctor's more often."

"Fine, then I will go with you," he said firmly.

"No, WuJian. As we did with the monthly sessions, I don't want you to go and trouble yourself. Your career and shooting are more important to me than this minor bump in the road. You go on doing what you've got to. If there's ever an issue, believe me, I will call you."

And so, with that reassurance WuJian and I went downstairs to eat dinner as usual. I sat at my seat, more confused and worried than ever about what the future would hold. I didn't know if I would be okay.

I mean, going to the doctor once a week wasn't a big deal. It was the fear that each time I went they would tell me there was another big deal.

Would today be the day I needed immediate surgery?

Would today be the day they said my heart was inoperable?

Would today be the day when there would be no more of me?

I didn't know any of this. Those thoughts troubled and confused and scared me.

It is amazing when you get older what you think about. When you're young, you think you have it all, you know it all and you have all the time in the world.

Eventually, time creeps up on you faster than you ever expected. Even when you have happiness in your life time creeps up on you. Time doesn't differentiate between happiness and not being happy. The fact is, time moves either way. That's why so many people try to recapture their youth, so to speak.

All "recapturing their youth" means is trying to get back the time they wish they had. However, you can never get it back. You just have to enjoy the moments you have. Enjoy the moments with your children, enjoy the moments with your boyfriend or girlfriend, just enjoy the moments.

To me this was a wakeup call.

I needed to do more with my life. I could take more acting roles—that'd be great—but what would I do with the money?

I decided to start a foundation. I called it the Mary and WuJian Foundation. I didn't know if people understood what we were going to do. Heck, neither did I; I didn't know if it would do any good. But I did know that starting a foundation was very important to me.

On the first day of my new project, I went to town to get the paperwork to be able to do it. The next thing I did was build a staff and make sure they were able to handle the foundation's business, and the third thing was my decision that I was going to need to tell people not only about the foundation but my health condition.

I called up my sons and said, "I have something to tell you. I don't know if I should tell you in person; we'd probably be better off face to face."

They came to the house with stern faces, knowing that there must be something wrong that I wanted to tell them. We were all rallied in the living room. Bo and Bobby looked at me intently and asked, at the same time, "What is it, Ma?"

I sighed and said, "I have a health problem. I'm working through it with very good doctors. We're monitoring the situation, but I don't know what's going to happen."

They got all nervous. Their eyes scanned me up and down trying to make sure that I was okay.

"How serious is it?" Bobby asked with a frown.

"Well, it's my heart and I don't know what will happen to it. I was hoping to avoid surgery with the proper rest and medication and regimen." I talked quietly and slowly, trying not to make it too unbearable for my children.

"Ma, we're with you no matter what." Bo gave me a hug.

"Me too." Bobby also gave me a tight hug.

WuJian was simply watching calmly from the side, not saying much.

I felt so loved by my sons. I might have regretted marrying my first husband, but there was never a moment I regretted having my children, especially as I got older. I felt more and more of our strong family tie and how supportive they were of me.

I fought back tears and said, "I appreciate that, appreciate the support boys, and I know I'll pull out of this fine."

Their voices went a little shaky. "Ma, we're with you every step. Do you need us to come to the appointments?"

"That won't be necessary. WuJian offered the same thing; I immediately dismissed it. There's no need for you guys to worry as much as you are. I am telling you that I'll be fine, and I will beat this. There's no doubt in my mind that I can handle this."

To me, telling them it's not a big deal was more of a confidence booster to myself than anything else. The more I told people, whether it be my agent, my children or WuJian that I would be fine, I knew I would be.

That didn't mean that I was a fool. I did keep my appointments. However, I did know that the sense of self and the fact that I had a better attitude about things certainly helped my prognosis.

No one knows what their future holds. That became my mantra. You have to do what you have to, but also enjoy the moment. I tended to go out more with WuJian than ever before. We enjoyed each other's company each night.

I tended to look for roles that would pay good money, took those roles and then donated all the money to charity through my foundation. To me, it wasn't about any of it, it was about enjoying things that brought me pleasure, brought me happiness, and helped others as well.

With all the adjustments, I was able to accomplish more in those few months than I had done in a long time. I was very proud of that looking back. It was something I wished I had done sooner, wished I had done more of, and wished I had started doing before I got sick.

CHAPTER 27
The Foundation Takes Hold

It was never my intention to be someone who was so involved in the foundation. I enjoyed the idea of starting the foundation and seeing all the charitable endeavors that it could undertake.

Helping people in ways that I prioritized was something that WuJian enjoyed doing with me. However, the more I saw what was going on, the more it became necessary for me to be involved.

At first, I attended monthly meetings and gave my input. Soon, though, the foundation's staff would come to my house with questions that "just couldn't wait."

Which charitable causes do we support?

Which charitable foundations should we partner with?

What should be our primary purpose?

How would we continue to raise money?

All these questions kept me busy day after day, night after night. I got calls from project planners and committee members. It had become a very complex organization in no time at all.

Within a few months, we had to rent a larger space in Hollywood. I tried to keep overhead to a minimum, because I knew that every dollar spent wouldn't be going toward charity. I suppose this is a challenge that often plagues most of the charitable dinners and corporations that try to attempt these things.

You often hear of Hollywood celebrities or athletes starting foundations. However, I do believe they don't understand quite what goes into a foundation until they're actually on the ground doing it. Everyone tends to have their own cause. For me, the issue was I didn't have a specific one.

Our foundation had a focus on my particular illness because it sounded reasonable. However, there was also divorced parents, children from overseas, you name it, I thought about it. I could relate to all of them in some way, shape or form.

It was quite important to me that I be able to convey the fact that there needed to be a singular voice in the foundation, and that voice should be mine. I hired a very shrewd woman, Lena, to be the head of our foundation, who understood my vision.

Lena was a middle-aged woman who had worked in fundraising for fifteen years. Besides Lena's and a few other workers' salaries, I was able to carry out the business of the foundation with as minimal cost as possible.

Don't get me wrong—Lena didn't come cheap. Her salary was quite high. However, the idea there was the fact that she was well worth it because whatever dollars she raised more than covered her salary and went a long way toward fulfilling the foundation's goals.

That to me was very important. After all, I worked hard for the money that I was providing for the foundation. I'm sure those that donated to the cause through my effort (and some might call it pressure) felt the same.

I had put pressure, if you will, on Mike and many of the Hollywood actors and actresses, producers and directors that I knew. Some rebuffed me politely, some donated minimally, and some gave huge sums. It was quite impressive to see the variance of the types of donors we got. I was quite happy with that.

Media outlets played a part in what we did as well. We wrote articles about the efforts we were making and the people we were helping. These gave tangible proof to the fact that our foundation was real, legitimate and honest. We were not like those who squandered money on lavish banquets for themselves. We were there to help people, and at the end of the day those people were the only ones with whom we were concerned.

Occasionally we did hire people who didn't have the proper vision. I immediately got involved to make sure those people didn't have a voice and eventually left the company.

If they couldn't see the vision that helping people was first and foremost, then they couldn't be part of our foundation. To me, having a foundation was about a legacy. It was about the fact that you had something that was beyond you. If people couldn't see that then they couldn't be a part of it. It was that simple.

One day I was having coffee with Lena in the office. I asked her, "Tell me… how are we doing this year?"

She tilted her head back and smiled. "Well, our fundraising efforts have yielded fruit. We've reached fifty percent of the amount of money we want coming in this year, and the effectiveness of our operations is so good I would say three quarters of every dollar is going to charitable causes."

I nodded with approval and said, "That's great. However, it's not good enough. We need to get to eighty-five percent. I realize that would be squeezing our overhead even further. There are so many causes I want to give to, which you're aware of. In fact, you've brought me a few yourself. Obviously there's not nearly enough money in the world to be able to provide for everyone. So, we do what we can, and I understand the effort you've made, but we must do even better. We need to help those in need. It has to be our priority."

She looked at me with sad eyes. "I understand that, Mrs. Maddin. Believe me, as someone who's on the forefront of the issue there's no one that understands it better than me. I completely understand the fact that we have to use every dollar as efficiently as we can. That is one of the challenges that charities and fundraisers have always faced—how much actually gets allocated to charity. I suppose you're right that in Hollywood they never think about those things; they think it's not important. It's the fact that their name got out there associated with having started a foundation. That was more important than the actual efforts made. I believe at the end of the day though, we can make it happen. We will go through the books, look at our overhead and see where our expenses are too much and cut down on those."

"Listen, Lena, if you need me to lean on some more people, I'm happy to do so. If there are more fundraisers needed, then let's do it. If it's wine tastings, you know, cocktail parties, cook sessions, whatever it is that will help us raise money I'm all for it. I am no stranger to dinners, but I know that you can't do them all the time; once a year seems to be fashionable. Doing them more than that has a negative effect. However, these little fundraisers like walkathons and things of that nature seem to produce massive results given the proper backing. I will back any and all efforts on behalf of this foundation."

I paused and said, "I do hope to one day bring my children into this endeavor as well. I hope that is not offensive to you; it's not my intention to replace you—it's simply a matter of having someone else's opinion. Others to bounce our ideas off of. At the end of the day, my children do come first. They're the most important thing. WuJian is also interested in helping. He has already donated plenty of money from his earnings. However, he wants to do more and be more involved. I do hope to bring them into the fold in the future. I hope that won't be an issue for you."

"Mrs. Maddin, anything that can help us grow and succeed is what I want. For me, having a charity is not something to take lightly; it is a responsibility to the people you're serving, as well as to the donors that you're taking the money from. Both sides must be happy that the money is being used wisely and well. If either side is unhappy then you're right, we aren't doing ourselves any justice."

I smiled and said, "I'm glad that we are on the same page. It is important that we get along. I value your work and really do respect the things you've done in this field."

"And I respect you as an amazing actress! All you've done deserves nothing less than our best. You have achieved so much in your career and having this legacy to leave behind is certainly something I hope to provide."

I laughed. "I hope you're not assuming I'm going just yet."

Lena shook her head. "Of course not. That was never my intention. It was simply a matter of saying that you will have something to look back on with pride, I promise."

We gave each other a hug and continued planning for the next dinner, which wasn't far off. The guest of honor was going to be a famous actor who did not agree to many public appearances. It was someone I could promote to my colleagues and others with money. It was a rare opportunity for them to be in this person's presence.

The weeks until the dinner flew by. WuJian was instrumental in helping me plan certain aspects of the evening and he worked well with Lena. I was also happy to have Bo and Bobby involved.

The amount of money raised was twenty million dollars. It was a record number for us, probably a record number for many institutions. I was really proud of the fact that we were able to do that.

I showed the attendees the diversification of the charity, and that their donations were not just going to one specific cause but to many causes that were dear to our hearts. They were so moved they ended up giving more than they usually did. I appreciated the fact that they understood what our vision was and that they were able to help us.

The dinner was a success and would only lead to more and more fruitful fundraising efforts. The foundation became something more than I ever imagined it would be.

I got to see the smiles of all those we helped. Whether it was the inner-city kid who needed an education, or the student in China who needed help for their college, or someone who had heart disease and couldn't pay their medical bills. Our foundation was able to help all those people, and I was proud of it. It was a legacy I truly wanted to leave behind, and I was on my way to accomplishing it.

CHAPTER 28
Choices Are Made for the Future

It was a long time before I finally decided to tell WuJian about my will. I didn't know how he would react. We had been married secretly for three years.

At some point we would probably have to tell my children that we got married. I didn't believe that they would receive this information well, especially the fact that we held a secret wedding in Italy to which they weren't invited.

However, I also needed to tell WuJian about my will and what was in it for him. I didn't know how to properly do this, and it was something that I had to think about for a long time.

Finally, one quiet evening, while it was just the two of us watching television in our bedroom, eating a light snack, I decided the time was right. After the snack, I turned off the TV and said, "WuJian, I need to tell you something important."

He laughed. "Mary, when you tell me things it all seems to be important. Somehow each thing, although it is always different, gets harder and more important."

"This is true, but I need to tell you that my will has been written."

He seemed unprepared for the topic and went completely still. After a short pause, he said, "I assumed you had a will but I did not think too much about it. I never needed or wanted to be part of your will."

I wasn't offended by WuJian's remarks. I was very grateful that he said what he did. It further proved to me that he was never after my money, even when I offered it.

I nodded with appreciation and said, "I know, and I understand that, and I'm sure your earnings through Hollywood now require no need of that. However, I did want to tell you I have put you in my will. I didn't want the most important man in my life to be left out. While my children do come first, and you know that, they are well taken care of and the foundation has its money as well. But I also love you tremendously. I want you to be taken care of. Again, I realize that your own Hollywood earnings far surpass your need; however, I wanted to show you my affection in my own way."

I pointed out the parts of the will where WuJian was involved. He got certain cars, he got one of our residences and he got twenty million dollars.

WuJian took my hand. "I am flattered that you would put me in your will. However, the twenty million you can remove. I have plenty of money. I don't want your children or any other endeavor to be shortchanged because of me. Believe me, I'll be well taken care of. You don't have to worry."

I shook my head and said, "I know that, but I still want you to have it. If you wish to give it to charity or do anything else after that it's your choice. I am happy with whatever decision you make, but I want you to know that it was your choice and that is what's most important. This is money that you will have, and you can do what you want with it. Please agree to this."

WuJian thought for a moment. "Okay, Mary, you're right. If that day comes I will take the money, but I will also do what I please with it. I hope you understand. Believe me, I don't intend to spend it lavishly and foolishly. You know me too well. It is my intention to honor your example and use it for good. You have started a foundation which I find amazing. I'm inspired by what you're doing with your life right now. It is truly a thing of beauty. I don't know if I could have ever done that on my own. You started a foundation from scratch, hiring the right people, working through it and being involved every day. This to me is a sign you're taking it seriously."

He paused. "I'm jealous of that fact. My acting jobs require too long days and nights to be able to pursue such a thing. The least I could do was to donate to your foundation so that you can have a cause. It was really important for me to do that. However, I know that's not my legacy. I look at you and see someone who'll leave this world having accomplished so much. That is something to envy. That is something I wish to achieve as well. I know that that is not something in my cards right now but something I wish to do eventually. It is important to me to be able to establish my own foundation. I hope you're not insulted by that. What causes I will support I don't know yet, but I do think that I will try to work with everyone I can."

"WuJian, I'm so proud of you!" I smiled. "I do think you will establish your own foundation one day. I do think that you'll be able to do this. Time will not allow you to right now, but there's time. Knowing that you will use the money I have given you in my will for a purpose you wish to fulfill is all the happiness that I want. It is so important to me to see you happy. You doing charity work really makes me happy."

The man I had fallen in love with understood how important it was to be able to do the right thing for people. Hollywood had not spoiled him.

In fact, I knew so many Hollywood stars who spent lavishly on all the wrong things. You name it, they probably tried it, justifying it by saying, "Hey, I worked hard for this money." I would laugh and say, "Fool. The money is going to be there well after you are since you have so much of it. Why not at least leave something to other people?"

I thought about how impressed I was with WuJian. Here I was giving him all the money in the world, or it seemed like it, and his only desire was to help others. He had understood I had seen a long time ago that all the Hollywood parties, drama, goods, cars, houses, and so on don't make someone happy. They certainly don't fulfill why we are here in this place in the Universe.

The Universe placed us here for a reason. The Universe doesn't randomly place people to use them up and then go away. It is important that people understand their role and use it well. If someone has the ability to earn money through acting or through other methods, they should not just use it for their purposes alone; they should use it to be able to help others.

I was so proud of WuJian. He understood this message and wanted to do the same. I had no doubt that he would blaze his own path in life. One that would make me proud to my dying day.

CHAPTER 29
The Lost Come Back

After I had my health scare, I became more cautious about life. I tended to be more careful in making decisions. If I were going out on a date with WuJian, I would make sure that we didn't stay out too late. I told him I needed my sleep and my rest. I became somewhat of a hermit.

WuJian's abilities in acting got noticed more and more. There were parties he would go to without me. I wasn't disappointed or upset because of this. In fact, I welcomed it. I wasn't sure if my life had changed because of my illness, or because I was getting older. At the end of the day this is what was meant to be I suppose. However, one day I got an unexpected call from my agent.

"Mary, it's been too long since you've been in a movie."

"You know my situation, Mike. I am very worried about my health. I don't wish to jeopardize it in any way. I want to be with WuJian for as long as I can and my children as well."

He sighed and said, "Listen to me Mary. Something I learned a long time ago—if you don't live life fully that is not a life worth living. You say you want to be there for them. You have so much to give to others as well. You don't understand what it means to people to watch a movie, or to see a play. I think you forgot everything. I think the fact that you became sick basically shut you down. You became a shell of yourself."

Mike paused and then raised his voice. "It's not the Mary I used to know nor the Mary I want to continue to know. You need to get out there and do something and that's why I'm calling. I came across a script that is super unique. You'd star as the main character again. It's a role you have not seen in a while. It's about an aging actress who ironically decides her life is not worth living because of her age. She laments the fact that everyone around her is so much younger and so much more beautiful. And, in fact, she tries to hide it through various things like drinking. At the end of the day she comes to realize that there's more to her life than just acting. With that she goes out and does many things. Sound familiar? I think it's the perfect role for you."

He slowed down his pace to make his emphasis. "It sums up your life in parallel. You feel you are an aging actress with health issues. You feel your life is declining; therefore, you are thinking it's not worth living. You are tremendously wrong. It's well worth living. This film is something you should consider doing. I recommend you read the script. In fact, I'm not taking no for an answer. Mary, you don't have a choice. I'm sending you the script today and you are going to read it. Pre-production meetings begin next week."

I wasn't in the mood to fight with Mike, so I said, "Fine. Just send me the script and I'll read it." He wasn't very happy with me because my tone said I wouldn't take it seriously.

He wasn't far off. I had no intention of actually doing this.

Until I started to read the script.

I fell in love with it.

In recent years, I took jobs more for the money they would bring in and more for the ability to help others, and the fact that others could benefit from my acting is something I truly wanted. However, this role spoke to me. It spoke to me in a way that a role hadn't spoken to me in years. It basically summed up my life, just as Mike had said. It was a part I couldn't say no to.

I called him back and I said with excitement, "Mike, I'm on board with this. I love this script. I think you're right—the script speaks to me. This is a perfect script for someone like me."

"I knew you would take it. I already told the production manager to save you the spot. I just had a feeling that you were really going to want this script."

I thanked him and hung up.

When WuJian came home I said, "You are not going to believe this. A script came my way that I actually love."

He laughed. "Well, many scripts come your way, Mary. You are bound to love at least a few of them."

"No. I'm actually the lead part in this role, and it's a role that speaks to me. It's about an aging actress who feels life is not worth living anymore, and suddenly has to realize there is so much more to life than just Hollywood."

He grinned. "You know what? You're right—that is the perfect script for you. I can't believe someone actually didn't think of it before. In fact, I can't believe you didn't think of this first… you could have become a screenwriter!"

"In all the years that I have been doing this, I never had any interest in becoming a writer of any sort." I laughed. "But I'll tell you what… I have put my input into scripts. Sure, I gave my opinions, but I never had any interest. The writers have such a demanding role, constantly being yelled at, constantly being criticized, it's not worth it. Being an actress when you get criticized, they do it in a very sensitive way, after all—you are the frail, temperamental actress. Unfortunately, when you are the writer you are considered not much of anything. It's sad because they are so talented, yet the reality is true."

With that, I sighed and continued. "Okay. It's time to begin studying the script." WuJian helped me prepare. I read it and it came back to me like nothing. I had good parts in recent years but pretty small in terms of lines. This was so much bigger.

The production meeting came around before I knew it. That day I drove to the set, extremely nervous, and in fact wondering if I was able to do this. When I got there the producer, a man named John, walked to me with open arms and said, "Hi, Mary! I have heard so much about you from Mike as well as seen some of your work. It's an amazing body of work that you put together. Your Lifetime

Achievement Award was well deserved! You were strongly recommended to us. It really was a no-brainer."

I smiled. "Thank you! I appreciate that. And let me tell you the script that you guys wrote is amazing. I fell in love with it. I can't wait to do the movie."

"Great! That's extremely important to us. We want someone involved who is passionate about the project. If not, there is no point in making the movie. This movie has to speak to the audience, as all the movies I produce must. The director is second to none. I think you have worked with him before. His name is Brandon."

"Brandon Jones?"

"Yes."

"Of course! I know him well. I have worked with him on two films. Really talented director. You are lucky to have him!"

The producer just laughed and said, "I think he is lucky to have us."

"Well, I'm lucky to have both of you." We both laughed.

As I was introduced to Brandon, I said, "It's been a while, Brandon."

Brandon gave me a hug. "Mary, I'll tell you something. I was the one who called Mike about the project. I said there is no one else who can play this role but Mary, Mary is perfect for it. In fact, she needs to be the lead or there's no point in making this film. Mike said, 'Really? If it's so good, send me the script.' I sent him the script that day, he called me back said, 'Brandon, you know what? You are one hundred percent right! Just put her down for it and I will make it happen.' I called the producers and said we're going forward with the project. Everybody was extremely excited."

Day one of shooting it all came back to me like a breeze. I put all my heart and effort into the script, having to do very minimal retakes. They say once you ride a bike you can do it forever; I suppose the same thing is true for acting.

Once you actually put your heart and your soul into the role, you know what it's like to remember the script, to live the script, and that is how I felt. Once the role spoke to me I was in. This role was truly for me. I did the first day of shoots like it was nothing. There was no work involved because to me it was so exciting. Everybody on the set was extremely happy about how the first day went.

The days that followed were just as amazing. They put together an extremely talented cast and crew. The movie itself did very well, eventually making millions. It's something I got critically acclaimed and nominated for. I won several awards, though I didn't get nominated for an Oscar. But I did get nominated and won several others, such as the Golden Globe for Best Actress.

It was truly gratifying to realize how much I missed the acting world. How much the little parts were not satisfying me. Some would say, "You're still in Hollywood, it's just that your lines have been reduced." To that I say, once you get to be a lead actress, the main person that everyone focuses on, it's never really the same. However much I enjoyed a line or two it was never the same as being a lead actress. It was truly exciting and something that I cherish.

I called Mike the day after shooting wrapped and said, "You know, after all this I truly believe that I could still do it. I have so much more to give. I think I can still do acting roles if major parts speak to you again. If they come across your desk, please don't hesitate to call me."

"Mary, I'm always thinking of you, you know that. After all these years don't you know I'm still never going to let you down?"

I laughed. "That's true." I thanked him and hoped that more parts would come my way again soon.

CHAPTER 30
The Teaching Bug Hits Me

I had been waiting for a month or two for Mike to call. He did call several times, but it was with very small parts. I was getting frustrated. Having wrapped up a successful movie, I really wanted to be the star again, something to fill my time and showcase my talent. However, it just wasn't happening.

Sure, there were occasional parts that seemed to fit, but it was never the main lead, never a script that spoke to me. After a month and a half, I felt depressed again.

WuJian did his best to cheer me up, taking me out, dragging me to award parties, and even suggesting another vacation.

I shrugged. "None of that will help. I appreciate everything you are doing my love, but at the end of the day this is not what would satisfy me."

"I understand." He nodded. "Having been in the movies and playing the leads myself, I can truly relate now to what it means to be the star. It's something that fills your heart and can't be explained to others. No one else would believe what happened, no one else realizes what it's like until you experience it for yourself."

"Exactly, WuJian. You get me."

Finally, the strangest thing happened.

I was in the library one day reading a book, doing some research on a small part I had taken just to keep my skills fresh. I noticed something. There was a sign on the wall saying, "Teachers Wanted, Local Acting School."

I stared at it for a few moments thinking, why would they highlight something like that here? Shouldn't it be in some fancy newspaper?

I walked to the librarian. "Can you tell me who put this up?"

She smiled. "Actually, it was me."

"Really?"

"Oh, don't be fooled by my day job. I actually do enjoy acting a bit here and there. In fact, I know exactly who you are, and I have been truly impressed with your work."

I smiled and said, "Thank you, I appreciate that."

Eventually I learned she was a local teacher of the Arts at night, while being a librarian by day to pay the bills. I understood that so much because when I was a struggling actress at the beginning, balancing life and expenses wasn't that easy.

"Listen, would you like it if I came down to the school to possibly do a demo for teaching?"

She laughed. "Demo? You would be hired on the spot! Your career speaks for itself."

"I appreciate that, but I do want to do this right."

"I understand. Why don't you come down tomorrow at about eleven a.m.? I'll make sure the acting principal is there. I would love to be there too but as you can see I'm tied to this chair for my day job."

I laughed and said, "I completely understand. I really hope one day you won't be tied to that chair."

"I certainly hope not," she said. We both laughed.

I went home excited by the fact that perhaps this could be something to fill my time. I went to the school the next day as promised.

I knocked, and the secretary answered the office door. She was a young woman who seemed to be in her twenties with beautiful curly hair.

When she saw me, her eyes went wide. She opened the door for me and asked, "Yes, may I help you?"

"I'm here for the acting teacher position."

She was standing by the door blocking me from going in. She looked at me up and down as if she was conducting an X-ray with her eyes, and then she asked amusingly, "Is this a joke?"

I laughed and said, "No, it's not a joke. I'm here for the acting teacher job."

"No, this is a joke." She shook her head.

"Why do you say that?" I asked.

"Because you are Mary Maddin, the famous actress!" She said it as if she were a detective finding an important clue.

I shrugged. "So?"

"People like you don't do things like this."

"What do you mean?" I frowned.

She tilted her head. "I've never seen a famous actor or actress teach anywhere in all my years. I think they do it as a charitable cause for maybe a week or two as a favor but never like this, applying for some job that was advertised in the library."

"Well, I guess I'm a little different." I smiled. "I really enjoy acting and I want to give back. I've tried to give back in so many ways, it's probably the only way that I haven't given back yet. Teaching is something that I've found interesting and relaying my ideas to others is so important."

"Well, if you're taking it that seriously then yes, please come in and have a seat." She moved to the side to let me in.

I made my way past her. "I certainly am, and I will have a seat, thank you." I found myself a seat next to her desk.

She went off to get the principal, who emerged from an office soon after. Her name was Eileen. She was an older woman who seemed to be in her sixties. She was slender, and she looked good-tempered and elegant. Upon seeing me she said, "Wow! I can't believe this! A famous actress is in here."

"I'm not so famous but an actress, yes." I stood up to greet Eileen with a genuine smile.

She laughed. "Humble too."

"Well, I try." I grinned.

I sat down with Eileen and we had an extremely close conversation. She was someone I looked up to immediately, someone who dedicated her life to young upcoming actors and actresses.

When it was all done, she looked at me. "Listen Mary, I can't offer you any type of job here. The pay is going to be way under your value. Heck, I can't even come close to the thirty thousand dollars a year this job surely deserves. But I can tell you this—the kids that we are teaching truly want to succeed in the arts."

I said, "Let me take the job. It's my hope that even if I could reach one person then I will be successful."

Eileen was shocked. "Really? I will say this. You will be able to mold and shape them and help them more than you know. With your help they will probably be able to get out of the projects or the bad situations they have in their lives. You will truly make your mark and they will appreciate it."

She then took me to see the classroom, where I met the students. Eileen whispered something to their supervisor and then announced to the students, "Welcome your new teacher, Mrs. Mary Maddin. She's a famous actress. Have you seen any of her work?"

They all shook their heads and said no.

"Yeah, it's probably been a while since my major movies, but I did have a movie recently," I said. "It's called *Aging Flower.* Have you seen that?"

They all laughed and said, "No. But we saw a preview for it."

I laughed too. "At least you saw a preview. Your first homework assignment is to go find the movie and watch it. Everything is available these days on videotape."

They all laughed and said okay.

"Great. Let's discuss it in the next class."

That night I went home and told WuJian all about my acting class. He laughed. "So now you are teaching? First you did a movie, before that you founded an organization that helped people in charitable endeavors, and now you're doing a teaching job."

"Yes, I'm trying to stay busy and motivated."

"Am I not enough motivation for you?" He winked.

I gave him a kiss and said, "You are more than enough motivation. The problem is you are too busy for me."

"Perhaps you're right." We both laughed.

When the first day of my teaching job arrived, I went into the classroom, having prepared some basic notes about what it meant to be an actress.

I started with, "Okay, kiddoes, whoever watched the movie please raise your hand."

They all raised their hands, and I said, "Wow! That's impressive. All twenty of you raised your hands. I'm very proud."

I paused and said, "Tell me, what do you think of the performance? You can be honest, don't worry—I'm not embarrassed. I've been told the worst in my career."

One of the children, named Joe, said, "I feel you were very good. However, I thought the lines at times were dragging."

I laughed. "Hmm yes, scripts sometimes can be dragging. It's all about the story. Sometimes you have to feel the story. The story takes time to develop. I can teach you that and why we do it."

On hearing that he said, "Thank you! I'd like to learn that."

Another student raised her hand and said, "Yes, the job you did was quite impressive. However, I didn't like the costume very much."

I replied, "Well, the costume was about the time it was set in. It's supposed to be set in the '70s. Everything about costume design is about setting and making you feel like you are actually in that time period. I can teach you about that as well."

A third person raised his hand. "I didn't like it much. I've got to be honest, I like action films."

"You mean like *The Getaway* or something like that?"

He laughed and said, "*The Getaway*? That's so '70s! I mean I like all the comic book stuff."

I raised my eyebrows. "Oh wow, I've never worked in that genre. That's not my style of acting. But, if they offered me the right amount of money, maybe I'd jump in." Then I laughed.

When I laughed the whole classroom laughed. I thought I was getting through to them.

In the first class I simply explained what it meant to be an actor or an actress, how Hollywood set up the designs, what went on in the early meetings, and what it was like to actually act in Hollywood. They were fascinated and took in every word. I truly felt like I got through to them.

It was amazing—the students actually listened to what I had to say. So many years I had to take orders from producers and directors. I was the one who had to always listen to what *they* had to say. Here were twenty students, who all had an opinion, yet wanted to hear what I had to say. It surely made me feel special and important.

I went home that day feeling very satisfied. It was my intention to remain for at least the rest of the semester and then take it from there. I looked forward to the new endeavor and enjoyed teaching very much.

CHAPTER 31
A Student Catches My Attention

It was about two months into my first semester teaching. I truly enjoyed it. It was such a rewarding experience for me to give back to students.

There was one particular student named Charlene. She was in her early twenties. Charlene had thick dark hair and big brown eyes. Her chin was slightly pointed, making her face exquisite. She was an amazing actress. She had so much talent, she reminded me of myself in my younger years.

One day after my latest assignment to critique a certain play, Charlene came over to me and said, "How did you do it?"

I frowned. "What do you mean?"

"I read about your early years balancing life and a family who didn't support you. How did you do it?"

I said, "Why don't you wait till all the students clear out and we can talk for a little bit. I have some time to stay."

After the class cleared out, I said, "Have a seat."

Charlene took a seat, and I sat next to her. She sighed. "It is so hard for me. I come home, my mom doesn't support my ideas. My father really doesn't care either way as long as I am happy. However, we are not the most well-to-do family and my mom wants me to go get a doctor's degree or a lawyer's degree or something like that. She wants me to succeed in a profession. She says acting is not a profession. At the end of the day, there are so few who make money and so many who fail; it's not worth trying. I was so broken-hearted and said, 'Mom, you don't understand, this is the only thing I ever wanted to do.'"

I smiled. "Let me tell you a story. My parents as you know didn't support me. My father worked very hard as a stage carpenter.

My mother was a seamstress and costume designer. They worked long hours and hated the Hollywood profession.

However, it did pay well enough to provide for me. It was something that was extremely important to them to take care of me. However, they didn't want to see this become my life. They didn't want me to work such long hours with so little reward. I ended up ignoring them and going my own way. Once they saw I was that determined, the success came. That, I think, is the same for you."

I paused and said, "I'm not saying to ignore your mother's wishes, because I realized early on that acting does come with its risks and perils. Your parents are right—not every actor or actress makes it, even the ones who are so determined. However, I must say that you have so much talent, you have the ability to do anything you want. You remind me of a younger version of myself. If I can help you in any way, I certainly will. If you'd like to learn more about some extra work and small parts I can make some phone calls. I think you would do really well and I think once you show your parents that this can become your way of life, that you can make money at it, they will support you. I'm not saying it will always be easy, because at the end of the day it's very hard to act. There are so many producers, so many directors, so many divas and so many things that go into making a movie. Plays are no easier."

Charlene was listening intently, her eyes focused on me and her frown slowly disappeared. I knew that I was getting through to her, that I was having a positive impact on someone's life.

I continued. "People don't realize when they watch a television show how complicated it is. There is so much more to it than what they see. Each step has its own challenges and each step requires its own design. If a person really wants to succeed they will, but they'll have to overcome so much to do so."

I paused again, so I was sure she was understanding each thing I was saying. "Getting an agent is super important. Not every agent will work with you. My agent is kind of old and has decided that he'd rather retire than work with new clients, but I can certainly ask him who he recommends these days and he can curry favor with."

I smiled and took her hand. "Hollywood is all about connections, right? I hate to say it. That's probably true for any industry, but it's certainly more so in Hollywood. If you don't know the right people, you'll never get anywhere. One thing I will say is that for people who are serious, people who really are good and talented, the world should get to see them."

Charlene grinned. "I really appreciate it, Mary. It's really important to me."

I laughed. "I'm glad you learned your first lesson, which was to call me Mary. Don't call me Mrs. Maddin. I'm not an old lady; at least, I don't feel like one."

"I really appreciate this. This really is great advice and an amazing opportunity. I wouldn't have sought you out except for my dilemma of my parents not supporting me. The world probably thinks I'm nuts because everyone around me is a professional. They seem to be doing all the right things, going to college, having the right boyfriends, marrying, even some of them having families. For me, it was never about that. I wanted to blaze my own path. It was about becoming a true actress and enjoying what I do and helping others do it as well."

I patted her back and said, "Charlene, you're on your way, and I'll tell you this—people will enjoy it. I enjoy it and I'm sure your classmates enjoy it, and I know the world will enjoy your acting once you start. From there I want you to focus—I can't say that word enough, focus is key. If you got distracted it will show in your acting. If it shows in your acting, people will not want to work with you. If people don't want to work with you, that'll be the end of your career. I've seen it more than once, and it's a sad thing. It really is.

I signed up for teaching you kids to give back. I didn't think that I would enjoy it as much as I have but seeing the rewards of giving to people like you means everything. It really is special to be able to teach, and it's my honor to mold and shape young actresses like yourself. I think you have a great future in front of you. Don't give up no matter what. Don't let people around you distract you and dissuade you."

I paused to make sure that she understood, and then I continued. "For me, it was more about dealing with my parents and showing them the reality; everything else fell into place. I don't say this to mean there were no other challenges in my life. Believe me, being an actress is a challenge on its own, but I don't want to discourage you in any way. Life will present many challenges once you succeed. That is a place you need to get to first. If you never get to that plateau, you will never be able to understand what I'm talking about. I want you to seek me out again in your later years when you have become famous, which I know you will, then I can explain to you all that has not gone into our conversation now."

I told Charlene again I would make a few phone calls.

When I got home, I immediately called Mike and said, "I have a girl for you. Her name is Charlene. She's an amazing actress."

"Mary, I told you I'm not taking any new clients. It's too hard for me. Work's getting in the way, and I want to enjoy what's left of my life," he replied. "For you, you know I'll do anything. But no new clients."

"Mike, I'm not asking you to take her on. I'm asking you to use your contacts to find her the right agency to work with."

"There are a few I trust but I don't know this Charlene. I'm not going to call in a favor for someone I don't know."

"You're right, that's true. Therefore, I want you to meet her. Why don't you come down to where I'm teaching? I have the students working on scenes that they'll be presenting. Kind of like a showcase.

It's scheduled for a week from tomorrow and you can watch this young actress at work."

"Really? I have to come down to your acting school?"

"What are you doing, playing tennis? You can wait a day, wait an hour, don't worry about it. I'll give you the VIP treatment. You'll have a front-row seat."

"How many people are actually coming?"

"You'd be surprised. The place sometimes gets full."

He laughed. "Acting school showcase? Is this where we are, Mary?"

"I didn't realize the reward of teaching, Mike, until I actually did it. I really do enjoy it. You know it's certainly not for the money."

"Yeah, that for sure," he said. "All right, Mary, I'll do it. I'm doing it just for you. I would never do it for anybody else."

We made a plan for the following week. I continued to work with all the kids, especially Charlene. I paid close attention to her look, her line delivery, the way she positioned herself, and the way she moved.

The day of the showcase we got everyone seated. It was a great turnout. I was more nervous than usual. As soon as I sat down, a familiar face sat next to me.

"Hello, Mary!" It was Mike. Mike had come to look at this famous actress that only I saw in Charlene. The showcase started and soon Charlene came onstage. I had chosen a scene to clearly demonstrate her talent.

Her voice was a little shaky, but her methods and mannerisms reflected a seasoned actress. Mike watched with delight and told me he liked the story. At the end of the showcase everyone cheered. I clapped and clapped and stood up saying, "Bravo! Bravo! Guys, Bravo."

I turned to Mike. "Really, what do you think?"

"I'll tell you, she has potential. She has a little bit of you in her," Mike admitted.

I laughed. "That's exactly what I said."

He thought about it for a few seconds. "All right. I'll tell you what. I know a producer that's looking for a girl for a bit part, maybe two lines. Also there's some extra work I can get her. I'll put in a word with the producer, tell him I think she's the right person. There are a handful of young agents I trust. Two in particular. I'll make a few phone calls. Can't promise anything, but I'll tell them that Mary Maddin is supporting her. Teaching her. When they hear that, they'll probably jump at the chance."

"Thank you. I really appreciated it." I felt like I wanted to jump up and down.

As the audience left I hugged each one of my students. I gave my Charlene an extra big hug and said, "Charlene, you were wonderful! You did such a great job!"

She frowned. "Really? You think so?"

"I know so." I smiled ear to ear. "Let me tell you something exciting. I spoke to my agent and he may have something for you. We'll talk at a different time."

She smiled and ran off.

The next day Mike called back and said, "All right, the producer wants to meet this girl, so she better be the real deal."

"You saw her for yourself, you know she's good," I said with pride.

Charlene went off to her first audition. I met her there for moral support. She came out beaming. "I think they liked me."

The producer saw I was in the waiting room and called me in. "Mary, so nice to see you again."

I nodded. "You as well."

"What have you been doing?"

"I've been teaching. There's one of my students."

He laughed. "I knew it. I knew the way she spoke. It sounds like you a little bit."

"Well, that's a compliment I think."

"Yes, of course it is."

"I think she can do this part easy, what do you think?" I whispered.

"Listen, there are twenty applicants; you know the deal. Every small, good part has lots of actors who can handle it, and we'll limit it down to as few as possible today. Off the record, though, I'll tell you what. I really liked Charlene. If you're saying she's the real deal I think we're going to give her a shot."

I immediately said, "You won't be sorry! If I can help you in any way with this movie, let me know; if you need me, I'm here."

"Don't tell me that unless you really want to do it."

I grinned. "I'm serious, I'm willing to do it."

The producer smiled. "You never know, you may get a call."

"No problem." I walked out of there feeling my heart filled with delight.

Turned out, a week later, Charlene got the part. It was her first professional acting role. She was so excited, she gave me a big hug. "Mary, without you I could never have done this."

As time went by, Charlene became a famous actress, appearing in many movies and even a few TV shows. She once told me that she had me to thank for all of her success.

I said, "No, you did it on your own. You just needed someone to show you how and open that first door. You had the courage to walk through it."

She wasn't the only student I was able to reach and help. There were more than a few over the three years that I taught. I was really most proud of this because at the end of the day it's one thing for me to be able to act, but another to be able to pass it on to another generation. It's something I really appreciated having the chance to do.

CHAPTER 32
China Appears in the US

With success in my teaching and a thriving charitable foundation, I was really busy, but I enjoyed it tremendously.

One day WuJian came home looking depressed. His face dragged, and his lips pointed down. His shoulders were sagging as if he had lost a battle. He sat on the living room couch as rigid as a statue.

"WuJian, my dear, what's the matter?" I sat down next to him.

"Mary, my father's here."

It was nearly four years since we had visited China, when WuJian's mother was sick. Since then we were so busy with our lives we kind of forgot about them. I raised my eyebrows. "What? Your father?"

He shook his head and said, "Yes, and I don't know why."

"How do you know this?"

"I received a call. He's in New York and he wishes to come here. But I would rather go there. The best would be if he didn't even come to the US in the first place."

"No problem. I'll come with you." I held his hand.

"Mary, I don't know what he wants. We never know what he wants. Him appearing in the US the first time… it's probably not a good thing. I'd rather keep you away from this as long as possible."

I saw his determination. I wished him well and said, "I love you. Hurry back."

He booked a flight for the next day and flew to New York.

The story he told me later was that his father was staying at an acquaintance's small apartment in Chinatown. His mother was sick, on the verge of death, and he didn't know what to do. He didn't really want to live there anymore and felt that he couldn't deal with witnessing the death of his wife.

Sitting on the living room couch with his father sitting across from him, WuJian frowned and said angrily, "I'm not quite sure why you're here. You never were a very good father to me in the first place. You sent me off to military school as soon as possible. You and mother were never around, so I'm not sure why you're here now asking for my advice. Besides, wouldn't a phone call have sufficed?"

He told WuJian, "I couldn't do that because I didn't wish to return home."

WuJian said, "Really? Who's watching mother now while you're here?"

"I hired a nurse who's with her all the time."

WuJian frowned and asked, "Is she capable of anything?"

"Unfortunately, no, she is not capable of much. In fact, she's barely able to move and doesn't recognize most people."

"So, you walked away from a painful situation and decided that it's easier to just not deal with it?"

He looked at WuJian and shook his head. "You don't understand what it's like."

"No, I don't, but try me."

"You watch someone deteriorate, someone you had such emotional attachment to, that became part of your life. When that person deteriorated to the point you can't even deal with them or look at them, it affects you every day. Day by day you slowly wither away, just like the patient you're trying to take care of."

WuJian held his head high. "Really? Is this your mindset? Well, if that's the case you have the wrong mindset. It was a woman who you loved for over forty years. You can't abandon her simply because it didn't work for you."

WuJian's father rubbed his eyebrows with his cupped hands as if to rub off all the pressure there. "You're right, but I can't do this. Every day the thought of going home drags in my stomach. I want to jump off the nearest building. It's not worth it for me to do this anymore. I can't live day by day knowing that when I get home this is what I will face."

WuJian scowled and raised his voice. "I can't have a relationship like you do. I would not send my kid off like you did. I can't abandon my wife when she's in her time of need. I know I will never do either of those things. I don't know if I will have a family, but I know one thing—if I had one, I wouldn't abandon my children. They are super precious, they are special. As far as my wife, I will never abandon her no matter what. Her pain is my pain."

WuJian paused to see his father silently lower his head to avoid eye contact. "Obviously, you can't say the same. What you are doing is selfish. You don't even understand why you have called me here. If you don't wish to go back to China and decide to stay in the United States, that's fine. But, again, why did you have to call me all the way to New York?"

"I did offer to go to California—"

Before his father could finish his sentence, WuJian cut him off and yelled, "That's not the point here. The point here is that you decided to tell me in person. You ran to the United States and abandoned my mother. I'm not sure how you expected me to react. Do you expect me to clap, do cartwheels? What was it that you were thinking I was going to do here?"

WuJian's father lifted his head to look at WuJian. "I didn't know, but as you are my son, I had to explain my actions. I knew that if you found out some other way it wouldn't be received well."

"Received well? See how well I'm receiving it now? What did you think would happen?" WuJian snorted.

His father sighed. "I do not know, but I knew it would be received worse. I see that my abandoning your mother in her hour of need is something that you cannot accept."

"You're right, so this meeting was pointless." WuJian's nostrils flared. He fell back on the couch and rolled his eyes with one arm on his forehead as if to say *I give up*. He decided it wasn't worth his time any longer to be there.

He got up to leave.

His father grabbed his hand and said with a shaky voice, "No, son. I don't believe this would be the last we see each other."

"I don't know if that's the case. I do know one thing—right now I don't want to be with you." WuJian looked at his father with a penetrating stare and said, "It's better if I do my own thing. I have some business meetings scheduled while I'm in New York, and then from there I'll fly home. I wish you well, Father. I wish that you made the right decisions in life and then you could live with no regrets. Remember the last part—LIVE WITH NO REGRETS." He said the last part word by word with pauses in between.

His father let go of his hand, his expression turning cold. "Really? You lecture me, WuJian, but what about you? Why have you not flown back to see her? I just told you your mother was on her deathbed. Would you fly home now knowing that?"

WuJian paused for a long time before he said firmly, "You and I are not the same. I didn't benefit from her love the way you did. I didn't benefit from her kindness, from her actions, or her simple things like dinners, house cleaning, long walks. I benefited from none of that. I was shipped away and told, 'have a nice life kid.' I didn't benefit from anything. I did my part, I did go say goodbye. Is there a sense of guilt on my part? Perhaps, but it's quite small. It should be a much larger sense on your part, and yet there is nothing. For that I wish you well and hope you have no regrets."

WuJian turned and walked out. He didn't see his father again after that. He didn't know what happened to him in life and he never regretted it for one minute.

WuJian went on to meet with several talent agencies in New York. After all, New York has a vast film and television industry. Not as big as California but certainly big enough.

He went on to meet with some local people from some of the cable outlets who were doing local shows. He had an interest in that. WuJian told them maybe the next summer he'd be back in New York to do a film shoot. They said, "No problem, we'll be in touch with your agent."

Two shows he got in touch with were actually receptive to him and he ended up doing work in New York.

He flew home as soon as his business was done. When he got home I hugged and kissed him and said, "Welcome home dear, how was your meeting?"

He related all I've told you here.

I looked at WuJian. "I'm sorry your father has done this. However, do you want to return home to China one more time?"

"Perhaps, but not now. I have a shoot that requires another four weeks. If she passes in that time, then it's meant to be. If she doesn't, then yes, I will probably go back at least one more time," WuJian said calmly.

"I understand. If you need me to go to China without you I'm happy to do so."

He shook his head. "That won't be necessary."

"Go back to filming and finish your shoot and then go from there." I gave him a comforting hug.

We both decided that that was the best plan forward.

CHAPTER 33

"Tragedy" Strikes WuJian

It had been about three weeks since WuJian last saw his father. He didn't mean to keep up with him and didn't.

WuJian never called or texted his father again. For him this was dismissive. It was his mother he felt bad for, although he didn't consider her his true mother. I felt very bad for him and didn't know what to do.

I brought it up on one occasion when we were discussing something while sitting on the couch. "Have you heard from your parents in any way?"

"My mother as far as I know is on her deathbed, or in some comatose state. There is no way she would be able to reach me. My father I have no interest in talking to anymore. As far as I'm concerned he might as well join with her."

With that being said, I saw the sternness in his face and decided it wasn't in my best interest to bring up the topic again.

Again, I felt very sad for him, having dealt with my own parents' deaths. I knew the sadness and emptiness that could occur. He didn't feel the same way, and this I knew so I didn't bring it up.

One day, as we were eating breakfast together, the phone rang. I answered it and said, "WuJian, it's for you, it's your father."

"How did he track this number?" WuJian's eyes opened wide in surprise.

I shrugged. "I don't know. It's unlisted but perhaps someone gave to him."

WuJian went to the phone and said hello. His father cried, "WuJian, my son, it's over; your mother has passed on to the next world."

WuJian looked intense but said with a calm voice, "Father, thank you for calling. I appreciate it." And promptly hung up the phone.

He was very quiet and seemed frozen for a few seconds. His shoulders and head were down, his eyes a bit wet looking from the side, but he didn't allow the tears to come out.

I patted him on the back as a way to comfort him. "Are you okay, WuJian?"

He turned around. "Yes, I'm fine Mary. Don't worry about it."

"Did your mother pass away?"

"Yes." His voice was a bit shaky.

The look in his eyes told me that apart from sadness there was a deep hurt in his heart that wasn't able to come out. There was so much pain—the hatred buried by years of neglect—that it was impossible for it to come to the surface.

I gave him a long hug. He hugged me back, but more robotically than was typical of him. He whispered that it wasn't in his heart that he felt this pain. There was simply the fact that someone he knew passed on to the next world. It was sad, but he moved on quickly.

I said, "If you ever do want to talk about this you're welcome to."

"There's no need. I didn't have anything to do with them when they were alive. I certainly am not when they're dead."

"Is there anything in your culture that honors the dead?"

"Yes, but there's no need for it. You honor a culture when someone appreciates who you are, you honor a culture when you have a connection, even if it's remote and far. People have long-distance relationships of all kinds, and yet seem to keep in touch," WuJian said. "However, my parents chose otherwise. I didn't initiate this, they did. When I was five, they sent me to a local military school, very young to be trained. It's a junior school, so little kids were there. In China it seemed like many. I'm sure in the United States it would seem like hundreds of classrooms, yet relative to the Chinese it was very small. As I got bigger I kept going through the different schools. As I've told you my parents had decided that they wanted to serve the country. My parents put the country first and me second. I made peace with that. As I grew up and had my own life, I buried any pain I had and showed no remorse."

After a short pause, he continued. "When I got to the United States you opened my heart again. There was a relationship that was devoted completely to you. It was never going to be about anybody else. They have chosen to come into my life only at the end when they are dying. It is not my fault that they have done this. In fact, I wish they hadn't."

As WuJian spoke I saw a pain that was finally starting to come to the surface. I don't think he would let it go past this, therefore the topic was closed from that point on. But I do know that probably somewhere deep in the recesses of his heart there was tremendous pain.

He never spoke to his father again as far as I knew, and obviously never mourned his mother. It was an extremely painful episode, one that made me reflect on the relationship with my own parents.

I got along with them well. Despite their early rejections, once they saw that I wanted to do acting they supported me to the fullest. They probably in their hearts rejected it, but knowing that it made me happy, they kept their mouths quiet. It was something I truly appreciated.

They didn't have to be this way. They could have pestered me and made it more difficult for me; however, that would have only pushed me away. I truly appreciated the way that they supported me all those years. I could never thank them enough. I did tell them on more than one occasion.

With the income I made over the early years I was able to pay a lot of their debt. You see, while they earned a lot of money, putting me through various schools and doing things they loved they accumulated a lot of debt. Once my career was established, I was able to quickly repay what they owed.

They kept insisting that I shouldn't. They said, "No, please don't do this. This is your life and your money, please use it the way you see fit."

I always waved my hand and said, "This *is* the way I see fit. Believe me, this doesn't shortchange me in any way and it gives me much happiness to do this act of kindness for you. After all, if it weren't for you I wouldn't be in this position in the first place. I truly owe you everything."

I had said that to them many times, and even when they were sick in their older age I kept saying it. I was thankful to be at their side when they passed away.

I wonder if WuJian ever thought about the fact that he wasn't there when his mother died. He planned to go to China after the shoot but that was never meant to be. He had the opportunity to go back and he had the opportunity to also know where his father was.

Was he still in the United States, or did he travel back to China to be with his dying or deceased wife?

I never got the answer, because WuJian never asked the question. I guess that was something that he just made peace with as well. For me, it was about supporting WuJian in his hour of need and that was all I did.

CHAPTER 34
Health Declines Again

I had made peace with the fact I was now teaching and working on my foundation. There were bit roles that came through but none to match the lead role I had a few years back. I wasn't depressed over this fact. In fact, I somewhat enjoyed it.

There was no pressure to act any longer, and although I enjoyed doing what I did, I didn't have to deal with all the coming and going. It was simply a matter of making sure I enjoyed what I did.

Teaching fulfilled my time and the foundation filled in the pieces as well. I had regular meetings with all the players in the foundation. I saw firsthand all the good we did, and it made me extremely happy.

However, one day as I got out of bed I began to feel faint again. I had been on medication as prescribed and going to regular doctor's visits. I never missed one.

Each time I was given a relatively clean bill of health; relative, because my condition would never go away. But the fact was I was able to live with it.

I never wanted to run a marathon at my age anyway. I made peace with that. I did regular walks, kept certain exercise regimens as prescribed to me and took my medication. That was all I could ask.

However, on this particular day, I felt very dizzy. I had to sit back down. It was the first time in years I'd felt this way. In fact, this fainting spell was the first time since the bus stop.

WuJian had already gone downstairs to prepare for the day. I yelled for him and he came running. "What is it, my dear?"

I took a deep breath. "WuJian, I'm sorry to say I feel faint today. I don't think I'll be able to teach my class. I need to ask a favor—can you call in to say I won't be at class today?"

He nodded. "Of course, and we're going to the doctor's."

"No. *We're* not going to the doctor's… *I* am. You need to finish the shoot. You're a week away from a wrap and it has to get done."

"There is no way I'm leaving you with this. This is not a good sign."

"I will handle it."

After going back and forth for what seemed like forever, he finally relented and said, "Fine, but as soon as the shoot is done I'm coming."

"No problem. I'll call you."

I arranged for the driver to take me and the maid to escort me yet again to the doctor. When I went in, Doctor Earl asked, "What's the matter Mary? Our visit's not for a couple days."

"I hate to say this doctor, but this morning I tried to stand up and felt very faint. It wasn't an easy situation, it was like the bus stop, only worse. However, I've never missed my medication, nor my exercise, nor my doctors' visits. I can't explain what's going on."

"Neither can I. Let's run some tests."

I submitted to a wide variety of tests, including an EKG. After he studied the results, Doctor Earl said, "Mary, your heart is out of rhythm. It looks like there could be a blockage. I don't know how bad it is, so we have to do more tests. Your heart is declining, I'm sorry to say. We could do bypass and that will make things better temporarily, but I have to be honest—your heart is starting to give up."

I sat down. "I don't understand… Isn't there more medicine you can give me? Perhaps there's something else you can do. There has to be a way for this to be fixed. I mean, just give me some more medicine. Let's prescribe some physical therapy and get on with it."

Doctor Earl looked stern. "I'm afraid it's not so simple, though I wish that were the case. Believe me, if what you truly needed was more medication, I would have written the prescription already.

However, the reality is that's not the case. Sorry to say, Mary, we're going to have to schedule surgery as soon as possible."

I was in denial, but understood what he said. I asked for the next step.

"The next step is to confirm my diagnosis through an MRI and then once we know for sure we will schedule the procedure immediately. Please tell those you love what is happening," he said. "I must warn you, this isn't a guaranteed success. The outcome could be amazing, or it could be nothing or it also could be fatal. I have to present to you the worst-case scenario as well as the best, which is that you come out completely healed and able to live for many more years. Worst case obviously is that the procedure is fatal."

I gasped. "Tell me doctor, how much is the chance for each?"

"Well, from the amount of surgeries I've done I put this at a ninety-five percent success rate. That five percent is sticky, and I have to tell my patients. I dread telling that one, especially to someone like you that is a very valued patient. But I must be honest."

I nodded and said, "Thank you for your honesty. Let's schedule the next steps."

When I left the doctor's office, I went to the fountain in the hallway and got a cup of water. In fact, I took two cups of water. I couldn't handle the news.

My life was taking shape and I finally found something that made me happy. I had an amazing man in my life. I had a teaching job I loved, and a foundation that was doing very well. I had even been in an acting job in recent years that I truly enjoyed. If one more were to come around perhaps I'd be happier. I wasn't ready to relinquish this world.

I truly didn't want to.

I decided not to call WuJian and tell him the news just yet. If I did he would leave the set immediately. Who knew if they had another two or three hours to finish their shoot for the day. I was not going to be the one to ruin that. I thought to myself, *Today is not the day that I am to pass. I can at least let him finish what he needs to.*

I went home and laid down on my bed. I told the maid not to disturb me unless WuJian came home.

A few hours later the maid knocked quietly on the door. "WuJian is pulling into the driveway."

"Thank you, I appreciate it."

I slowly got out of bed and made my way downstairs. When I got to the bottom, WuJian came immediately over to me and gave me a hug.

"Mary, is everything okay? You didn't call me today." He held onto my shoulders, examining me.

"Everything is fine. However, it seems I'm going to require surgery," I said softly.

He frowned in disbelief. "What? That doesn't mean you're fine, and why didn't you call me?" He gave me another hug and then led me to the living room where we both sat down.

"I didn't want to trouble you. There was no point, considering the fact that the surgery wouldn't be happening today. They have to run two more tests tomorrow and after that it looks like it'll be scheduled for next week."

"How much recuperation will this require?"

"I was told about two weeks, and after that there will be a very strict recovery schedule."

"No problem. I'm taking a leave of absence from the shoot."

"How many days are left?"

"It doesn't matter."

I said, "It matters to me, and if there's a week left you must honor that."

"There's exactly a week left."

"Then finish your shoot. We will do the surgery after. If I even need it—we won't know until after the tests."

"I will go with you tomorrow, and there is no arguing with that."

"Very well. I am sure the director can manage without you for a day." I smiled.

He immediately called the producer to say that he couldn't be there the next day because his wife was ill, to the point she required surgery. However, he would be in the day after and finish the shoot.

I went to the doctor's with WuJian and they ran a battery of tests. The diagnosis was confirmed, stating I needed surgery. We scheduled it for the end of the next week. It would be the day after WuJian finished his shoot.

Each day I rested, trying not to do too much. I didn't want to test my body more than was needed. Each day WuJian ran home to make sure I was okay, and he called several times a day in between takes. He was extremely worried.

I appreciated and adored his dedication. However, I worried what kind of toll this would take on him. Would he be able to act with the perfection required?

Would he be able to do everything he needed to?

I didn't want to be the cause of his unhappiness.

The day of the surgery I was quite nervous. I could barely move or get out of bed. WuJian helped me to the car and of course we had someone drive us.

As we entered the hospital, Doctor Earl was waiting. "Mary, don't worry, I've had tremendous success with the surgery. There's nothing to fear."

I was slightly more relaxed after that.

The anesthesiologist came in to the surgical room and put me out. Four hours later I remember being wobbly and slowly opening my eyes to look around. The surgery had gone well. The doctor proclaimed it would be successful. I breathed a deep sigh of relief, thanking the doctor and holding WuJian's hand as I woke up slowly.

For the next few months I had physical therapy, occupational therapy, and a diet change. My entire life seemed to shift.

I had to take a leave of absence from my teaching and from my involvement in the foundation. It was extremely depressing to me that I had to do this. These were two things that I really loved. However, I understood that my health came first.

WuJian was by my side the entire time. He didn't leave for a moment. He had two or three acting jobs that he could have done in that time, but he turned them down.

Mike came to visit me, as did some other close friends, and of course my children and grandchildren were always around.

Sometimes there were too many people around. The noise sometimes stressed me out. When that happened, my sons were quick to remove their families from our presence and to let me rest.

Bobby hugged me and said, "Ma, we can't lose you just yet... you have to go on."

I laughed and said, "What's the matter? You don't think I wrote you into the will?"

They frowned and Bo said, "It's not about that. We can live on our own. The issue, Ma, is that we want you around and to be happy and guide us. Your presence is the guiding light in our family and needs to continue."

My heart was warmed to hear my sons speaking those kind words. I had no idea why I was so lucky to have such wonderful children.

I said, "I appreciate that boys and I love you very much." I truly meant it—my children were my biggest rewards in life, and WuJian as well. Many times when I couldn't tolerate the noise and pressure of too many people around, WuJian was the only one there with me. He kept me company and I couldn't imagine a life without him.

I slowly began to recuperate and regain my focus. After about three months I was back on my feet fully and able to walk around. I was able to make decisions on my own, but I felt as if I was never going to be the same.

Things would quickly deteriorate after that, and from there it would continue to only get worse. It was but a brief shining light after the surgery for the next four months. After that there was a slow decline for three years. I was a realist, knowing that I did not know how much longer I had in this world and I intended to enjoy every moment that I had.

CHAPTER 35
An Ultimate Test

After my recuperation, I noticed a change in WuJian.

He became more and more devoted, yet more and more apart. This contradiction confused me greatly. I felt him very loyal in terms of making sure I was well taken care of, making sure the maids and everyone else did their jobs.

However, the love and affection I seemed to have felt previously before the disease wasn't there. I was extremely concerned by this. I wasn't sure how to handle it.

One day I called Mike and asked him to come over. When he arrived, I said, "Mike, have a seat."

He sat down. "What's the matter, Mary?"

"Well, it's WuJian. I feel like he's pulled away from me. I'm not sure if you got that sense."

"Well, Mary, to be honest, I'm not around that much, so I really couldn't tell you. I mean, from the outside it looks pretty difficult. I mean, you know you are sick and not as well as you need to be. I think he just didn't know how to handle that. From my perspective, the fact that he still remained here said a lot about him. I mean, if it were me as a younger man and my wife was an older woman, and my wife wasn't feeling well and required being taken care of, I don't know if I'd be able to handle it for so long as he has."

I nodded. "I appreciate the information. However, for some reason I just think there are other reasons he's pulled away from me."

Mike thought about it for a minute. "Listen, Mary, if you really do feel that way you need to be up front and direct with him. I am pulling for you and I am sure you'll get well soon; however, the reality is both of us are not getting any younger. You need to ask him for the truth. If he's willing to stay with you for the long haul or he's going to pull away. It's not up to you. He has to make that decision for himself, and only he can answer you honestly. Sorry to be the bearer of bad news with that advice. Like I said, I'm pulling for you and think you're going to do really well. But if it's in your heart that he is not the same person you married, then you need to confront him about it."

I thanked Mike for the advice and wished him well. After he left, I started to think about what he had said. It's extremely frustrating on the one hand to have this type of confrontation in my current state. I was recuperating nicely; however, I was far from one hundred percent.

For me to be in a position where I had to have extra stress is not something I really wanted. However, I knew that every day that went by that I didn't have an answer about the situation would only make it worse. Stress would increase and eventually take a toll on my health. I couldn't afford that type of situation.

I decided that when WuJian got home I'd have an upfront conversation with him. The rest of the day I tried not to think about what had transpired. I tried not to think about the fact that I would confront WuJian that night about the situation.

Finally, WuJian came home after another long day on the set, I was relieved to see that he was in a happy mood. He joined me on the living room couch. "Oh, Mary, you're up and about. I didn't think you'd be out of bed."

"Yes, I'm feeling a little better and decided it was in my best interest to be able to not only do the rehab but to be able to walk around the house a little bit. Every day I do that I feel like I'm getting stronger."

WuJian smiled. "I'm really happy, Mary. That's great news for us!"

I smiled too but then I became serious. "WuJian, I want to ask you a question. Something serious and I hope you don't mind."

WuJian looked me in the eyes and nodded. "Of course. You know you can ask me anything."

I sighed. "I know we've been together for nearly thirteen years, but it seems like a short while. We have become very close, as close as I've ever been to another man, but if I'm being honest, I am concerned. I want to ask you... are you planning to stay with me forever?"

After hearing this question, he became very puzzled. He froze and frowned. "I don't understand the question. I married you, didn't I?"

"I know that, but in my current state of being sick, it feels like you distance yourself from me."

He stared at me, not wanting to answer the question one way or the other. Time seemed frozen and my heart was beating faster than ever.

I felt like that response confirmed what I had feared. That he was planning on leaving.

I said calmly, "WuJian, if you plan on leaving, do so quickly because I don't want to deal with the situation. I need to recuperate and get over the pain."

"Mary, I think you're misunderstanding this. My response wasn't to confirm your theory that I was planning on leaving. It was rather to confirm the fact that you're someone I felt extremely close to, more than I've ever felt before. I couldn't be here to watch you in this state." His eyes filled with tears.

"I knew that I was responsible to be near you and help you in any way I can. However, emotionally, seeing you in this state breaks me. I know that if I seem broken to you, it makes it much worse on your health. I could never do that to you. I can't be the cause of any additional health issues that you have. Mary, I want to be with you till the day that one of us passes on. It was never my intent to leave you and never will be."

Tears welled in my eyes as well and I gave WuJian a big hug. "Thank you! That's all I needed to hear. I don't need to hear anything more. Your loyalty is one thing, but your heart is another. Giving over your heart to me, myself giving my heart to you, was my intention the entire time. It is throughout this journey of life and through everything I've been through that we have come this far and have been able to do this. I am so in love with you and can't believe that I have found the perfect soulmate… No matter the age, no matter the situation, I love you dearly."

Tears streamed down my face. WuJian helped me wipe my tears while he couldn't stop his own.

I gave him a big kiss and we went to our bed to continue talking while lying down. It had been a long time since the two of us had spoken, especially on this level. It had been a lot of polite conversation and easy questions for many weeks. It was as if we were living apart while being under the same house, and in fact the same room.

However, after this conversation and after being able to have such a frank discussion with him, I was able to fortify our relationship. I think he felt comfortable opening up to me about all of this.

It was a weight that was lifted off our shoulders. I couldn't believe how we were able to talk so openly. I don't remember the last time I was able to do so frankly with someone I cared about so much. I was really happy that we were able to have this conversation. I knew then that we would be together forever.

CHAPTER 36
Living My New Reality

There comes a point in time where someone needs to accept the situation that they are in. I know that seems very philosophical but it's the truth.

For me it was a matter of accepting the fact that I wasn't the same person I once was. I tended to think back to my youth when I had all those acting jobs lined up. Each role would be a job unto itself. I would throw myself deeply into the role and actually tried to become the person I was portraying. It was a tiring, draining yet rewarding experience; each time I felt stronger than the one before, and each time I would build upon creating the character from what I learned from the previous one.

It was truly amazing to watch as I looked in the mirror and saw my reactions, my facial expressions, my hand mannerisms becoming part of the character.

I felt like I passed that on to WuJian as well. I would see him at night looking in the mirror practicing with his hands and face, repeating gestures over and over as he memorized lines. He had learned this from me and I was proud to be able to do this.

One thing I did notice was the fact I couldn't do what I used to in the sense that I couldn't run around as much as I wanted to. I was never really one to party hard, as I've stated before.

I tended to avoid Hollywood parties. Functional gatherings I felt were just a trivial thing for people to show off their nonsense. However, with my foundation, I found the need again to attend parties and fundraisers and other types of events. I felt that my justification was that I was being rewarded.

However, after my illness and the recuperation and strength that were required and the new adjustment to my exercise regimen and diet, I often felt weak and tired. It wasn't something I enjoyed but something I accepted.

I did try to get out, but it tended to be maybe once or twice a week. I felt like I harbored a little bit of resentment, as someone who was forced to live in a situation that they didn't want to.

It was very tough for me to be in this position, especially because I knew WuJian deserved better. He deserved a woman who could be at his side no matter what.

I always encouraged him to go out to any events, any gatherings, any acting workshops, anything that involved the profession he enjoyed. I told him, "My health shouldn't ruin your life."

He looked me in the eyes and said with determination, "Mary, on the contrary, your health is what has become my life. If it's important to you it's important to me."

I didn't want to fight with him too often. I picked my battles and at times I would actually demand that he leave.

In those days I felt this keen sense of satisfaction. It may sound weird to have the man of your life out and about. It was actually rewarding to me because I knew he was doing something he needed to and something that he enjoyed. He was being held back because of me and I knew it. Any way that I could release him from those bonds was important to me.

I became more and more dependent on my maids and butlers and their kindness was helpful. They dared not speak to me a word about it, but simply came running as soon as I demanded.

I wasn't a very demanding person by nature, so many a time I tried to do things myself. When I felt like I hit a wall and could no longer do that I called them. They understood this and at times tried to anticipate when they might be needed. In those cases, they were actually there before I even thought of it.

I appreciated their extra effort and kept thanking them. The same message was conveyed every time. They all said, "No need to thank me, ma'am—this is our job. You have been loyal to us and have allowed us to be in your home for so long. The least we can do in your hour of need is to repay the debt."

I laughed and thought in my head, *well at least they're getting paid, so I guess* it is *their job.* On the other hand, they had become like family to me in so many ways. I don't want to simply think that I rang a bell and they came running. I wanted it to be more of a relationship they felt they could enjoy and actually want to participate in. Perhaps that was something that was insane for me to think. However, I did believe in my heart that these people had become family to me.

I really did try to get used to my new reality. If I wanted to go to the grocery store for whatever reason, I had a chef to do it, so I would send him instead. Every time I went out of the house I thought to myself, is this something I need, or want?

If it was something I just simply wanted, then I usually wouldn't do it. However, there was one thing that I did enjoy doing more than anything else and wouldn't give up.

Part of my exercise regimen required walks in fresh air. I had a few parks that I truly enjoyed. Even on days when I wasn't feeling one hundred percent I walked anyway. For me it was more about the fact that I just enjoyed it and it was healthy at the same time. Each time I took a walk and came back I felt more refreshed.

WuJian would try to spend time with me on those walks when he could. I completely understood the realities of Hollywood, all that it entailed, and I appreciated any time he had to give me.

I didn't want to break that bond for him and therefore I knew that I had to let him do what he needed to. However, many a time he insisted on coming with me or he would just show up at the park.

At those times I felt remorseful and happy at the same time. Remorse of the fact that I had caused him to be away from doing what he loved, but I was happy with the fact I had his company.

WuJian and I would talk about life as we walked around and simply talked about the things we envisioned, or the things he and I had accomplished. I told him how proud I was of the fact that I had taught so many students by now that actually had accomplished things in the acting world. I felt responsible for their success and cherished the knowledge that they became better actors and actresses.

I enjoyed the foundation and all that it accomplished. I was amazed beyond my wildest dreams. I told WuJian that I thought that I was put on this earth for these types of things, that and to meet him. I said I had no regrets and I enjoyed everything I'd been doing.

WuJian stared at me and said, "Mary, I'm not ready to let go of you just yet. You're not going anywhere. Stop talking like you're on to the next world already."

"I don't know about that, but I feel like I have at least one toe in the next world," I laughed and said.

He grabbed me by the arm and he said, "Well then, I'm going to pull that toe back into this world because you're not going anywhere."

We went back and forth for a few moments on that issue and both of us accepted the fact that the situation had definitely changed and would never be the same.

For my part, I found peace and made terms with what was happening. As much as it bothered me I simply enjoyed every moment that I had. WuJian, for his part, tried to balance becoming more devoted but on the other hand trying to keep his own life and his career. It was a very tough balance and one that I commend him for attempting.

When I was younger, had I been presented with that challenge I don't think I would have done as well.

Had I ever been tested by the ones I loved?

I don't know. In fact, the only test I had was when I was a young actress in Hollywood. At that time my parents were sick, but they did unexpectedly die, so in both cases I didn't have the chance to be tested in that way, on that level, as WuJian was. I never got the opportunity to be tested by balancing work and taking care of an elderly person.

My fear was that, had I been tested that way, I don't think I would have passed. I would have simply ignored everything else but my acting.

I really did accept my new reality, and in fact in some ways embraced it for the fact that I would cherish life and live life to its fullest for as long as I could.

CHAPTER 37
My Bucket List

As I began to get sicker in the two years after the surgery, I realized there were so many things I had yet to do in life. It was truly amazing to think about how much I accomplished, yet at the end of the day it all seemed too little. There was so much more I wanted to do in life.

I told WuJian about all my ideas and he said, "Mary, I think there's a lot you could still do. However, you need to be careful. If you take too much on too fast, you'll become too sick and you'll eventually not be able to do any of them."

I sighed. "For my limited time I want to be able to accomplish so much."

"Well, maybe you should prioritize your list. What's most important to you? Is seeing the Swiss Alps very important? Can you fly? Can you sit on a plane for so long?"

I thought about what he said. "You're right, WuJian, I think I need to sit down and look at the list."

After supper one night I sat down with the paper and listed twenty to thirty items that I thought were important. Some of them were as simple as seeing new landscapes, beaches, and beautiful scenery. Some were making sure that my foundation distributed funds to certain charities and others were getting to meet famous people that I never had the chance to. Last, I made sure that I had the right priorities for each one.

For example, to me, seeing a beautiful mountaintop was extremely important. To that end we did make a trip the next week to the Swiss Alps. WuJian was able to clear his schedule and go with me.

It was very comforting to me to have him along. Having his company in these last moments of my life was extremely important.

When we got there, we checked into a beautiful five-star hotel. I loved it. It overlooked the mountain tops. I took in the view and took in the beautiful clean air. It was cleansing for me, almost a relief.

A part of me wished that it would never end and I would not have to return to the real world. Returning to the real world meant I had to accept my limitations. That was something I didn't want to do.

I turned to WuJian as we sat on the porch one night, sipping cocoa. "WuJian, isn't this amazing?"

"Yes, it is. I never want to leave."

I nodded. "I feel the same way."

However, I knew that life was calling us back. My kids would be worried about me. They wanted me near. I knew I couldn't abandon them. I didn't know exactly how much time I had left, but each moment that I had I'd experience it to the fullest.

We traveled to other places on my list. We saw beautiful beaches, amazing grass fields, and even traveled east and saw the trees in Vermont during the fall.

If you've never seen Vermont in the fall, you've never seen anything like it. Trees become beautiful color paintings one next to the other, like a beautiful rainbow flowing softly. I would take walks on their trails and it made me amazed by what nature had to offer.

I wished I had spent this time in nature when I was healthier. I should have taken more time to enjoy the little things in life. With each passing day I knew my story was coming to the close. My "movie" was wrapping up.

I knew I didn't have a lot of time, but I did take some time to make sure my foundation was set up properly in the event of my death. To me that was very important.

I spoke with Lena and made sure she had the means to be able to continue after my passing. I spoke to WuJian, who agreed to be in charge, provided my children would also be involved. They had been there from the start and deserved to be. I acknowledged that and decided to make Bobby senior director at the Foundation.

After a family dinner soon after, I turned to Bobby. "The foundation is especially important to me and to my legacy. I want you to be able to carry this forward."

He nodded and said, "Ma, I know how special this was to you. This foundation meant so much. I'll continue to do the good work and make sure it helps so many people."

After teaching for several years, I saw how many inspired actors and actresses needed help. There was little good guidance and direction out there so I established a workshop, free of charge, that provided weekend classes.

I then made sure I hired the right teachers and paid for it myself. I turned to Bo this time. "Bo, I need you to make sure that my workshops continue after my passing."

He nodded. "Ma, I understand. I will continue to make sure the right teachers are in the right places."

"I can't thank you all enough for how much you've helped me." I gave Bo and Bobby a big hug.

The final thing I wanted to do was to call my agent. "Mike, I can't thank you enough for everything you've done for my career. It was extremely important to me that you were there to help me along the way."

Mike was choking back sobs. "Mary, you know I don't really cry much; however, you're going to make me do it now if you continue with this. I'm not going to like it."

I laughed. "Well, Mike, that's just what you're going to have to do, because I'm just going to keep thanking you."

I went on to thank Mike for the next half hour about how much he helped me in my career, how instrumental he was, how he pushed me to the right projects. He steered me away from bad influences and was able to guide me when I didn't know how to guide myself.

Eventually, he did break down. "Mary, I have to be honest with you. In this business I don't trust many people, but you I seem to trust implicitly. You're the one client I could always depend on to follow my advice. If I thought a role was right, you took it, even if you didn't always one hundred percent agree with me. You made my career more than I made yours. It went both ways. I can't thank you enough for what you've done, and I'll miss you terribly. Your time is not up yet, Mary. I know there's more you can do. Don't give up yet."

With that I said, "I know, Mike, I'll fight for as long as I can, but I'm sensing the end is near, and therefore I want to make sure that I thanked you while I was still conscious."

To that end, Mike thanked me also. We both hung up with tears in our eyes.

I was able to at least accomplish many things of my bucket list. I didn't think I would get to everything, which I didn't, but each time I put my pencil through something on my list I was quite happy. I said to myself, *at least I was able to do all of this in my lifetime.* I could go on to wherever the next world was, knowing that I had actually done that.

Finally, I turned to WuJian one night and said, "WuJian, I have to tell you. I loved you for all my life and I am so glad I found you."

He waved his hand. "Mary, let's not talk about this now. You're not going just yet and I'm not ready to let go, so let's have a conversation about anything else. Let's save this one for another day."

I said, "No problem. I understand." We were able to talk about anything and everything. We kept things light and simple.

Around my family it seemed to be the same way; Bo and Bobby were just not ready to let go. Their families were the same. Each time I brought up my passing they brushed it off by saying, "Ma, you're not going anywhere, so what we are talking about here?" I understood that no one was ready to let go.

I don't know if *I* was ready to let go, but at the end of the day I was a realist. Somehow, I was always a realist when no one else wanted to be. I knew my time was running out, so for me, it was natural to always say goodbye.

But for them, they didn't accept that and therefore, they didn't want to hear it. I understood and said, "Okay, I will wait for another day if I can."

I prayed I had the chance to properly do that when the moment was right.

CHAPTER 38
A Tearful Goodbye

It was a Monday morning in 1993 that I never would forget. It would be my last Monday morning. I woke up in such terrible pain that I couldn't move. I turned to WuJian. "I'm just not going to be able to move today. Please summon the doctor."

The doctor came right over. "Mary, I don't know, it's not looking good. I can give you some medication to help you. Would you like to go to the hospital?"

I shook my head. "No, there's no point."

The doctor sighed. "Very well. I understand. I'll give you something for the pain."

"Just a little bit. I don't want to lose my clarity of thought. If I do that, I won't be able to properly talk to people."

WuJian was there by my side every moment. He had turned down many acting roles in my final year, and he put all his attention on taking care of me.

I turned to him after the doctor left. "WuJian, now is the time to say goodbye."

He wept and said, "Mary, no, it's not yet time."

"No, this is the time. I will probably lose clarity at some point or maybe consciousness, so I will say it now."

I reached for his hand and slowly touched it, rubbing it gently.

"WuJian, my love, you have been there for me from day one since I found you. No man has ever been this close to me my entire life. I don't think I would have ever found you if I had not taken that second trip to China. There's a blessing from the Universe that you came into my life. I'll never forget that moment I met you, and all that we've accomplished together. Those things have become so much a part of me that I don't know how I would ever live without them; I can't remember the day that I did. I can't say how grateful I am that someone like you was able to help me. My children have meant so much to me, but you have meant much more in very many ways that I could never explain to them, or anyone. I just want to simply say I love you and I will never forget you, and wherever we end up in the next world you'll always be with me..."

I started to cry, really sob, which I had never done before. I tried to remain strong at each step. I put on a brave face to everyone so that they wouldn't know my pain.

Now I couldn't hold back. He seemed to understand I was in my final moments and I knew it well too.

WuJian wasn't very emotional in general. This time he couldn't help it; tears streamed down his face.

He hugged me tight. "Mary, I will never forget you because there will be none like you in my life. I have never felt so close to someone so fast for so long. My parents as you know were never around, and I could never form a proper relationship. There was no one else in my life I trusted, but you I trust completely and wholly. I've never left your side because I never felt the need. I never wanted to. It made me a better person than I ever thought I could become. You showed me that there's light at the end of the tunnel. You showed me that you can balance having everything but helping the world. I will never forget these lessons and will take them with me for the rest of my life, no matter what happens to me. Our souls are meant to be together and I guarantee you we'll see each other again in another light."

He hugged me tighter and gave me a kiss on the forehead. His tears poured down his face like water gushing from a well. He wiped his tears and lay down beside me. For the next hour we barely spoke. I lay there in tremendous pain, not moving much.

After an hour I finally turned to him with the little strength I had left and said, "WuJian my love, please invite Bo and Bobby and their families; it's only right that I say goodbye."

He nodded his head, wiping away the tears, and said, "I understand."

Bo and Bobby and their families arrived within an hour. When they came in they saw me in such terrible pain, laying there half motionless.

I said to my boys, "Come close to me." I gave them hugs and kisses and said, "I'll be in another world soon. Please take care of your families and stay strong for each other. Always get along and never forget where you came from. Never forget that there's more to this world than money. Never forget that without giving back there's nothing to the world. I had to learn this all too late in my life, and I want you to start while you're still young. Put yourselves in positions to succeed both financially and with the ability to give back. Bobby, you'll continue my foundation and help others and Bo you will lead the acting workshops. Don't ever forget your responsibilities. I want to thank each of your families as well."

I gave their wives and grandchildren each a kiss and a hug. "Grandma loves you and will never forget you. You're so special to me."

Everyone was crying, even the grandchildren seemed to understand, at their young age, that their grandmother was on her way. After about another three hours of talking, tossing and turning, my strength at last went out.

I felt my soul going over to another place. I felt myself looking back at WuJian and the children and grandchildren and somewhere out there, Mike, as I went up and up into the Universe.

There's a funny feeling when you look back and look down at your life and feel yourself being pulled away and trying to remember and search for those you loved.

I can't explain it to anyone reading this, because they are still here. It's only as you get closer to being One with the Universe again that you seem to understand that everything had a perfect reason. You begin to put it all into proper perspective after leaving the physical plane.

WuJian and I were truly in a love destiny—we were meant to be together from the moment we met. Our souls were intertwined throughout countless lifetimes. Each of us couldn't have accomplished what we did without the other.

The Universe had to take its time to put us together, so things became clear only when it actually happened.

I looked further and further back as I pulled away from my life, and I saw the true destiny of WuJian and I, and how our love was truly destined to be.

CHAPTER 39
To Honor Our Mother's Work

It was about a month after our mother passed away when we decided the best way to honor her was to keep alive the legacy that she asked of us. It was very important to her that we maintained the workshops and foundation.

Bo and I made sure that we were involved in both entities. I know mother assigned us each one part, with myself working on the foundation, and Bo doing the workshops.

However, we both decided it was important to be able to handle both items. To that end, we made sure to attend weekly meetings with the foundation and acting workshops. We had our own lives to live and our own families, but we made sure to stay in touch regularly.

If there were any complications that arose, we always thought about what Mother would do. If she was going to do something important but hard, she would do it directly without beating around the bush. We tried to mimic her as best as possible. We were far from perfect at it, but at least we knew that we were trying to do what she wanted.

We enjoyed going to the acting workshops on Sundays and watching how the actors eagerly learned their craft. The teachers would instruct them how to position themselves, how to talk properly, how to present themselves, how to try out for roles, how to handle rejections, and all of the things that went into being a Hollywood actor or actress.

We learned so much from that. We learned that there's so much more to being an actor or actress than simply showing up on a movie set saying, "Here I am."

We learned you had to carefully position your resumé and headshot, learn how you properly speak, decide how many roles you tried out for, and which roles to take. So many things, all of which our mother put into perspective, all of which she chose the right people to handle for her.

Speaking of which, her agent Mike went frequently to the workshops. He thought this was the best way he could honor our mother. He would go and say how hard it was to break into the business, yet he would try to give examples of the best agents and how to approach them. He would work with the students on their resumés to see if they were good enough, tighten them up where he could, and try to get them small acting jobs so they had something on their resumé to show people.

This time of Mike's was priceless. Here was a really successful Hollywood agent teaching them the real ropes of the business. Not every agent wanted to do this. Most of them were so busy trying to hustle everybody, trying to get clients and get parts for the clients that they didn't have time to give back. Mike was a seasoned veteran on his way out, and at that point he was pretty much retired and wanted to get more and more out of his life. Part of that was the workshops. We were truly appreciative of all his efforts.

At the end of the day mother's vision was successful. The foundation gave millions and millions for charitable works all around the world.

It became a cycle, a positive cycle for change. A cycle that involves someone giving their money and time once they became successful, and being role models for others to do so.

At the end of the day we know that mother is proud of us, and how we've helped her endeavors and taken care of our families. We guided them by the same principal, always—teaching them to learn to enjoy the moments that they have, and we always came back to help those in need.

We know that you're smiling down on us from heaven,
Mother.

CHAPTER 40
WuJian's Legacy

I wouldn't do our journey justice if I didn't write about my dear Mary. I can't summarize my life without her; it was too hard, and too painful. I had not opened myself up to someone in that way ever, and I would never do so again.

As I write this, though, I would like to focus on one part of it. I did remember the end and how Mary gave back. To me, that was the most important thing.

However, I didn't feel in the right place in the United States, no matter how many acting roles I had. I never was truly satisfied, I never felt like I could be part of that again without Mary.

I did keep in touch with Mary's children for a while. They were special to me. However, I never really wanted to be a part of it anymore a few months after Mary passed on, because they reminded me of her. It was like putting salt on my wounds. I missed Mary terribly.

Mary left me twenty million dollars. That, together with my earnings from my acting roles, was more than enough for myself.

Through that money, I went back to China. I invested wisely and became even more wealthy. I decided that it was time to give back and implement the lessons Mary taught me well for the fifteen years I was with her. I made sure to establish a foundation and gave a great deal to the poorer part of China.

Most people know how populated China is, but most people don't know just how deep the poverty runs. If you look at the average family, they live on so little.

In comparison, in the United States the poor would be considered rich. It is a shame that this is not publicized, but I think it's because no one wants to truly believe that it exists. Therefore, it's easier to sweep it under the rug to obviate that effect.

I became the coolest bachelor, if you will, who focused on charitable endeavors and events. Yes, I planned the proper parties and proper events, only to attract other like-minded individuals and hope that they would give as well.

Sometimes they would give and sometimes they wouldn't. For those that joined me in my endeavor, it was very rewarding. I liked inviting people or things I didn't expect. I had to try and then when I did it, it was very rewarding and exciting.

We were able to give a lot of money to charity; billions of dollars in fact. We were able to rescue so many people from so much sorrow, and I continue to smile to this day.

I never did have any interests in marrying anyone ever again. Perhaps to you this would seem very strange. Beautiful young women threw themselves at me. I never could know if they were throwing themselves for the money or for any other reason. So I rejected them.

To me, my life was about honoring a legacy taught to me by Mary. From that day when Mary passed on, I set my heart on continuously giving. I put myself into motion to do so endlessly.

I never did have any children of my own, but I considered the children who benefited from my charitable work all the children I ever needed.

Each time a smile came across the young girl's or boy's face, my whole life lights up. I was able to restore their smiles that they so deserve. That was my child, that was enough for me.

Each time I did that I would look up in Heaven and see Mary and hopefully she's proud of me, thinking I'm doing a good job here.

Each time I would go and buy myself something I'd make sure I bought somebody else the same. What I mean is, let's say I bought myself a nice car. I'd buy twenty cars for other poor people. If I spent a lot, I'd give the same amount through my foundation.

For me it wasn't about hoarding money. What's the point of that? We all end up in the same place at the end of the day. Can't take it with you as they say.

It was a lesson I seemed to learn every day. Each time I did more and more charitable work I realized that this is really what I wanted to do with my life.

Acting perhaps was the vehicle, but it was a lesson taught by Mary that I needed to learn. I've been doing that ever since. Each time I hope to do the same thing, to make Mary proud.

I understand the lesson she taught me. She sits with me throughout my entire life. She completed my destiny.

ABOUT THE AUTHORS

Sue Maisano:

Sue is a Chinese American writer, healer and meditation facilitator. Sue was born in a small Chinese village and spent 23 years there. Then fate led her to the US and marriage, and is now a proud mother of 3 children.

She believes that you are an infinite multidimensional being here to grow. Sue found her passion in writing, healing, and leading workshops. **A Love Destiny** is part of a project to demonstrate the power of the mind.

Visit Sue's website MindRealities.com for healing and empowering messages.

Sue's other books include:

THE HEALING JOURNEY: How a Poor Chinese Village Girl Became an American Healer

The Nature of Mind Realities

Charles Rappaport:

Charles is the "channeler" of **A Love Destiny**. He has heightened abilities to meditate and tune in to higher consciousness and dictate the book automatically. **A Love Destiny** was drafted through Charles meditations.